The song ended and .... and falling more rap..... ..... the frenetic music. They conferred briefly then started again, this time side by side, their legs kicking out with amazing speed and dexterity. Watching them jive was like watching *Dancing with the Stars,* but better, because I had a front-row seat.

Dana splayed her hands on Yuri's rock-hard abdomen and he thrust her up in the air. Her long legs, covered in black leggings, whirled around and around while remaining at Yuri's waist level. Their performance was mesmerizing.

Yuri suddenly bellowed a sound reminiscent of the roar of a wounded elephant. Dana flew out of his arms and slid across the varnished floor. She landed in a sprawl, her face dark with anger that quickly changed to horror.

Yuri clutched his chest, his face as white as a bridal gown. He staggered a few steps then crashed to the floor.

★

Previously published Worldwide Mystery title by
CINDY SAMPLE

DYING FOR A DATE

DYING FOR A DANCE

CINDY SAMPLE

WORLDWIDE®

TORONTO • NEW YORK • LONDON
AMSTERDAM • PARIS • SYDNEY • HAMBURG
STOCKHOLM • ATHENS • TOKYO • MILAN
MADRID • WARSAW • BUDAPEST • AUCKLAND

This book is dedicated to my mother, Harriet Bergstrand,
the best mother a daughter could ask for,
and my children, Dawn and Jeff, who have turned into
the most amazing adults.

Recycling programs
for this product may
not exist in your area.

DYING FOR A DANCE

A Worldwide Mystery/December 2012

First published by L & L Dreamspell

ISBN-13: 978-0-373-26827-6

Copyright © 2011 by Cindy Sample

Printed in U.S.A.

Acknowledgments

It takes a village to write one of my books. Many thanks and hugs to my critique group for their astute observations and unfailing support: Kathy, Norma, Pat, Rae and Terri. Thanks to friends who were willing to read the early drafts and provide excellent suggestions: Bonnie, Jaci, Julie, Kelly, Liana, Liz, Matt, Nora and Peggy. Also thanks to those experts in homicide investigation who shared a few helpful tips: D.P. Lyle, M.D., and Wayne Farquhar. Thanks also to Sisters in Crime (Sacramento and Northern California) Sacramento Valley Rose, California Writer's Club and NCPA for their support. My editor, Cindy Davis, has to be the most patient editor in the world, as are publishers Lisa Smith and Linda Houle.

Thanks also to Matthias Mengelkoch and Tom Novi for their generous donations to the Sacramento Opera and the El Dorado Women's Center. You both make great characters.

Special kudos to Tony Nguyen, Jim Clark, Tania Chegini and Ricardo Salazar, the instructors who have spent countless hours attempting to mold me into a graceful and competent ballroom dancer.

And last but certainly not least, thanks to those fans from around the world whose emails make this journey so much fun.

ONE

I DIDN'T THINK MY NIGHT COULD get any worse. But when I stumbled on a dead man with my broken shoe heel stuffed in his mouth, I realized it definitely could.

I was valiantly attempting to learn the choreography for my best friend's New Year's Eve wedding. Although Liz envisioned a bridal party version of *Dancing with the Stars,* after tripping my instructor for the third time in ten minutes, I decided the routine looked more like *Dancing with the Dorks.*

My twenty-one-year-old Vietnamese instructor, Bobby Nguyen, epitomized a ballroom dancer—tall and slender, graceful and flexible. Despite his attentive coaching, I remained cardboard stiff and clueless.

"C'mon, Laurel, remember what I told you," he said. "Bend your knees and make your thighs do the work."

I glanced down at my thighs. Obviously, work wasn't included in their job description.

The mirror-lined walls of the Golden Hills Dance Studio reflected my image multiple times. Shoulder-length reddish-brown hair grazed my aqua V-neck sweater. Black tummy tuck jeans provided much needed slenderizing, and my brand-new silver shoes almost made me look like a dancer. Presentation is everything, especially when you have no clue what you're doing.

Frank Sinatra's version of "It Had To Be You," wafted from the speakers. Dimitry and Anya, a pair of instructors, glided by us, their synchronized movements mesmerizing to watch. I eyed them with envy. If I wanted to look as graceful as a gazelle, I had to stop charging around like a rhino on roller blades.

Bobby positioned himself with his head held high, shoulders down, right arm resting in the middle of my back. Per his instructions, I thrust out my chest, sucked in my stomach and tightened my butt.

"Let's do it," I said.

Bobby's soft tenor intoned the fox-trot count in my ear. "Slow, slow, quick, quick."

I repeated it to myself…slow, slow, quick, quick… ACK!

The stiletto heel of my right shoe slipped out from under me and I slid across the waxed floor, crashing into Dimitry and Anya with all the grace of a defensive linebacker. Bobby rushed over to assist me as I attempted to extricate myself from the tangle of arms and legs.

"Sorry." I shot an apologetic smile to the instructors.

As they rose to their feet, I overheard Dimitry refer to me as a "klutzsky." I had a feeling the words Anya muttered in Russian didn't translate into "nice dancing." The couple disappeared from the dance floor, probably in search of safer terrain.

My thirty-nine-year-old body hadn't done the splits in at least thirty-six years. With Bobby's assistance, I struggled to my feet.

"Are you okay?" My teacher's eyes had darkened with concern. Dance protocol recommends that you keep your partner upright, at least most of the time. I swayed to the right and discovered that my heel was no longer connected to my right shoe. One hundred fifty dollars worth of sexy silver stilettos down the proverbial drain.

"I'm okay, but my shoe isn't." I glared at the offensive

heel lying a few inches away. "Bobby, this just confirms I'm not meant to dance the wedding routine."

"No, all it confirms is that we need to practice more. Remember, you've only been dancing for a couple of weeks. Do you have other shoes you can wear to finish our lesson?"

I nodded. "I came right from work so I'll change into my black heels."

Bobby gave me a sympathetic hug and I waltzed—okay, I still didn't know how to waltz—so I clumped through the enormous dance studio toward the back of the building where the cloakroom and the studio owner's offices were located. As I walked past the office, I heard raised voices from behind the closed door.

Crack! The sound of a slap reverberated from the room.

Dimitry, the dance teacher I'd crashed into earlier, stormed out of the office, slamming the door behind him. His elegant hand didn't quite cover the scarlet mark on his high Slavic cheekbone. He scowled at me then rushed away.

This studio was proving to be more drama-filled than the daytime soaps.

I entered the cloakroom, dropped my broken overpriced shoes into one of the small cubicles assigned to footwear, slipped into my black faux leather pumps and headed back to the main dance floor for more fox-trot torture.

Forty uncomfortable minutes later, my private lesson with Bobby was over. My bunions ached and my toes hurt from being stomped on multiple times—by me.

I entered the cloakroom and exchanged smiles with an attractive dark-skinned student named Samantha. She zipped up her jacket, picked up her shoe tote, and exited the room. I buttoned my black leather jacket and grabbed my purse. That's when I discovered my dismembered shoes had disappeared. I looked inside every one of the tiny cubicles and pawed through the oversized gray wastebasket outside the door, in case someone had accidentally thrown them away. *Nada.*

My silver shoes had danced off without me.

I couldn't believe someone had taken them. Liz's wedding was only three weeks away and now I would have to buy a new pair instead of merely repairing one shoe. At this rate, I would need a second job to pay for the honor of serving as matron of honor.

As I left the studio and walked through the parking lot, my mind rapidly calculated my additional wedding expenses.

I barely noticed the pink and lavender cotton candy clouds stretched across the twilight sky.

I did notice the man lying on the ground, a pool of blood under his head.

My silver stiletto heel jammed into his mouth.

I definitely noticed him.

TWO

Screams erupted and I swiveled around to find Samantha and her friend Nanette standing behind me. Samantha's screams subsided to a whimper although her dark eyes remained huge and frightened.

"What happened?" asked Nanette, an elderly woman who also took private dance lessons with Bobby.

"I don't know. It's Dimitry. He's um, I think he's d-dead," I stammered.

"Are you sure? I'm a nurse. Let me check." The short, fireplug of a woman marched over to Dimitry, placed her fingers on his carotid artery, waited a few seconds then shook her head. "You're right. He must have hit his head. Hey, what the heck is this thing in his mouth?"

I reluctantly joined her for a better look. Although I had hoped to find my missing shoes, the last place I expected my broken heel to turn up was stuffed in a dead dancer's mouth.

"Do you think we should remove, um…it?" asked Samantha. She leaned forward but before she could touch anything I placed a hand on her arm.

"Leave everything alone until the rescue people get here," I said.

"I'll go inside and get help." Samantha ran back into the studio. I rummaged through my purse, grabbed my cell and dialed the emergency operator.

The dispatcher and I were still in conversation when a horde of dancers erupted from the studio. Within seconds, they surrounded the body. A tall, slender woman I recognized as Anya pushed through the crowd. Her turquoise satin halter top bared sculpted muscles. When she crouched next to the body, her short black skirt bared almost everything else.

"Dimitry, darling," Anya shrieked. Tears coursed down her cheeks as she lifted her arms to the darkening skies. The dancer extended the palms of her hands as gracefully as if she were performing in front of an audience.

In reality she was. At least fifteen people were now gathered around the body listening to Anya's lamentations as she rested her head on her dance partner's chest. The crowd pushed closer and I worried about getting trampled by the spectators. Suddenly the onlookers moved aside, making way for a short fair-haired woman whose T-shirt covered a bowling-ball sized belly, indicating she was at least ten months pregnant.

"Let me through," shouted Irina, Dimitry's wife and former dance partner.

Anya impaled the recent widow with a gaze so hostile the hairs on my arms stood up like rows of dominoes. The tall, svelte dancer rose and slid gracefully to her feet. Pivoting on one very long bronzed leg, she glided back in the direction of the studio.

Irina knelt next to her husband and placed her right palm on the victim's pale cheek. As she leaned in, my heart skipped a beat. How tragic. She was about to kiss her husband for the last time.

Or maybe not.

"You son of a…" she screamed. She plucked the silver heel from his mouth and threw it across the parking lot with the force and speed of a professional shortstop. It arced through the air, ricocheted off the lid of the Dumpster and landed in front of Nanette, who scooped it up and stuck it in the pocket of her jacket. Irina continued to berate her dead spouse in unintelligible Russian phrases, punctuated by an occasional American expletive.

Bobby, with the help of a dark-haired instructor named Gregor, finally dragged her away from Dimitry's body. Her diatribe against her dead husband grew fainter as the men forced her back into the studio.

The shrill cry of sirens announced approaching vehicles. A dirty white El Dorado County Sheriff's Department patrol car squealed to a stop alongside the curb on the main road. Two uniformed men jumped out of the car and hurried in our direction. Seconds later, an ambulance whizzed around the corner, its brakes working overtime. Two paramedics jumped out of the back and raced over to our gathered throng.

"Stand back. Give him some air," shouted the older short-haired deputy, a heavy-set guy whose face resembled a bulldog but without the charm. Nanette marched up to the officer, the gray bun on the top of her head not quite reaching his armpit.

"He doesn't need any air," she proclaimed. "I'm a nurse and I already checked. He is one dead dancer."

One of the paramedics crouched next to Dimitry. After a brief examination he nodded to his coworker, evidently agreeing with Nanette's determination.

"Who called the dispatcher?" the deputy asked, his platinum buzz cut gleaming under the lights of the parking lot.

I slowly raised my hand.

"Did you see what happened?" he asked.

I shook my head. "He was lying on the ground when I first spotted him."

So it *could* have been an accident. But the odds of my heel *accidentally* landing in his mouth seemed on the low side.

"Okay, people, I'm Deputy Katzenbach." Buzz Cut introduced himself then pointed to his younger, slimmer and cuter companion. "This is Deputy Montana. We'll be taking statements from every one of you. Wait inside the studio until we're ready." Groans and mutters ensued from the spectators.

"You. The one who found the body." Buzz Cut pointed his index finger at me. "Stay here by me."

I gulped and nodded. Montana, the young black-haired deputy, shepherded the rest of the audience back into the studio. Some of the dancers grumbled, while others trudged slowly and silently back into the building.

I gazed at their retreating backs and wondered if any of them were acting suspiciously.

How would I know if they were?

Deputy Katzenbach conferred with the rescue workers then gestured for me to follow him into the studio where pandemonium reigned and the noise level exceeded that of two three-ring circuses.

I contemplated the impact of the dancer's death on the studio. Dimitry was their star, the man who garnered first-place dance competition trophies by the dozens. Not to mention the new clients he brought in by the droves. His alluring topaz eyes, broad shoulders and muscled thighs attracted more female dance students than the other teachers combined.

Not that I'd noticed. Much.

I was taking lessons for one purpose only—to learn Liz's *perfectly orchestrated* wedding routine. She had commanded each member of her wedding party to first learn the fox-trot routine with a professional instructor. Then one of these days the entire bridal party would attempt to dance it together.

Hopefully before the wedding day.

The reality of Dimitry's death suddenly hit me. I blinked back tears and thought about the students who would be devastated by his loss. As I glanced around the room, I noticed one of his more accomplished students, Paula, a middle-aged brunette, sitting on the lobby sofa, attempting to comfort the pregnant widow.

Paula caught my eye and motioned me over. I tapped Buzz Cut on the shoulder. "Excuse me, Deputy Katzenbach. Can I—" My words were cut off by the crackle of his radio. The deputy turned and stepped a few feet away. He glared at me but didn't stop me from joining Paula and Irina. I walked over, perched on the couch's maroon crushed velvet arm and leaned in. "How's she doing?" I mouthed.

"She's in shock and so am I." Paula gently massaged Irina's back. The widow hunched over, her hands twisting a sodden handkerchief.

"I can't believe Dimitry is dead," Paula said in a low voice. Her eyes traveled up to a two-by-three-foot framed photo, which hung on the wall behind us. It displayed Dimitry and his dance partner locked in one of those intimate embraces evocative of the rumba, the sexiest of all the Latin dances. The pose was so suggestive, steam practically radiated from the photo.

Irina followed our gaze; her body stiffened. The widow had danced professionally with her husband both before and after they wed, but once she became pregnant the doctors insisted she stay off her feet, and specifically off the dance floor.

The man and woman in the erotic pose were none other than Dimitry and Anya, his new professional partner. Irina struggled to her feet. She attempted to climb on the sofa, but her enormous belly interfered with her ascent. She knelt on the soft cushions, grabbed hold of the padded back, and pulled herself up.

For a long moment the new widow stared at the picture of her deceased spouse as tears coursed down her cheeks. With her belly resting on the back of the sofa, Irina reached down and with difficulty removed one of her tiny size five shoes. Having borne two children myself, I could empathize with the swollen feet of a woman with an impending delivery date.

Smack. The heel of her shoe bounced off the framed photo, making direct contact with Dimitry's face. Her voice rose to a screech as she once again hurled invective at her deceased husband's image. Worried the glass might shatter, Paula and I ducked.

A sinewy arm reached out and plucked Irina off the sofa. She collapsed into the arms of the new arrival.

THREE

IRINA FLUNG HER ARMS AROUND the neck of Boris, the studio owner. Even hugely pregnant, the widow still looked tiny in the arms of the six-foot-five former championship dancer. He stroked her curly blond hair and murmured in her ear, their conversation so intimate it made me feel like an intruder.

I backed away into a rock-hard male body, stomping with full force on his shoe. I whirled around to apologize for mashing yet another dancer's foot. My heart catapulted up to my eyebrows when I realized my victim wasn't a dancer. It was Detective Tom Hunter, my ex-boyfriend, assuming someone you dated only two weeks could be identified as a boyfriend.

Two weeks emblazoned in my memory bank. And on my lips, because somehow between solving murders in San Francisco, and now here in El Dorado County, Detective Tom Hunter had mastered the art of kissing to perfection.

"Laurel, what are you doing here?" Confusion mingled with pain as he gazed at me with Godiva-brown eyes that made me contemplate something spicier than a box of chocolates.

I straightened my spine and attempted that suck-in-your-gut and lift-your-butt thing which brought me almost an inch closer in height to his six-foot-three frame.

"I'm taking a dance lesson. Are you here because of the, um…Dimitry?" My attempt to remain poised and collected failed as I choked up, once again picturing the poor victim lying in the parking lot.

Tom started to speak when Deputy Katzenbach's boom box voice cut him off. "Hey, Hunter, about time you got here."

"I just received the call, Deputy," Tom responded in a voice cooler than an Eskimo Pie. His eyes quickly scanned the room. "Have you interviewed everyone in the studio?"

Katzenbach shrugged. "Nah, we were waiting for the hotshot to arrive."

Tom's shoulders tensed. No love lost between these two. I attempted to sidle away, but Buzz Cut clamped his rib-roast-sized paw on my shoulder. "You'll wanna interview this gal first. She claims she discovered the body."

I bristled and reached up to shove Buzz Cut's hand from my shoulder when Tom removed it for me.

"Get me a list of names and contact numbers for everyone who was in and outside the studio tonight," he ordered the deputy in an authoritative but measured tone of voice. "Find out who can corroborate the presence of anyone else and during what time period."

Katzenbach jutted his bulldog jaw in my direction. "What about her?"

"She'll be questioned by me. Is there a private room I can use for interviews?"

"Yeah, Boris Gorsky, the owner of this place, said we can use his office." Katzenbach pointed to the rear of the studio. The deputy's gaze flickered back and forth between Tom and me.

He started, as if a lightbulb finally clicked inside his brain. "Hey, you two know each other."

Must have been only a forty-watt bulb. It certainly took him long enough.

"We've met," Tom snapped. "I'll interview Ms. McKay right now. Bring me that list as soon as possible."

Dismissing the deputy, Tom guided me a few steps toward Boris's office then paused. "Wait here a minute. I need to talk to Deputy Montana."

He strode to the other end of the room where the professional dancers were segregated. The young good-looking deputy sat next to two of the female instructors at one of the small tables lining the side of the studio. The women leaned forward, their hands moving in tandem in that graceful pose invented by Fred Astaire, the third finger positioned lower than the other three fingers.

I wondered how many of the students knew Fred had invented that style to disguise his overly large hands. As Liz, my bawdy British friend would say, "why would he cover up a bloody great asset like that?"

Montana held a thick yellow pencil in his right hand, evidently in an attempt to interview the witnesses, but he appeared so mesmerized by the glossy-haired beauties that I doubted he'd scribbled any notes on his pad. One of the women placed her palm on the deputy's right forearm. His face reddened and he dropped his pencil under the table. When his head popped up, he made eye contact with Tom Hunter. Montana jumped to attention with the alacrity of a young recruit.

This seemed like an opportune moment to call home and warn the kids I'd be late. I yanked out my cell. My sixteen-year-old daughter answered on the third ring. "Hi, Mom, what do you want?"

That's my daughter. All business. "I'm still at the studio, honey. There's been a…" A what? An accident? A murder?

"I can't hear you," Jenna said. "Too much noise in the background. Don't forget to bring home milk." The dial tone buzzed in my ear as my daughter terminated the call.

Brevity was the order of the day when it came to conversations with Mom. Especially if her boyfriend, Michael, was on the line. It was refreshing to see my studious daughter acting like a normal giggly teenager these days.

The last thing I wanted to do was inform the kids I'd discovered a body. Jenna still hadn't forgiven me for becoming involved in a murder investigation several months ago. It's tough enough surviving the teen years much less having one's mother considered a murder suspect.

I snapped my phone shut and dumped it back into my purse. The noise from across the room had increased in volume. Four females now demanded Tom Hunter's attention.

Anya was no longer wailing over Dimitry's demise. Instead, the gorgeous dancer perched on top of one of the tables, long legs crossed seductively, her left foot, encased in a copper satin sandal, moving to its own beat. Two other female instructors, Tatiana and Wendy, clad in minimalist dance attire of brightly colored abdomen-baring tops and gauzy black skirts, appeared more interested in ogling the detective than sharing relevant information.

Nanette was also trying to get Tom's attention but having little success amid the tall dancers. It would take more than a nudge from the elderly woman to distract the detective from the scantily clad females surrounding him.

Ouch! The stiletto point of Nanette's shoe jabbed the detective's foot, right above the leather of his cordovan loafers. Tom yelped, but she had definitely found a way to get his attention. Nanette reached into her pocket and handed something to him, which he dropped into a plastic evidence bag. She whispered into his ear and pointed across the dance floor at me.

Me? Why was she pointing at me? And what had she given him?

Tom's jaw tightened as he looked in my direction. Katzenbach approached the men, a brown paper lunch bag in his hand. The three officers moved away and held a mini confab as they looked at the item Nanette had given Tom. Then each peered into the bag. Katzenbach threw a suspicious glance in my direction, my definition of suspicious being a downright nasty look.

Deputy Katzenbach led Nanette away and Tom headed in my direction, the brown paper bag clutched in his left hand. Despite his forbidding expression, my body tingled with the anticipation his presence evoked.

Although stumbling over a body was *not* how I envisioned him coming back into my life.

"What's in the bag?" I asked.

"Evidence." His voice was curt and the hand pressed against my back wasn't as gentle as before. Tom propelled me down the corridor leading to the back office. He flicked on the wall switch illuminating four pale gray walls lined with framed photos of gorgeously attired female ballroom dancers, posed with… Hmmm.

All the photos featured Boris. I had never been in his office so I hadn't realized what an oversized ego the studio owner possessed. Despite his immense size, he was supposedly an amazing dancer, combining dexterity along with extraordinary strength.

Although Boris's muscles had turned a little flabby, as evidenced by his increasing girth. Possibly one too many piroshkies?

My stomach growled a visceral response to the visual of those tasty Russian dumplings. Tom pulled out one of the chairs for me then went around Boris's desk and sat in the owner's massive black leather chair. The detective shoved both hands through his thick chestnut hair. Despite my angst at being involved in another murder investigation, I couldn't help noticing he was letting it grow longer. It looked good on him.

My stomach grumbled again. "Sorry," I apologized. It was way past my dinner time.

"You can say that again," he muttered.

"What?" My stomach and I spoke at the same time.

"Laurel, what is it with you and dead bodies? I can't believe you were the one who found him. And that nurse, Nanette, insisted it couldn't be an accident because the victim had the heel of your shoe in his mouth. What the heck is she talking about?"

He frowned as his gaze slid down to my black pumps. "Please tell me you're not wearing shoes tied to a potential crime scene."

I rolled my eyes. Really, he could give me more credit than that. After our last experience, I was practically a pro when it came to crime scenes.

Not that that was anything to brag about.

I pointed at my Nine West heels. "These are my street shoes." He looked confused so I proceeded to explain.

"When we dance ballroom, we wear special shoes with suede soles. It helps us glide across the floor." At least it helped some of the dancers. It wouldn't matter if I danced in jogging shoes since I hadn't mastered that gliding thing yet.

"Okay, but tell me what this pair has to do with the victim?" Tom aimed the contents of the brown bag in my direction.

I glanced inside the bag. My silver dance shoes?

My blue contact lenses almost popped out of my eyes. "Where did you get them?"

"The crime scene guys found the bag in a Dumpster in the parking lot." He reached into his jacket pocket and pulled out the plastic bag I'd seen him holding earlier.

"Nanette pulled this heel out of her pocket and gave it to me. I still can't figure out how this pair of shoes is tied to the accident."

"Trust me, this was not an accident." I pointed to the broken heel in the evidence bag. "Someone crammed that heel into the victim's mouth."

FOUR

Tom smothered an expletive and glared at me. "Laurel, what have you gotten yourself into now? Back up and tell me everything."

"I was planning on it," I said, miffed, "but you didn't give me a…"

"Every. Last. Thing."

Fine. I shared every frustrating detail of my dance lesson, including crashing into the dance pros, and the disappearance of my shoe heel that magically reappeared in Dimitry's mouth. What I did *not* share was how devastated I was when the man facing me disappeared out of my life without a word.

I had reached the point where I'd discovered Dimitry's body in the parking lot when the door to the office slammed into the wall. Deputy Montana fell through the doorway, almost crashing into my chair. I half expected to see a bevy of female dancers in hot pursuit.

Tom frowned. "What's the problem, Montana?"

"The woman. The wife. Baby."

The wrinkles between Tom's brows formed parallel lines. He looked at me in confusion.

"Irina, the victim's wife, is pregnant," I clarified.

"Now. She's pregnant now," the deputy yelled. "I mean, she's having the baby now. Her water broke."

We jumped out of our chairs and reached the door at the same time. Tom politely gestured for me to go first, but once we reached the hallway, the two men in their rubber-soled shoes moved a lot faster than I could in my heels.

Irina's screeches of fury when she discovered her dead husband had been horrible. Her cries during labor were worse, resembling the hideous keening of some of the female singers tossed off *American Idol* during early tryouts. She reclined on the sofa in the reception area, her left palm pressed against her belly, her forehead covered with crystalline dots of perspiration.

Samantha leaned over the pregnant woman. The student grimaced but she let Irina squeeze her fingers as a powerful new contraction began. Nanette stood next to Samantha, scrutinizing her watch.

Waaaaagh! The high C emitted by Irina caused the mirrors on the walls to rattle.

"Less than a minute between contractions," Nanette announced. Her gray bun bobbed up and down with every word. "I think this critter's ready to pop."

Tom turned to Montana. "Where are the EMTs?"

The deputy looked panicked. He motioned to Tom and they withdrew from the group surrounding the widow. I didn't see any reason not to join them so I did.

"The ambulance just left," Montana said.

"Why didn't you have them turn around?"

The deputy's face reddened. "Because her husband is in the back. Of the ambulance. Sir."

Okay, now that's awkward.

Waaaaaaaaaaaagh! Irina increased her shrieks by a few decibels. I glanced at my own Timex watch. About thirty seconds since the last contraction. If memory from my own two labors served me correctly, Nanette was absolutely right. The baby was on his or her way.

Tom got on his cell, calling for another ambulance. He sent Montana back to interview the seven instructors who were huddled on the opposite side of the studio, waiting to be questioned. They were surprisingly quiet for a change. I eyed the svelte female dancers, doubting any of them had ever given birth.

Although I might be jealous of their gorgeous bodies. I was still trying to lose the weight I had gained with my last pregnancy.

Seven years ago.

The doors to the studio flew open. The sight of a pair of El Dorado county emergency technicians pushing a gurney brought a collective sigh of relief from everyone in the studio, except Irina.

"No!" She pushed the first EMT away when he bent over her. The other, older paramedic leaned in to assist his partner.

"Go away." She kicked at him, barely missing his chin.

"Hey." He jumped back a few feet for self-protection. Nice to know ballroom training would come in handy if I ever needed to assault anyone.

With her legs thrust apart, Irina pointed down at her belly. "I haff to poosh!"

Tom crouched next to the red-faced Rambo. His soothing voice settled her down. Nanette squatted next to him. Between them, they were finally able to talk Irina into walking down to Boris's office for some privacy. The two medical technicians followed at a safe distance.

It didn't look like there would be room for anyone else in Boris's office, not that anyone had asked for my assistance, so I collapsed in one of the chairs lining the perimeter of the studio. The two deputies were still taking statements. My gaze shifted from the row of teachers to the students sequestered together, waiting their turn so they could go home.

I shivered, realizing any one of them could be a killer.

My dark musings were interrupted by loud cheers coming from Boris's office, followed by high pitched wailing. The baby sounded like a miniature version of his or her mother.

Evidently, I wasn't the only one curious to see the new arrival. The female instructors ignored Montana's protests to stay in place and rushed to the office, hovering outside the door like a flock of brightly feathered exotic birds. The stiletto-heeled dancers blocked the doorway and I couldn't see into the room. My stomach rumbled with hunger as I wandered back into the main studio.

Anya's satin turquoise outfit glittered among the more somber clothing worn by the male instructors gathered together. She appeared to be the only female not interested in the arrival of the baby. An hour ago Anya had been sobbing over the dead man's body. Now she laughed and flirted with Yuri, another instructor, her arm draped familiarly over the handsome dancer's shoulder, her slender fingers stroking his thick, tawny-brown hair.

The sultry dancer's attention shifted suddenly to the entrance of the studio. She froze in place, staring at a tall, slim woman who was attempting to gain entry. The look of hatred that marred Anya's beautiful face brought the blood in my veins to a freezing halt.

Deputy Katzenbach appeared to be in a heated discussion with the new arrival. When the woman turned her head, I recognized the short stylish black hair and profile of Dana Chandler, the wife of the president of Hangtown Bank, my employer. Although we occasionally crossed paths in the ladies' room when the bank held its annual holiday party, we definitely did not travel in the same social circles.

Did she and Mr. Chandler take dance lessons at this studio? It was difficult imagining the short, rotund CEO ballroom dancing with his tall, elegant wife. What was even harder to visualize was the two of them attempting the rumba.

Either vertically or horizontally.

The clatter of a gurney on the wooden floor resounded throughout the studio, jerking me back to the present. The paramedics grinned as they conveyed their charge across the room. Irina waved one regal hand at her devoted subjects as she gazed lovingly at the newborn, swaddled in a white blanket, resting on her chest. Tom and Nanette both wore pleased expressions on their faces. There was nothing like the birth of a child to soothe the memory of a recent death.

Tom moved toward the front entrance, so I followed. I was hungry and tired and ready to go home. Surely he must be done with me by now. Dana slumped against the wall, a stunned expression on her face. Even from several feet away, Deputy Katzenbach's voice boomed as he chastised the new arrival.

"Listen, lady, I don't care if you're married to the President of the United States. We have a crime scene here and enough suspects to fill a football stadium. You can't come in, so go home and let us do our job."

Tom's tone of voice was less truculent, but equally firm. "I'm sorry, ma'am, but you can't enter the building. We'll be tied up for the next few hours interviewing everyone as it is. If you leave your name and number, I promise to call you tomorrow."

Dana straightened her shoulders and regained her customary regal posture. "Detective, I cannot understand why you won't let me share my thoughts about Dimitry's death."

"Yeah, Tom, you should listen to Dana," I interrupted as I joined them. The more information he possessed, the better for everyone. And the sooner I could go home.

"Laurel, it's nice to see you again but a shame we have to meet under such tragic circumstances," Dana said. "I've tried to share some important information with these gentlemen, but they don't seem to be interested."

"I'm sure Detective Hunter would be thrilled to hear anything you can share about this murder," I replied.

"Ladies, no one has determined this is a murder," Tom said, his face drawn. "Trust me. We'll be investigating all possibilities."

"I would certainly think you'd want to know about the letters Dimitry received," Dana replied.

"Letters?" Tom asked.

"Not just letters. Death threats."

FIVE

"WHAT DO YOU MEAN BY DEATH THREATS?" Tom guided Dana out of hearing range. After investigating me for four weeks and dating me for two, he should have known that wouldn't stop me from eavesdropping.

I ambled over, bent down and played with the back strap of my heel, adjusting the metal clasp as I listened in on their conversation.

"Dimitry received the first warning about three weeks ago. The note was typed on plain white paper and left in an envelope up front." Dana pointed in the direction of the reception desk.

"Did you see the note?"

"No, he told me about it."

"And the reason he confided in you?" The suspicion in Tom's voice was evident to me although Dana didn't seem to notice. Of course I'd been on the wrong end of his interrogations a time or two.

Marriage to a successful bank president must have honed her instincts because Dana paused for a moment as she contemplated her explanation. "Dimitry has been my dance instructor for over three years. We became friends—very good friends. He felt he could trust me."

Tom nodded his acceptance of the explanation. I tossed it around for a few seconds and decided to accept it, too. After only a few weeks of dance lessons with Bobby, I felt comfortable confiding in him, much like the personal relationship with my hairstylist.

"Dimitry received three different notes," Dana said. "Each one more threatening and disturbing than the previous one. He really freaked out when the third letter arrived."

"Did you see any of them?"

She shook her head. "He told me he tore the first one up, thinking it was merely a childish threat. The verbiage was vague. Something like, 'stop if you know what's good for you.' The second one was stronger, phrased more like 'this is the last time we're going to warn you.'"

"When he received the third note, the threat seemed far more obvious, is that correct?" Tom prompted with his gentle investigator voice. The one he used to catch his suspects unaware.

And his girlfriends.

"The third note said, 'you're a dead man.'"

"Was it in Russian or English?"

Dana paused for a minute, her expression perplexed. "I never thought to ask. I assumed it was in English." She placed her palm on his forearm and blazed a dentist-enhanced pearly white smile in his direction. "Excellent question, Detective."

Tom nodded, ignoring her. He was used to women simpering over him, flattering him, and plain throwing themselves at him. Must be tough trying to solve crimes when your female suspects are all chasing after you.

The heavy tread of a paunchy deputy halted their discussion. Katzenbach's expression was as frazzled as the khaki shirt threatening to escape from the regulation belt that couldn't quite contain his nonregulation-sized stomach. Under his breath, I heard him mutter something about, "crazy Sputniks."

Tom intercepted Katzenbach. "Are you talking about the Russian dancers, Deputy?" he asked him in a sharp tone.

"All they talk is gibberish. I can't figure out a thing they're saying. How am I supposed to know if they're telling the truth or not?"

The deputy once again reinforced my low opinion of him. I felt like telling him off, but decided it would be wiser to keep my comments to myself. In the few weeks that I'd taken lessons in the studio, I had discovered that the professional Russian dancers were smart, funny, and ferociously loyal to their friends.

Tom looked fried, but who could blame him? In less than two hours, he'd contended with a murder, a birth, death threats, and an ex-girlfriend. Tom motioned for Deputy Buzz Cut to follow him out of earshot of Dana and myself. She tapped her right foot while maintaining her graceful posture, either the result of her ballroom dance training, or twenty-plus years of community service.

This was probably the only opportunity I would have to chat with her alone. "Do you compete, Dana?"

She nodded. "A few years ago when our youngest entered college, I experienced empty nest syndrome. One night when I was watching *Dancing with the Stars,* I thought, why not? I certainly wasn't getting any younger. I took tap and ballet as a kid, but I'd always wanted to learn how to ballroom dance.

"You don't need to spread this around the office," Dana grinned at me, "but Gordon isn't exactly light on his feet. He has as much rhythm as a grizzly bear."

I visualized the portly president lumbering through the office. "I guess you don't need rhythm to run a successful bank, do you?"

"No, all you need is…" It must have dawned on Dana that she was fraternizing with the staff because she suddenly clammed up and started rummaging through her purse.

I glanced over at El Dorado County's finest. Deputy Katzenbach's expression had changed from frazzled to furious. The deputy squared his shoulders then strode to the back of the studio.

Tom turned back to Dana. "Mrs. Chandler, I'll contact you tomorrow regarding those warnings the victim received." He reached into the pocket of his charcoal slacks and pulled out a business card. "If you remember anything else, please call me at once. My cell number is on this card."

"Thank you, Detective. Dimitry's death is a tragic event, and I will do anything in my power to help you. As will my husband, of course. As President of Hangtown Bank, he has tremendous resources." She slipped the detective's card into an oversized Prada handbag that didn't look like it had been purchased from a street vendor, and gracefully exited the studio.

"So...dare I ask why Deputy Katzenbach looks so annoyed?" I asked the detective.

Tom grinned and my heart rate ratcheted up a few notches. The detective's presence was having a greater impact on my emotions than discovering Dimitry's body. I wasn't sure what that meant, other than I was more accustomed to dealing with dead bodies *than* lovers.

"Since the heel of your shoe was in the victim's mouth, Katzenbach decided you're guilty."

I blanched. "What do you think?" I asked, my voice barely audible.

"You're still a suspect but you aren't the only one." His expression was weary as he pointed to the remaining dancers waiting to be interviewed. "Not to mention the killer could have taken off before you found the body."

"Are you going to interview everyone here tonight?" Given the Russian dancers' volubility and poor English, the interview process could turn into an all-nighter. I glanced at the instructors. Gregor fidgeted in his chair, twirling his dark ponytail in his hands. Bobby sat next to him, solemn and watchful. Yuri and Anya had switched from the seductive rumba to a paso doble, far more suitable to the somber atmosphere in the studio. Dancing must provide a way for them to cope with the recent tragedy.

"Our goal is to interview every one of them." Tom sighed, undoubtedly thinking of the long night ahead for him.

"What about me?"

"You're free to go."

I blinked. "I am?"

Tom nodded. "I know where you work. Where you live. And where you're going to be Saturday evening."

SIX

NEVER DOUBT THE ENCYCLOPEDIC memory of a homicide detective. I'd almost forgotten the elementary school holiday program was scheduled for this Saturday. Tom's daughter, Kristy, and my son, Ben, were in the same second grade classroom. Despite their initial meeting, which consisted of a soccer confrontation between the super-sized little girl and my undersized son, they had formed a close friendship.

Since my interrogation was over, at least for now, I could head home. Paula stood in the reception area, a shiny gold key chain in her palm. Dimitry's talented student looked forlorn, a feeling I sensed most, if not all of his students would soon experience.

"Are they done with you?" I asked.

Paula nodded as she slung her large leather carryall over her shoulder.

"What an ordeal," I said.

Her lower lip trembled. "It's so horrible. I simply can't imagine dancing with another teacher."

Uh-oh. Was Paula implying she also had been involved in a romantic relationship with the deceased dancer? I was beginning to wonder if Dimitry spent more time practicing his hip thrusts in the bedroom than on the dance floor.

Paula noticed my questioning look and shook her head. "No, nothing like that. Dimitry and I are... I mean, we were, supposed to compete on New Year's Eve at the Holiday Ball in Lake Tahoe." She sniffed. "It's one of the biggest dance competitions in the country."

"What a shame you'll have to miss it. What level are you competing at?"

"In the Pro Am open gold division."

Impressive. The Pro Am division paired an amateur like Paula with a professional teacher. Competing in the gold category meant Paula had previously won first place in the lower bronze and silver levels.

"Wow. I didn't realize you were competing at that high of a level. What kind of dances do you perform?"

"All the International Standard dances."

I must have looked puzzled because she elaborated. "It's like American Smooth but with one extra dance."

"American Smooth?" These ballroom dancers spoke an entire language of their own.

She smiled and her eyes lit up. You could tell ballroom was her passion. "In American smooth you perform the fox-trot, waltz, tango, and Viennese waltz. International Standard is a European version of the same dances. The style is different because you always remain in a closed hold with your partner. You also perform one additional dance called the quickstep."

Quickstep? I didn't know what that dance entailed, but I was having enough problems with the "slow slow" concept of fox-trot. My clumsy feet would never catch on to something called quickstep.

"Why don't you compete with Bobby?"

Paula's keys clanged together as they dropped to the floor. She chuckled as she bent over and scooped them up. "Laurel, it's not that easy to switch partners. Plus Bobby has only been dancing five years himself. Dimitry and I have been practicing ten to twelve hours a week for the past three years trying to get me up to this level."

Ten plus hours a week? If I practiced that much I'd be as good as…

I looked down at my bunion-enhanced size nines. Nah. No amount of practice would turn me into Ginger Rogers. Or even Paula.

She sighed and went back to her key jangling. "I'll talk to Boris and see if he'll compete with me. Did you know he was a world champion ten years ago?"

I knew Boris had won some competitions, but not at that level. So those photos in his office did represent a successful dance career and not just an uber-sized ego.

The crime scene technicians were still hard at work in the parking lot, taking photos from different angles under bright floodlights. My eyes grew teary again. Even if the rumors were true and Dimitry cheated on his pregnant wife, the man did not deserve to die.

We arrived at my car. Paula and I hugged each other goodbye, females bonding through a tragic event. I remained deep in thought as I pulled out of the lot, my periwinkle Prius directly behind Paula's black Mercedes SUV. Based on her car of choice, Paula could easily afford so many private lessons.

My own lessons with Bobby cost fifty dollars an hour. As the top teacher in the studio, Dimitry charged seventy-five an hour. Paula must really be motivated to compete. If Liz hadn't insisted on paying for my private lessons, I wouldn't have been able to afford even one hour with my teacher.

Who would have thought when Liz and I met at college, two escapees from a drunken frat party, that twenty years later I would be dancing at her wedding. Although this time, I hoped my escort would skip the fringed lampshade on his head.

Liz and Brian had met through a local dating agency called the Love Club. I'd joined the same dating service with far less success but I was thrilled they had found one another. My best friend had waited a long time to find her Prince Charming and she deserved to live the fairy tale of "happily ever after."

As I drove home, I mulled over the events of the evening. Irina's furious response to her husband's bizarre death saddened me. Having suffered the pain and rejection of my ex-husband's infidelity, I could empathize with her in that respect. But her violent reaction seemed extreme by any standard. Was her anger merely the result of a hormone imbalance due to her pregnancy? Or was the fiery widow capable of killing her unfaithful husband?

Could a marriage go so wrong that one partner was willing to murder the other?

These negative thoughts swirled through my mind as I approached the house that my ex-husband, Hank, a contractor, had built shortly after Jenna's birth. Despite our marriage disintegrating more than two years ago, Hank had agreed that I should remain in the house where our children had been raised. Lately, it seemed like creaks and cracks were appearing in our home on a daily basis.

I twisted my head to the left to check for traffic and my neck creaked in response. My body was also starting to show its age. And I was still a few months shy of forty. Ballroom dancing was lauded for improving balance, brain acuity, and plain old weight control. I'd be thrilled if I could see improvement in any one of those areas.

Actually, I'd be thrilled if I could put my panty hose on while standing.

I pulled into the driveway of our Craftsman-style home, squeezed the car into our filled-beyond-capacity two-car garage, and entered the house through the connecting garage door. The hallway and kitchen were both dark. My children used to burn electricity with the willful abandon of millionaires, but now that they'd been taught the benefits of "going green," it was all I could do to get them to use a sixty-watt bulb in their bedrooms.

Ben's latest ploy to avoid doing homework was his claim that by not using electricity he was helping the environment.

Nice try, but his mother wasn't born yesterday. I hit the light switch, which illuminated the bright yellow kitchen walls. My rooster clock glared at me from its perch above the sink displaying the time as nine-thirty. Ben should be in bed, but Jenna was probably still up studying. My daughter was only a junior, but she had already decided she wanted to be an astronaut, or at least the first person to build a vacation home on the moon.

My seven-year-old just wanted to know if the man on the moon was bald.

I climbed the stairs then pushed open the door and peered into Ben's room. Beams of moonlight glinted on the posters lining his walls. Batman and Superman posters were intertwined with ferocious dinosaurs. A poster of a Tyrannosaurus rex hung over his bed. With its jaws wide open, the T rex looked poised to devour my son for a snack.

It never ceased to amaze me how Ben could sleep surrounded by creatures that were right out of *Jurassic Park*. He lay there breathing softly, hair tousled, deep in a young boy's sleep, his arm wrapped around his cat. There was no way I was going to disturb my son. Or Pumpkin. I'd never met a cat that slept less than Pumpkin, our newly adopted calico kitten.

Light beckoned from under Jenna's closed door. I knocked quietly then turned the knob.

The pink end of an eraser-tipped pencil grazed her upper lip as she gnawed on her lower lip. Her cornflower-blue eyes squinted slightly as she focused on the fine print of her textbook. It might be time to have her eyes examined in case she'd inherited my myopic genes.

"Hi, honey," I said softly.

She nodded without looking at me, the auburn tresses that curled halfway down her back swinging in unison with the movement of her head. When my daughter focused on a task, she wasn't easily distracted.

Good, I could drop the *D* bomb and she might not even notice. In the McKay household, the *D* word unfortunately meant "dead body." After my involvement in that murder investigation a few months ago, I felt obligated to disclose what happened at the studio tonight.

"Bobby and I worked on my fox-trot."

"Mmm-hmm."

"He said I could be the next Ginger Rogers."

"Mmm-hmm."

The next response would determine whether she was focused on her homework or her mother.

"I found a dead man."

"Mmm-hmm."

I closed her door and walked down to my own bedroom. That was way easier than I anticipated.

SEVEN

AFTER DREAMS OF DEAD DANCERS and tall dark detectives, I woke up Friday morning, my head pounding with questions. Had the detectives determined what happened? Would the entire studio be closed and considered a crime scene? Would I get out of my dance lesson on Saturday?

The most important question was whether my best friend would let a murder interfere with her carefully orchestrated wedding plans. I already knew the answer. A resounding no.

The doorbell pealed as I put the finishing touches on Ben's sandwich, an easy task which consisted of a swipe of grape jelly on one slice of whole wheat bread, and a slap of creamy peanut butter on another. Thank goodness for the simple taste buds of seven-year olds.

The front door slammed. I could think of only one person who would barge in this early on a weekday morning. As the muffled voices grew louder, my suspicions were confirmed. I shoved Ben's pathetic sandwich into his blue-and-red plastic Spider-Man lunchbox and snapped the lid shut. The last thing I needed was to be admonished yet again on my domestic skills. Or lack thereof.

"Morning, Mother. A little early for house calls, isn't it?" I pointed to the clock over the sink. "We have to leave in five minutes, and I'm running late."

"Of course you are, dear," she responded. "If you organized the children's lunches, wardrobe and homework assignments the night before, you wouldn't always be running late, would you?"

If I would stop discovering dead bodies, I would also have time to become more organized. I bit back a response, wondering if my mother had heard what happened at the studio the previous night.

Tom Hunter's former partner, Detective Bradford, whom I'd dubbed "Tall, Bald and Homely," had recently retired from the El Dorado County Sheriff's Department. Bradford and I had developed a mutual dislike of each other, which could either be attributed to his desire to incarcerate me for murders I did not commit, or the fact that he was now dating my mother.

Much as I hated the thought of my mother cavorting with the newly retired detective, she might have access to all kinds of supersecret sheriff stuff. My stomach churned as I visualized the two of them intimately sharing information. On a positive note, my mother seemed mellower since they'd started dating. She was no longer the uptight woman who had harassed me my entire life.

A sudden roar disturbed my reverie. It appeared that my uptight mother hadn't totally turned over a new leaf. The buzz of the dust buster drowned out further conversation as my powerful minivac inhaled a few scattered bread crumbs from the floor.

How many women do you know who scoop up dust bunnies while clad in a designer black wool suit, pearl necklace and pearl earrings? Wearing three-inch heels?

I snatched the dust-busting machine out of her hands, clicked it off and yelled at the kids to hurry up. "Mother, we have to go. Did you come here for a reason? Or is annoying your daughter on today's to-do list?" The minute the words left my lips, I felt bad. My mother meant well but she always made me feel like an incompetent child.

She flicked a speck of dust off her sleeve. "Judging by the looks of this place, I should drop in every morning. One of your neighbors is listing her house with me. I thought I'd stop by before I met with her and spend a few minutes with my grandchildren."

She raised an eyebrow. "And perhaps find out why my daughter is a murder suspect once again."

I felt my cheeks turning rosy. "Oh, yeah, about that. Did your, um…did you hear about it from Bradford?"

Now it was my mother's turn to blush and my turn to chuckle. It was kind of sweet that my sixty-two-year old widowed mother had found romance once again.

Although why she settled on that crotchety former detective was beyond me.

Mother grabbed a sponge from the sink, dampened it and began wiping down the white tile counters. Sigmund Freud would have a field day with her. Was her attempt to expunge stray crumbs from the counter reflective of her desire to tidy up her daughter's messy life?

She rinsed the sponge, flicked the faucet off then turned to face me. "Robert said someone died at the dance studio last night and you were involved. I was worried about you, sweetheart. What happened?"

I looked at the clock. Two minutes until departure time.

"A Russian dancer at the studio was murdered. Well, probably murdered. I had nothing to do with it and… Hold on." I ran to the foot of the stairs. "Ben, Jenna, now!"

"Do you think you're a suspect?"

"I have no idea. But my shoe may be the murder weapon."

Before she could ask me to explain my cryptic comment, the melodious tones of two siblings engaged in conversation erupted from the staircase.

"Twit," Jenna yelled.

"Fathead," her baby brother shouted back.

I waited for the refrain.

"Mom," they shrieked in unison as they burst though the doorway.

Ah, the joys of parenting. Mornings like this made stumbling over a dead body seem like a minor inconvenience in comparison.

"Ben destroyed my calculus homework." Jenna threw a crumpled piece of lined paper at her brother. It bounced off his chest and floated to the floor like a wounded bird.

My young son graced me with an impish smile, the one he used on his mother when he knew he was in trouble. "I was practicing origami. We learned it in school yesterday. I can fix it." He picked up the paper and attempted to smooth out the wrinkles.

Jenna grabbed it out of his hand. The sound of ripping paper reverberated through the kitchen. She stuffed the torn homework in her backpack and screamed at Ben, threatening to cram him in there next.

We would never make it in time for my errant son to catch the school bus. My mother's maternal instincts kicked in. Whether it was her desire to assist, or merely prove once again that she is a superwoman, Mother grabbed Ben, his Spider-Man lunchbox and his quilted parka, and marched him to the front door. "Laurel, I can drop Ben off at school and still get back in time for my listing appointment."

I breathed out a sigh of relief. "Thanks, Mom."

I shook my finger at my son. "Young man, I'll deal with you tonight."

Mother zipped Ben's jacket and turned to me. "I'll also do a little research into that matter we were discussing earlier."

We exchanged conspiratorial smiles, all mother/daughter angst forgotten. Sometimes my mother can be the most annoying woman in the world, but she always comes through in a crunch.

The drive from Jenna's beautiful woodsy campus to Main Street in Placerville was a quick ten-minute trip. The quaint gold rush town, formerly known as Hangtown, is the headquarters of my employer. During the gold rush, the local townsfolk took advantage of two huge California oaks to eliminate a few pesky troublemakers. Now the town is simply known as Placerville, named after the placer deposits of gold found in the hills.

Hangtown Bank was a gold mine itself. Owned and run by a local family for over one hundred years, the bank concentrates on bringing in deposits from foothill residents and using those funds to make home loans. Management eschewed the crazy loans that had brought down the mega banks and Wall Street investment firms a few years earlier.

Thanks to their conservative but gold-plated investment strategy, the bank recently received the distinction of number-one-rated bank in the entire state of California. Not bad for a family-owned lending institution.

I flung open the double glass doors at eight on the dot. Vivian, our surly fiftyish receptionist, was hooking on her headset. I saluted the seven-foot-tall burled wood bear the president moved into the lobby upon the request of his wife. Rumor had it Mr. Chandler originally purchased the bear for their house. He might know how to run a bank, but interior decorating was *not* his forte.

"Good morning, Vivian." I smiled and gave her a cheery wave.

Vivian snarled her good morning. When it came to ferocity, she and the bear could be soul mates. The tellers were already readying their cash drawers for the onslaught of bank customers. I strolled down a hallway lined with wildlife photos taken in the Sierra Mountains, then past a few gray tweed cubicles, until I reached my own workstation.

A few years after Ben's birth, my ex-husband's income as a contractor was sufficient for me to quit my manager position at one of the bank's branches. Two years later, when Hank decided it was more fun to nail his *client* than nail her shingles, we split up. At that point, the only available position in the bank was mortgage underwriter, but I was thrilled to have a job again. Before the ink on the divorce papers dried, I re-entered the workforce—another single working mom.

I threw my purse into my desk drawer. My phone rang and I mumbled a hello into the receiver.

"Are you trying to ruin my wedding? Why did *you* have to find a dead man?" shrieked the bride-to-be. "The sheriff cordoned off Golden Hills Dance studio so we can't rehearse tomorrow. What bloody bad luck!"

"Ah, Liz, considering the circumstances, you could be less callous about the situation."

Her sigh echoed over the phone. "You're right, luv. You don't think I'm turning into one of those Bridezillas, do you?"

Liz is my best friend. Who was I to tell her she had passed the Bridezilla stage weeks ago? My girlfriend had waited until she turned forty before she agreed to tie the knot with her perfect man, Brian Daley, an El Dorado County Assistant District Attorney. And the perfectionist whose friendship I'd cherished for over twenty years would accept nothing less than perfection when it came to her special day. Fortunately, Brian was more than happy to accommodate his fiancée with her fairy-tale wedding.

I quickly reassured her. "The studio shouldn't be closed for long. Dimitry was found in the parking lot so I doubt they'd need to keep the inside of the studio off-limits for more than a day or two. Once they search the place for clues… Omigod."

"What is it?"

"I remembered an argument I overheard between Dimitry and someone else halfway through my lesson. I forgot to mention it to Detective Hunter last night."

"Tom Hunter was there? Do tell. Did you want to melt into his arms when you saw him?"

Maybe. A little. "Nope, it was all business between us."

She snorted. "As in monkey business?"

"No. As in murder business."

"You better not be a suspect. We don't have time for that."

Like I did?

"Did you hear that the broken heel of my right shoe was stuffed into Dimitry's mouth? The sheriff's department confiscated both shoes. There's no way I can afford to buy another pair."

"Eeuw. Brian didn't tell me all of the details. Gross." She paused for a minute to ponder the implications of my bridesmaid apparel being taken into official custody. "The wedding is more than two weeks away. If they return your shoes, you can superglue the heel back on."

"Superglue the stiletto heel someone shoved in a dead man's mouth?"

Liz either needed a copy of Miss Manner's book on wedding etiquette or D. P. Lyle's guide to forensics.

"Okay, maybe that's not the best option. Don't worry. We'll come up with something. Can you meet me here at the spa? We have so much left on our to-do list."

We agreed to meet on Monday for lunch at the yummy health-conscious café in her beautiful Golden Hills Spa. Then I hung up the phone and laid my head down on the one and only uncluttered spot on my desk.

Our to-do list?

I could barely "to-do" my own maternal and professional activities these days. If you added in shopping for Christmas presents, attending the kids' various holiday events, and baking cookies for the annual holiday exchange, three weeks was not enough time to get ready for Liz's New Year's Eve wedding.

The ring of the phone interrupted my ten-second pity party. Probably Liz with an addendum to her to-do list.

"What now?" I barked into the receiver.

The voice on the other end barked back a response. A baritone response.

"Ms. McKay," said Mr. Chandler, the bank president. "Come to my office."

My bark was reduced to a mouselike squeak. "Now?"

"Now." The phone slammed in my ear as the president of the bank ended our conversation.

Could this also be the end of my career?

EIGHT

As I TRUDGED UP THE STAIRS TO the second floor where the executive offices were located, I racked my brain trying to think of any loan files I might have screwed up. One bad loan could significantly impact the bank's bottom line. Was I in danger of being fired over a poor underwriting decision?

By the time I reached the executive level, my spirits had sunk lower than my heels that were sinking into the plush gray carpeting. The management team worked out of large glass-fronted offices, furnished with mahogany desks and matching credenzas. Black-and-white framed prints of scenes from nineteenth-century Placerville were hung along the hallway. I paused to examine a photo of former President Ulysses S. Grant ambling along Main Street. Back in the day, this town was quite the burg. Unfortunately, the former general and president had no advice to share this morning.

Belle, Mr. Chandler's assistant, frantically waved at me to hurry up. It was time to face the big boss. I thrust back my shoulders, pasted a suck-up smile on my face, and entered his spacious office. The short, portly, silver-haired president stood up from behind his massive desk and gestured to one of the navy tweed visitor chairs. I settled nervously into the uncomfortable and undoubtedly pricey seat, in a pose I'd perfected whenever I landed in trouble in school—hands demurely folded, legs crossed at the ankles.

Mr. Chandler lowered his charcoal-gray pin-striped frame into an oversized leather executive chair. His desk was not only totally devoid of the clutter that covered every inch of my own desk, it was devoid of anything. No papers, pens, or mugs. An ocean of shiny mahogany stretched between us.

"Ms. McKay, I understand you've stumbled over yet another...corpse."

"I didn't stumble over it, I mean him, that is Dimitry..." I said, flustered. "I strolled by and he was lying there. Dead." My hands fluttered hopelessly as I tried to explain the circumstances in a more cogent manner. Not an easy task when confronted by the big boss.

Mr. Chandler cleared his throat. "Yes. You seem to have a knack for that, don't you?"

I stared at my nails, most of which were chewed down after last night's ordeal. Normal people develop a knack for knitting. Writing. Painting.

How come I have a knack for finding dead bodies?

"I guess Dana, I mean Mrs. Chandler, told you what happened to Dimitry."

"My wife was most distressed. Ballroom dancing is her passion. Or at least her latest passion." He frowned again. I couldn't tell if the frown was directed at me, at Dana, or at her latest hobby.

"As you can imagine, I am not pleased with your involvement in another unseemly incident," he said, his expression not masking his displeasure. "It was difficult enough explaining to the board when you became embroiled in that fraud scheme two months ago."

Hold on. I was the one who saved the bank from being

defrauded. Not to mention the perpetrator tried to murder *me*.

"Our board of directors would be quite displeased should the bank's name be mentioned in regard to this little matter. Don't you agree, Ms. McKay?"

Hmmm. I agreed that the board probably wouldn't want the bank mentioned in conjunction with a murder, but was Mr. Chandler implying the life and death of a dancer didn't equate in importance to the life and death of a bank?

I stared at my hands, worried that I might say something that would get me into more trouble. "No, sir. I mean, yes, sir."

"Good. I can see we're on the same page. I'm relieved to know you will not risk the bank's reputation, again, by interfering in areas not of your concern." He stood up, still unsmiling, and gestured toward the door. The meeting was over.

I stood and exited the office, not sure whether to be angry or relieved. What a weird meeting. He might think we were both on the same page but I wasn't sure we were reading from the same book.

Belle was away from her desk but she might know what her boss was alluding to because I didn't have a clue. I grabbed a lime-green pad and scrawled a message asking her to call me later. Her phone already held a sticky note so I stuck mine next to the other one.

The writing on the other note was barely legible. It read, "*schedule meet Det Hun.*" A phone number was scribbled below. A cell number unrecognizable to most people, but which was easily identifiable to someone who had dated Detective Hunter.

So Tom had called the president. Did that mean he was checking up on me? Dana? Mr. Chandler? Or maybe it meant nothing at all. Tom was active with several local charities. He could have been soliciting the bank for a donation.

Yeah, right. And I didn't have two left feet. I knew what he was up to. There was an investigation afoot.

I ran down the stairs and turned the corner. Smack into my underwriting assistant, the man who thought of himself as the Watson to my Holmes. Although it was more like the Hardy to my Laurel.

"Sorry, Stan, you okay?"

"Fine. What about you? I heard you received a summons from El Presidente." Stan looked concerned, as any responsible underwriting assistant would. "Did we screw up any loans?"

"Nope. He wanted to discuss Dana and her dance partner."

We reached my cubicle, and Stan dumped several four-inch-thick loan files on my desk. He dropped into my visitor chair, crossed his khaki-covered legs, and pushed his wire rims up his pointy nose. The soft gray eyes behind the clear glass lenses looked puzzled.

"Mr. Chandler called you up to his office to talk about his wife and her dance partner? Do I detect some yummy gossip?" Stan's eyes popped out in anticipation of a little bank dirt.

"Of course not. Dana would never lower herself to have an affair with Dimitry. Not that it's even possible."

"Is Dimitry gay? Can you introduce me to him?" My assistant rubbed his hands in anticipation. "Most of those ballroom guys are so straight. What a waste."

"Sorry, Dimitry is unavailable. Permanently."

"Hey, nothing in life is permanent except death and taxes." He snorted then his eyes met mine. "We're not talking taxes here, are we?"

I shook my head.

"So this Dimitry guy is dead?"

I nodded.

"Tell me you didn't find him?"

What could I say? In the words of our fearless leader, I have a knack.

NINE

BY EIGHT O'CLOCK THAT EVENING, I discovered that while
I have a knack for finding dead bodies, I do not have
a knack for designing costumes, particularly costumes
that involve the design and construction of fake antlers.
Mangled wire hangers littered the family-room floor. Discarded pieces of misshapen brown felt were stacked in a
raggedy pile at my feet. On top of the pile rested Pumpkin, the Halloween-hued kitten my ex had given the kids.
The jury is still out as to which of the two creates more
headaches for me. The cat, or my ex.

A flash of blinding headlights illuminated the room. It
was too late and too cold for anyone to be out selling mag-
azine subscriptions. Her highness must be making a house
call. For once, I was pleased at my mother's predilection
for unannounced visits. If anyone could design reindeer
headwear, she could.

The front door creaked open. Number 23 on my to-do
list. Buy some WD-40. The sound of my mother's trilling
laugh was off-putting. She never trilled alone. The deep
voice resonating from the entry immediately confirmed
my suspicions. So did the knots that formed in my stomach. Mother had arrived with her boyfriend, Tall, Bald,
and Homely. And Crabby. And Suspicious. His negative
traits could fill an entire chapter.

I still couldn't figure out what my classy mother saw
in the man. He wasn't anything like my sweet, perpetu-
ally cheerful father, the wonderful man who had died too

soon, leaving behind a young widow to raise two children alone. I wished my brother didn't live 2,500 miles away in Hawaii. He'd have Bradford out of my curly hair and out of my mother's life in no time.

Bradford and Mother sauntered into the family room holding hands. Pumpkin took one look at the happy couple and dashed out of the room. Smart cat.

My mother's face glowed and she looked a decade younger than her sixty-two years. As I studied her smiling visage, my stomach slowly unclenched. Was my dislike for Bradford really due to the way he tormented me during the murder investigation? Or did memories of my beloved father keep me from accepting their relationship?

Or something darker? Could I be envious that her relationship with *her* detective lasted far longer than my relationship with *my* detective? I pushed those somber thoughts aside for another day when I would have sufficient time to lie on a couch and let a Jungian therapist solve my maternal issues.

I untangled my legs and stood up. Ouch. My thighs ached from sitting cross-legged on the carpet. "What brings you here so late?"

"We have some important news—what on earth are you making?" She bent over and picked up one of the jagged-edged scraps, dangling it from her fingertips.

"The students in Ben's class are supposed to dress up like reindeer," I replied, "at least from the head up. You're going to the concert tomorrow night, aren't you?"

"Of course. You know I wouldn't miss one of my grandchildren's performances." She grabbed a hanger, a piece of fabric and the stapler. Within seconds, sturdy brown felt antlers appeared out of nowhere. Barbara Bingham, the Houdini of home-made magic and childhood memories.

"There you go." She handed the felt masterpiece into

my less-than-capable hands then joined Bradford, who stood leaning against the doorway.

"Can I get either of you anything?" I forced a smile at the grim-faced former detective. Even though he was retired, he probably maintained his contacts within the sheriff's department. He could be a useful ally if Dimitry's death was officially declared a murder and I officially became a murder suspect. Again.

Bradford shook his head, but my mother smiled. "We have some wonderful news to share with you and we brought a bottle of champagne to celebrate."

"News?" For a minute I was puzzled then I grinned in relief. "Oh, you must mean I'm off the hook. Not a suspect in Dimitry's murder. That *is* an excellent reason to celebrate. Thanks, Bradford. I don't think I could survive another murder investigation."

He snorted. "I don't think the sheriff's department can survive another murder investigation if you're involved. But that's their problem."

Mother's arched brows joined together as she directed one of her royal-highness looks his way.

His face reddened. "Sorry."

"This has nothing to do with the murder, dear," she replied.

"So what's the big news?" And why were her hands flailing in the air like a novice orchestra conductor?

Oh, crap. The lights in my ceiling fixture illuminated something shiny on her left hand. To be specific, the fourth finger of her left hand. I grabbed my elegant mother by her elegant wrist and zeroed in on the two-carat diamond blinding me with perfectly cut prisms of light.

If the diamond had been residing on any other hand, I would have been mesmerized by the beauty and simplicity of the emerald-cut setting. Instead, my jaw dropped to my knees and I fell into the sofa cushions. "But, you barely know each other," I said.

Awkward seconds passed as I tried to eke out my congratulations but I just couldn't do it. The creak of the front door brought the arrival of my kids and an end to my silent agony. The babble of my two garrulous children, who had attended a holiday party at one of the neighbors, grew stronger as they approached the family room. "Is Grandmother here? Her car is in the driveway."

Ben catapulted into the room ahead of his sister. He immediately raced to the big man's side. "Hey, Detective Bradford, what's up?"

Bradford's face lit up at the sight of my young son. They bumped knuckles *mano a mano*.

"Did you bring it?" Ben squealed as he bounced up and down. Bradford reached into his pocket and pulled out a shiny brass object. He handed it to Ben. My son's eyes grew wide when he realized he held an official sheriff's department badge in his hand. He wrapped his arms around the detective, thanking him profusely. Since Bradford is almost six foot six that meant Ben was hugging the detective's tree trunk-sized thighs. Bradford's smile was a sight to behold. What happened to the crotchety detective I was acquainted with? And when had these two become bosom buddies?

Jenna ambled into the room. Her eyes zeroed in like a laser beam at the large diamond glittering on her grandmother's finger.

"Wow, nice rock. Way to go, Bradford."

"Isn't it lovely?" Mother said. "Robert has such excellent taste." She smiled at her darling granddaughter. At least one family member appreciated precious gemstones.

"Hey, can I be in the wedding?" Jenna asked.

Wedding? I had barely absorbed the news that my

mother was engaged. My brain hadn't processed the fact that an engagement normally led to an official ceremony.

"Of course, you can be in the wedding," Mother responded. "In fact, I want all three of you to participate in the ceremony. Why don't we go into the kitchen and discuss some of the details. Ben, you come, too. I brought some of your favorite cookies."

The three of them disappeared, leaving Bradford and me alone in sullen silence.

Bradford eyed me warily. He must have realized I wouldn't be thrilled to have him become a member of our close-knit family. My stomach clenched when I realized the detective would soon become my stepfather.

"Um…congratulations," I mumbled.

He pointed to the sofa. "Laurel, sit down. I need to discuss something with you."

I reluctantly moved, sitting as far from Bradford as possible, not easy considering that the oversized detective took up half the sofa. Years of service with the sheriff's department had etched deep Shar-Pei lines in his face. I could not understand the attraction he held for my mother. She, on the other hand, was obviously a catch for him.

"I realize you're…not pleased with our news, but you need to know how much I care for your mother. I've never met anyone as intelligent, gracious and thoughtful as Barbara. And for some strange reason, she's in love with me, hard as it is to believe." He smiled ruefully. "For either you or me."

His smile seemed sincere and so did his sentiment.

I shook my finger at him. "You better treat her the way she deserves. Otherwise you'll have me to contend with."

"Trust me, I know. You're as relentless as a pit bull."

"Uh, thanks." Was he complimenting or criticizing me?

"It's going to take tenacity and teamwork to get you through the coming weeks."

I sighed in agreement. "This wedding is going to be difficult for me."

"I'm not talking about the wedding. Guess whose shoe was officially declared a murder weapon?"

TEN

So much for a quiet Friday evening. My heart rate ratcheted up to Mach 1 levels as the detective's comment sank in. Bradford's revelation put my mother's announcement in perspective. A wedding is a joyous occasion. Involvement in a murder? Not so much.

As my heart rate slowed back down, the wheels in my brain churned faster.

"Okay, I know my broken heel was found in Dimitry's mouth, but that didn't necessarily mean my shoe killed him. How did the lab guys figure out how he was killed? Did someone whack him with the sole?"

Bradford shifted uncomfortably on the cushions. My sofa wasn't built for men his size. Neither was my mother's dainty Chippendale furniture. Did their impending marriage mean that a pair of matching Lazy Boys was in her future?

Focus, Laurel.

"The shoe with the missing heel wasn't the weapon. It was your other shoe," he said. "The base of the stiletto heel still had traces of blood on it, which the crime scene guys identified as the victim's. And the shape of the heel matched the size of the wound. According to the Medical Examiner, Dimitry may not have died immediately from the impact. He could have walked away and later lost consciousness as pressure from the trauma built in his brain."

"So someone might have hit him in the studio. Then

he could have walked out to the parking lot, not realizing how severe his injury was?"

Bradford lifted his bushy eyebrows. "Excellent deductive reasoning. Or is there something you need to share with the authorities?"

I held up my hands in protest. "Not me. I know nothing. So the person who assaulted Dimitry might not have intended to kill him. Do you think it was an accident?"

"I don't think anything. I'm retired, remember?" He sighed and glanced in the direction of the kitchen, where we could hear mom and the kids giggling. "Your mother was worried about you being a suspect yet again, so she asked me to ferret out whatever information I could get from Hunter."

I slumped back into the sofa cushions. Bradford's news was not improving my mood.

"Since your shoe appears to be the murder weapon, *you* are unfortunately a person of interest." He paused a moment in thought. "I have to ask, was there any reason why you wanted to hurt this guy?"

"Of course not. I barely knew him. Our only actual contact came that day when I collided with him and Anya during my lesson. Dimitry yelled some Russian obscenities at me and called me a klutzsky. That's not a reason to murder someone and he's certainly not the first person to tell me I'm a klutz."

Bradford's shoulders shook; he appeared to be biting back laughter. Wise move. I gnawed on my thumbnail. Where were Mother and the kids with those cookies? If I didn't have something edible to chew on while I worried about this latest revelation, my few remaining fingernails would be history.

Our mother-daughter telepathic communication appeared to be in working order. Jenna walked into the family room bearing a plate of iced snickerdoodle cookies. The scent of cinnamon and sugar provided a much-needed lift for my flagging spirits. My mother carried three crystal flutes brimming with champagne on an embossed silver tray—since it came from my kitchen, it was a cheap aluminum tray. Ben handled the heavy lifting. A cookie in each hand.

Mother smiled at Bradford and me. "You two seem to be bonding."

"Bonding over bodies," I replied without thinking.

Ben's intermittent bionic hearing kicked in. "Bodies?" he squealed. "Dead ones?"

Jenna dropped the plate of cookies on my glass-topped coffee table. The china plate hit the table with a clunk, sliding across the slick glass before landing on the floor. Snickerdoodles splattered everywhere.

"Jenna!" I bent down, scooping up crumbled cookies and chunks of vanilla icing before our kitty appeared in search of dessert.

With her arms crossed over her chest, my daughter shot me a look that would have scared a lesser woman. "Mom, are you involved in *another* murder?"

My opinion of my future stepfather elevated a few notches when he jumped into the fray in an attempt to calm my infuriated daughter. He unfurled his massive body from the sofa and put an arm around her shoulders. "Jenna, you have nothing to worry about. Your mom happened to be at the dance studio when someone got hurt and later died. It's merely a coincidence."

She narrowed her eyes at me. "Okay, if you say so. But you know how she is. Before you know it, Mom will think she has to find out who done it, and some crazy dude will be chasing after her and trying to kill her. Again."

Tears welled in her eyes as she dropped to her knees and

started rounding up the scattered cookies. "Sorry, Mom," she mumbled as she stood, apologetic but still fearful. I could see it in her eyes and in the tenseness of her body.

"It's okay, honey." I brushed my lips against her pale cheek and held her close to me. "Your reaction is completely understandable. Like Bradford said, I unfortunately happened to be in the wrong place at the wrong time. Wearing the wrong shoes."

"Huh?"

"Believe it or not, one of my dance shoes was the murder weapon."

She stared at me in disbelief. "Promise you'll stay out of trouble."

I nodded, expecting another lecture, but she merely tilted her head. "Otherwise Grandmother and I will have to ground you."

Her comment brought a round of laughter. I grabbed one of the flutes from the tray and offered a toast to the happy couple. After a few sips of excellent champagne, I started to mellow. Maybe Bradford wasn't such a terrible person after all. Perhaps we just got off to a bad start when he investigated me.

Ben stayed glued to the retired detective's side, playing with his shiny gold official sheriff's badge. My mother watched the two males, her eyes shining with love.

She obviously cared deeply for the man. My daughter appeared to respect him. It wouldn't hurt to have a former detective on my team.

Especially when a shoe-stealing murderer lurked out there.

ELEVEN

SATURDAY MORNING I AWOKE WITH a hammer pounding in my head and a blender churning in my stomach. When would I learn that my body couldn't handle the intoxicating bubbles of champagne? Even if I only drank one or two glasses.

Or was it three?

After a breakfast consisting of coffee, toast and four aspirin, Ben and I took off for our usual Saturday whirlwind of domestic chores, including the purchase of a new pair of shoes for him. My son didn't need to advertise our pathetic financial condition by standing on stage wearing dingy gray frayed sneakers.

Our shopping trip was a huge success and by 5:30 Ben was dressed for the performance in a red cotton shirt, beige cords, and his new black Nikes, decorated with glow-in-the-dark reflectors. I almost talked him into a forest-green vest dotted with reindeers, but he refused on the grounds it might incriminate him as a dork.

Mrs. Saddlebeck, Ben's second-grade teacher, had requested that parents drop the students off an hour before the seven o'clock performance. During the brief ten-minute drive to his school, Ben serenaded me with every verse of "Rudolph the Red-Nosed Reindeer." Twice.

The corridors of the elementary school bustled with children. The younger girls dressed in holiday attire. Ruby, emerald and sapphire velvet dresses trimmed with lace and ribbons, over white tights and shiny black patent leather shoes.

The older girls sported pastel-colored T-shirts, a significant number bearing the likeness of Justin Bieber, worn over short black skirts. Even ten-year-olds have discovered that black is slimming.

Ben and I strolled into his classroom, hand in hand. *Bedlam* was too tame of a word to describe the noise emanating from the room. Mrs. Saddleback, whose smile appeared freeze-dried on her face, seemed oblivious to the antlers flying over the scratched oak desks. Ben raced into the room, his own homemade head-gear poised for flight.

Before he could propel his antlers across the room, I grabbed his arm and brought him to a halt. "Stop right there, young man. I have too much time and material invested in your costume. Find something constructive to do."

Ben crossed his eyes at me then plopped the antlers back on his head where they belonged, at least for the next two hours. He sauntered to the back of the room where a couple of girls, one tall, one small, were chatting and giggling. The tall girl with the pixie cut waving her hand at me was Kristy, the tow-headed daughter of Detective Hunter.

I waved back, wondering if Kristy's father was in the vicinity, or if her grandparents had brought her to this event. The widowed detective tried to attend as many school functions as possible, but the life of a homicide investigator didn't allow much time for extracurricular activities.

Particularly extracurricular activities that involved dating. As a single mom, I agree that kids come first. I only wished he could have found time to include me in his life. Or at least explain why he stopped calling. Our children didn't object to us dating. Kristy liked me and Ben thought Detective Hunter was one awesome dude.

Ben's mom thought he was, too.

I left the classroom and walked into the gym, determined not to demean myself by looking around for Tom Hunter. Halfway up the bleacher steps, my neck started to prickle. As if someone was staring at me. I looked to the left and then to the right. There he sat. Two rows up.

He crooked a finger, causing my heart to palpitate and my feet to stumble.

I missed the next step and landed on all fours, scraping my right hand on the rough wooden stairs. Crimson droplets oozed out of the tiny cut at an alarming rate. Within seconds, the detective stood next to me, holding my wounded palm in his large callused one.

"See what you made me do." My hands verbalized my frustration by fluttering a trail of bright red dots on the wooden stairs.

"Me? All I did was try to get your attention. I can't help it if you're a kl…" His voice trailed off as he realized his size twelve loafer was about to be inserted into his mouth. His face reddened. "C'mon, sit by me and let me see what I can do about your, um…injury."

Tom rested his palm on my back as he guided me toward the bleacher seats he had requisitioned. The mere touch of his hand made my body tingle. Unfortunately, our relationship hadn't progressed to the point where we tingled together. Assuming I could even remember how that tingling thing worked. It had been a long time since my divorce.

Two very long years.

We reached his seats, and as he sat down, his muscular thighs touched my own soon-to-be-muscular-if-I-can-ever-get-to-the-gym thighs. I felt like swooning then realized my injury had metamorphosed into a gushing red river.

"Lift your arm up and press this against your palm."

Tom reached into the pocket of his jeans and pulled out a clean handkerchief. "That will keep the blood from streaming out of your hand and splattering all over the gym."

Some bedside manner. You could tell he spent more time dealing with dead bodies than distressed damsels. I elevated my right arm and pressed the handkerchief against the wound. The dripping halted immediately.

"You were right." I pointed with the index finger of my left hand to my now almost normal right palm.

"It happens occasionally." He smiled and nudged my knee with his. "But not often enough when you're involved."

Before I could respond with a brilliant retort, the squeal of a microphone shriveled my eardrums. The principal gave a quick introduction, thanking the teachers, students, and parents who had turned out in droves to attend the annual holiday show. The lights dimmed and soon the sounds of the season, as performed by the kindergarten through fifth-grade classes, resonated throughout the gym.

Since Ben is on the small side, I worried I wouldn't be able to locate him among the other twenty-nine students in his class. Thanks to his new shoes with their blinding orange sidebars, and his front row position, I singled him out and took a couple of shots with my camera.

Thunderous applause greeted the second-grade rendition of "Rudolph." All the students donned red noses at the end of the song. Even after the song ended, I still couldn't get the melody out of my mind.

We were in such close proximity, I sensed Hunter slipping his hand into his left pocket. He took out his cell and I realized his phone was the source of the continuing chorus of "Rudolph the Red-Nosed Reindeer." He tossed me an apologetic look as he conversed with his hand clasped over his other ear to drown out the clamor.

He snapped the phone shut and shoved it back into the pocket of his jeans.

"Duty calls," he said.

"Do you need to go help someone?" I asked, concerned about potential vehicle accidents on icy roads this time of year.

"Nope," he said. "But there is a strong possibility I may arrest someone."

TWELVE

THE BAD NEWS WAS THAT TOM HAD to leave the program early and go interview a suspect.

The good news was that I was not the suspect. Despite my attempts to weasel information out of him, he clammed up without sharing any clues to the person's identity. His only comment was a request that I inform his parents they would have to take Kristy to their home tonight.

The rest of the holiday program flew by like a four-hour foreign film. After the fifth graders sang what seemed like the thirty-ninth chorus of "Jingle Bell Rock," the audience gave all the classes a standing ovation. I left the auditorium with the other parents and followed the crowd back into the hallway then down to Ben's classroom.

Ben and Kristy played tic-tac-toe on a blackboard while Mother and Bradford chatted with Kristy's grandparents. I informed them that they would be babysitting their granddaughter tonight due to Tom's unexpected phone call.

Tom's announcement that he might end up arresting someone was a huge relief to me, although obviously not to whomever he was investigating. While I was curious to know the outcome, with my life no longer cluttered with allegations of murder or second-grade holiday programs, all I had left on my plate was my best friend's wedding. And bridal shower. And Christmas shopping.

A piece of cake. Wedding cake, that is.

WHEN I ARRIVED AT THE BANK Monday morning, the lobby exuded holiday cheer. Blue and burgundy ornaments decorated the fourteen-foot Noble Fir, cut from one of the local Apple Hill Christmas tree farms, while boughs of aromatic pine branches hung from the oak teller stations. Even the wooden bear looked less forbidding than usual. Sporting a red-and-green plaid scarf around his neck and a red velvet fur-trimmed Santa hat on his head, the bear looked ready to serenade our bank customers with Christmas carols.

With visions of sugarplums and dollar signs in the form of my annual holiday bonus dancing through my head, I hummed my way down the hallway. I was practically rocking around the Christmas tree when I suddenly came to a halt. A plain sheet of white paper rested on my keyboard.

LAUREL, GO TO MR. CHANDLER'S OFFICE AS SOON AS YOU ARRIVE. DO NOT STOP FOR COFFEE.

Do not stop for coffee? Do not pass Go? I looked around to see if Stan or Mary Lou, my cubicle neighbor, were trying to be funny but neither of them was at their desk. Mary Lou's desktop was clear of any paperwork, so she probably hadn't arrived yet.

The red message light on my phone flickered. It seemed prudent to check voice mails first. At seven-fifteen, Mr. Chandler's secretary had left an urgent message for me to come upstairs the minute I arrived in the office.

Fine. No coffee. No dawdling, although I wasn't sure how I would carry on a rational conversation with the bank president without an infusion of caffeine.

A strong wave of déjà vu swept over me as I climbed the stairs to the executive office. My sensation of being sent to the principal's office increased as I mounted each stair tread.

Belle sat at her desk, typing. As I approached, she looked up and a smile of relief crossed her angular face.

"Thank goodness. He's been pacing his office." As usual, Belle was immaculately dressed in a creaseless black pinstripe suit. One of these days I would have to find out her secret, although I had a feeling we didn't buy our clothes at the same shops since my wardrobe came from stores whose names ended in "mart."

"What's the problem? Am I in trouble?"

Belle shrugged, her face as puzzled as mine. "I have no idea. He didn't say why he wanted you. He just said to get you up here ASAP."

She pointed in the direction of the president's office. "Go."

I thrust back my shoulders and headed down the hallway to beard the dragon, or in this case, the president. Actually, I'd rather face a fire-eating dragon than Mr. Chandler. My career could be at stake. Again.

The door to Mr. Chandler's office was closed. I peered through the glass window fronting his office. He sat behind his desk, the phone cradled to his ear.

I tapped on the glass. He looked up and waved me in. The president's face was eggplant-purple; he looked ready to explode. I opened the door and sat down immediately. He slammed the receiver down and glared at me.

"Umm, good morning?" I didn't know what else to say because it didn't look like a good morning for our fearless leader. Mr. Chandler blew his breath out and unclenched the fists that had been resting on his glossy, uncluttered desk.

He grimaced at me. Or maybe that was a smile. Having never seen Mr. Chandler smile before, it was difficult to discern the difference. "Thank you for coming," he said.

Like I had a choice? Not that I was about to utter those words out loud.

He leaned toward me, his voice so low I had to scoot

my chair closer to hear. "The police have discussed the possibility of arresting someone for the murder of that dance instructor."

I nodded. After Tom's abrupt departure Saturday night, an arrest didn't surprise me.

Mr. Chandler's eyes burned a hole right through me. "The person they are considering is my wife."

THIRTEEN

NOW THAT WAS A SURPRISE. I couldn't believe I'd heard him correctly. "They want to arrest Dana? *That* wife?"

Despite the fact that his spouse risked going to jail, Mr. Chandler still managed to paste a supercilious look on his face. "Yes, *that* wife," he snapped.

"I'm sorry. But I'm stunned. Why Dana?"

"I have no idea. The District Attorney isn't overly fond of me since I didn't support him in the last election." He stared glumly at his manicured nails. "He probably wasn't too happy we rejected his loan application, either."

I frowned. "You think the D.A. wants to prosecute Dana because we rejected his loan? The sheriff's department wouldn't consider arresting her unless they had sufficient evidence that she killed—"

Mr. Chandler balled his hand into a fist and pounded the desk. "My wife did not kill that, that…gigolo."

Hmmm. I never would have thought of combining the words *bank president's wife* and *gigolo* in the same sentence. Was he implying that Dimitry and Dana not only tangoed together—they also tangled together? And even if they *had* moved their samba hip rolls off the floor and under the sheets, what did any of this have to do with me?

Mr. Chandler's face had turned even redder than the dark cherry desk he continued to pound. If I didn't calm him down, Dana would become a widow as well as a murder suspect.

"Maybe they've misinterpreted some of the evidence. Detectives suspect the wrong people all the time."

Now that was a subject I could discourse on at length.

"Exactly. I knew you would be able to relate to their incompetency at investigating. Obviously, they don't know what they are doing. Dana is incapable of harming anyone. She's so compassionate she never even spanked our children."

"Do you have any idea what evidence they have against her?"

"Two detectives showed up yesterday morning and interviewed her at our house. I gather her fingerprints were on the murder weapon and they found other incriminating evidence they were unwilling to share with me." His hands trembled as he looked at me in disbelief. "I was afraid they were taking her down to the jail but when they left all they said was that she better not leave town."

Jeez. I couldn't imagine the stylish diamond-studded Dana Chandler wearing steel bracelets. But I was still mystified why Mr. Chandler requested my presence. He looked so miserable I reached out and rested my palm on top of his.

Evidently he hadn't asked me up here for a little tea and sympathy because he yanked his hand out from under mine. So Mr. Chandler didn't want my sympathy and no one had offered me any Darjeeling. Why *had* he called me to his office?

"I'm sorry about Dana's predicament but I'm sure it will be rectified in a few days."

"Her name must be cleared immediately. My standing in this community is critical to the soundness of this bank."

True. In a small town like ours, reputation was everything. I wondered how he planned to resolve this situation.

"I certainly can't expect those bumbling county detectives to look for any other suspects," he said, "especially when the D.A. is pushing them. This is an election year and he's going to make the most of it.

"Someone needs to clear Dana's name. Someone with excellent analytical abilities. Someone who will give one hundred and ten percent to the bank."

His gaze drilled through my retinas.

"Someone like you."

FOURTEEN

M E? T HE WOMAN WITH THE KNACK for discovering dead bodies and getting the bank's name mentioned in the local newspaper's crime report? I was his number one choice for Nancy Drew? The first thought that filtered through my brain was what the heck did he put in his morning coffee?

My response was not one of my most clever deductions. "Huh?"

"Laurel, I need your help." He swiveled in his chair and stared out the window as if pondering what to say next. When he turned back, fear shone in his gray eyes.

"I'm terrified for my wife. And I admit I'm concerned how the bank will be impacted by this negative publicity. I realize I never gave you proper credit but you showed amazing tenacity when you solved our fraud problem."

"Thanks." I was stunned and surprised by the compliment.

"Dana mentioned you're friends with that detective. I think his name is Hunter?"

I nodded warily.

"Maybe you could put in a good word for her. She said you're also taking dance lessons. I would be grateful for anything you can find out when you're at the studio. I—" His extension rang, interrupting our conversation. He grabbed it and answered, "Chandler." He motioned for me to exit his office and I was out before his hand had stopped shooing me out the door.

I trod down the stairs in a daze. That the president

thought I was competent enough to keep his wife out of jail should have been a big ego boost, but what if I failed? I glanced around at my coworkers in their cubicles. If Dana was arrested, would that impact the bank's reputation? Could it eventually lead to bank employees losing their jobs?

Employees like me?

With visions of unpaid bills piling up in my head, I slumped in my chair and stared at the stack of loan files awaiting my decision. No matter whether the economy was in a recession or an inflationary period, people still wanted to close on their home purchases before the end of the tax year.

Decisions, decisions. Underwriting or detecting?

Despite my concerns, an excuse to interfere in a murder investigation won hands down over examining employment verifications and bank statements. Not to mention that the image of Dana Chandler clad in a baggy orange jumpsuit just seemed wrong.

I wondered how long it would be before they removed the crime scene tape from the dance studio. I didn't have long to ponder. My cell phone blasted out the tune to "Here Comes the Bride."

"Sweetie, they're reopening the studio tomorrow," Liz said. "Isn't that fabulous?"

Fabulous for detecting. As for dancing—not so much.

Between my friend's British accent, which seemed to intensify whenever she grew excited, and the poor reception on my cell, I could only catch occasional phrases of what she said.

One comment jumped out at me, however. "Practice our choreography?"

"Yes, it's time for everyone in the bridal party to try the routine together. You must know your part by now."

"Liz, I can barely figure out when to move forward or back, much less quick, quick and slow. No, I don't have the choreography or the footwork down yet."

"If Bobby's not a good teacher then let's dump him and get another instructor. Maybe Yuri. He's almost as hot as Dimitry, may he rest in peace."

"I doubt the hotness of the teacher has anything to do with my ability to learn the fox-trot. When I dance, I look more like Lucille Ball than Ginger Rogers."

"I'll schedule another lesson for you and Bobby for to-morrow night. Meanwhile, rent some old Fred and Ginger videos. That should do the trick."

My best friend was dreaming if she thought a few hours of watching that famous Hollywood duo would turn me into an overnight dance sensation but Liz hung up mid-protest. A tuneless whistle outside my cubicle announced the impending visit of Stan, arms loaded with manila file folders.

"Those better not be new loans to underwrite," I said.

"Nope, I'm on my way to the doc department to drop them off. I heard you were upstairs hangin' with the big-wigs again." He waggled his eyebrows at me, Groucho style. "What's going on? Are you getting a promotion?"

"It depends on how you define promotion." I hesitated, unsure if I should share the information about Dana with my assistant.

"C'mon, spill. You know you want to. I promise not to tell."

I motioned for him to sit. He dropped the files on the floor then plopped into my guest chair.

I leaned across my desk and spoke quietly. "Dana Chandler could be arrested."

"Arrested?" Stan yelled.

"Arrested?" shouted Mary Lou, my cubicle neighbor

who was also a senior underwriter. Her chair squealed as she jumped up, joining us in less than two seconds. "Laurel, were you arrested again?"

My reputation desperately needed a makeover. "I wish people would stop staying that," I said. "I was never *formally* arrested. Merely a person of interest."

Mary Lou appeared confused, but she was a blonde goddess. Confused looked good on her. "Who was arrested? Anyone important?"

Stan and I exchanged looks.

He shrugged. "I can't remember. Did you see the big box of Annabelle's chocolates that one of the title companies dropped off in the break room? The truffles are disappearing fast."

"Nice one," I said, as Mary Lou's footsteps receded down the hall.

"So what's the deal with Madame El Presidente? Did she bop the dancer? Or merely boff the dancer?"

"Don't be crude." I frowned at my friend. "Dana Chandler is a classy lady. Just because she took lessons from Dimitry doesn't mean anything sordid was going on."

Stan wrinkled his nose. "Sure, there's no reason why the sophisticated Mrs. Chandler would be wooed away by a handsome, muscular dancer when she has Mr. Chubby Cheeks to go home to every night."

Oh, well, when you put it that way…

"It gets worse." I sighed with so much gusto some loan conditions blew off my desk. "For some reason Mr. Chandler decided my deductive abilities should be used to find the murderer."

Stan's eyes lit up. "Awesome. Another case for us."

"Us?"

"Sure, remember how much I helped last time?"

Not really. But at this point I would take whatever

assistance I could get. Stan was officially on my payroll for his usual fee. *Nada*. We'd better come up with a plan because by tomorrow night I needed to be not only a dancing diva but a detecting diva.

I WALKED THROUGH THE PARKING lot of the Golden Hills Dance Studio on Tuesday night, my thoughts far, far away. Over a half century away. The previous evening, I'd sat through a Hollywood dance movie marathon. With Christmas in less than two weeks, the networks featured a few familiar classics like *Holiday Inn* and *White Christmas*. The vision of Vera Ellen clad in red velvet and white ermine fur, singing and tapping to the music of Cole Porter, enthralled me. Equally amazing was her nineteen-inch waist. If learning the fox-trot produced that kind of a result, I was hopping on the ballroom bandwagon.

My chest constricted as I drew close to the spot where I'd discovered Dimitry's body. I tried to avert my eyes but failed. Dark splotches splattered the cracked asphalt.

Oil stains or bloodstains?

Once inside, I released a sigh of relief, hoping everything would be back to normal. Ten minutes later I found myself wondering what the definition of normal was for a dance studio whose premier instructor had been murdered.

The haunting strains of a plaintive rumba echoed throughout the building. Rumba is frequently described as vertical sex. Anya, now coupled with Yuri, slowly slid down her partner's leg, her taut, bronzed arms caressing his muscular thigh.

As the last notes of the song ended, Anya arched her back in a full back bend, her mane of ebony curls grazing the floor. I wondered if all that blood rushing to her head was good for her. Appraising her muscular yet lithe frame, I decided it must be good for something.

Yuri stared at Anya with admiration in his dark eyes. And possibly a tinge of lust.

Shoot. Even I was ogling her. How many years of practice would it take to achieve that level of sexuality and flexibility? At the rate I was going, the only men lusting after *me* would be retired ballroom dancers, their remaining strands of white hair flying as they chased after me in their walkers.

A loud snap of my partner's fingers woke me from my reverie. "Laurel, concentrate. We need to practice." Bobby shook his index finger in my face to emphasize that he meant business. "We have to get the grapevine footwork down."

If it were up to me, I'd be enjoying the fruit of the grape instead of the convoluted dance steps named after the vines. "Sorry, too many things swirling in my mind," I muttered.

Bobby's face was somber. "We need to start swirling together. Liz called Boris this morning and berated him for your lack of progress. He threatened to fire me if you don't learn the routine by the end of the week."

"Oh, Bobby, I'm sorry. I told Liz you've done everything possible to teach me the steps. My stubborn flat feet are the culprit."

Speaking of flat feet…

"Were you interviewed by anyone from the sheriff's department?"

He sighed and released his hold on my upper back. Good, I could relax, as well. The proper fox-trot pose gave me a neck and back ache. I briefly pondered whether Liz would entertain a much looser hip hop version of "It Had to Be You," but I snapped back to reality when Bobby answered my question.

"The detectives talked to all of us pros."

"What kinds of questions did they ask?"

Bobby stared up at the ceiling for a few seconds before responding. "I don't know what they asked everyone else, but they wanted to know if I knew of anyone with a grudge against Dimitry."

I could tell from the expression on his face that he knew something but couldn't decide if it he should share it with me. "C'mon, Bobby. You can tell me."

Bobby's café au lait skin darkened. "You haven't been taking lessons here very long, so you wouldn't be aware of this, but Dimitry wasn't the most popular guy in the place." He paused and his fists clenched involuntarily. "At least not with the other male dance instructors. As far as the women…" Bobby shrugged. "He was in high demand with them."

"Can you think of something specific Dimitry did that would make someone mad enough to kill him?"

"Hey, I'm easy. Chill is my middle name. As for the other teachers, instead of holding master dance classes once a month, Boris should implement anger management sessions."

Wow. Multiple dancing suspects.

With my head bent, deep in thought analyzing Bobby's words, I barely noticed the freight train heading in our direction.

FIFTEEN

As Anya and Yuri barreled down on us, only Bobby's agile reflexes kept me from being trampled to death. Or squashed into a samba sandwich. I glared at the receding backs of the couple as they continued their hip swiveling promenade around the studio.

As far as I was concerned, I'd already spent far too much time in a horizontal position on the dance floor. If I wanted to be horizontal, there were far better choices of venue. *And* partner.

Thoughts of a handsome detective snapped my brain back into investigative mode. "Bobby, do you have any idea who might have killed Dimitry?"

His lips parted, and I waited breathlessly for my teacher to share the name of the murderer. Always the consummate professional, Bobby intoned, "Slow, slow, quick, quick."

I sighed and wished we could adjust our tempo to medium, medium, medium so I could concentrate on detecting instead of dancing. I rested my left hand on his bicep, arched my back, stretched my latissimus dorsi muscle and kept my eyes focused above the watch on my left wrist. Supposedly this little trick would help me maintain the proper form. Before I started dancing I'd never heard of lat muscles. Now I knew if you held the proper pose, a variety of body parts should hurt.

Some hobby.

We danced across the varnished floor. The wall mirrors reflected my image, which looked more like a spastic zombie than a ballroom dancer. Perfect for the "Thriller" video, but not so much for a wedding.

How had Ginger done it? Maybe if I wrapped a feather boa around my neck, I could create the illusion that I was a dancer. Would my dancing improve if I donned a gorgeous ball gown made of swirling chiffon skirts strewn with sparkling crystals?

Could the proper attire impact my ability to learn ballroom? Possibly, although some students went a little overboard, I thought, noticing a peculiar-looking guy standing by the front desk chatting with Anya. His black ruffled shirt exposed most of his hairless chest and his tight black trousers were, well, tight.

The guy bore a strong resemblance to Stan except for a tiny pencil moustache perched above his lips. I squinted in his direction and our eyes met. Oh, jeez. This was my assistant's concept of blending in?

Stan put his finger to his lips and I nodded back. There was no need to admit the strange-looking dude was a friend of mine. Stan's presence distracted me and I forgot to pay attention to my dancing. Before I knew it, Bobby was not only leading me in the grapevine formation, I was following him. Of course the minute I realized we were dancing well together, my heel stabbed my instep.

"Owww!" I hopped on my good foot.

"What happened? You were doing great."

I limped off the dance floor and collapsed in a chair. Bobby sat next to me as I pulled off my shoe and massaged my injured foot.

"Are you okay?" My young teacher's eyes showed his concern. I nodded and he quickly looked in the direction of Boris's office.

"Don't worry about him." I patted his knee. "There's no way we'll let Boris fire you because of me."

He slumped in his chair and shoved his hand through his spiky black hair. "It's not only that," Bobby said, his lips set in a thin line. He laced his fingers together and propped them against his chin.

"Hey, what is it then?" I looked in Anya's direction. "Girl trouble?"

He shook his head. "Nah, it's…okay, here's the deal, Dimitry planned on opening his own studio. He already had the space rented. He tried to solicit some of the other guys but like I said before, most of them couldn't stand his guts, although Yuri was considering it. Dimitry offered me almost twice the hourly wage Boris pays me, so I was seriously thinking about making the change. Anya and Tatiana had already agreed to follow him over there and of course they would have taken their students with them."

"Did Boris suspect anything?"

"I don't know." He shrugged. "Like I said, Boris called me into his office to discuss your progress. Then he made some comment about ungrateful dance instructors so I assumed he was talking about Dimitry and his efforts to solicit me and some of the other pros. I wouldn't be here today if Boris hadn't been willing to take a chance and train me. My background was strictly modern and ballet, but once I discovered ballroom, it's the only style of dance for me."

His eyes veered to the right and I followed his gaze. Speak of the devil. Boris stood at the end of the enormous floor, arms crossed, looking as happy as a KGB officer at a Girl Scout wienie roast.

How upset would Boris have been about his star dancer starting his own studio? Luring some of the instructors and many of their students away? Would he have been angry enough to take desperate measures to eliminate the competition?

I cast a quick glance back at Boris. His beady black eyes bore into mine. Definitely not someone I wanted to get on the wrong side of. The man looked far more like a member of the Russian Mafia than a world-famous ball-room dancer.

The strains of a sultry tango floated from the studio speakers as Anya led Stan out on the floor. I felt sorry for my pal. Tango was one of the trickier dances to perform with two slow steps followed by three quick ones.

My feet halted and my mouth dropped open as my buddy expertly maneuvered his professional partner into a *corte* pose. Who was this strange man dressed in black, sporting a fake moustache and adeptly steering the long limbed instructor across the floor?

Stan must have memorized some of the steps from the *Dancing with the Stars* shows he recorded each season. He actually looked like he knew what he was doing. All he needed was a black hat and mask and one would think Zorro had dropped by for a visit.

Or James Bond.

On second thought, after contemplating Stan's bizarre outfit—make that Austin Powers.

The sound of someone clearing his throat startled me. Boris towered over me, his expression as menacing as the villainous Goldfinger. What I wouldn't give to have Sean Connery or any of the former James Bonds standing next to me right now, a chilled martini glass in hand.

Or better yet, a glass in each hand.

"Good evening, Laurel," Boris said, his Russian accent highly pronounced.

"Um, hi, Boris. Nice to see you."

"Your dance…" His bushy black brows drew together. "She is progressing smoothly?"

That depended on your definition of smooth. If his definition meant galloping across the dance floor without a clue, well, then, yes, she *was* progressing smoothly.

Bobby's eyes locked with mine as he visually pleaded for support.

"The dancing is going great. Bobby is a wonderful teacher and very patient with me. I just need to practice more often."

"Da, I think maybe *much* practice would be good for you." He wrapped a muscular right arm around my waist. "Come. I have idea."

He half urged and half shoved me across the dance floor. As we drew closer to his dark office, his grip tightened, resembling the embrace of a boa constrictor. When he stopped in the doorway to turn on the light, I wondered if I should make a break for it.

Boris waved a meaty hand at me and pointed to a chair in front of his desk.

"Please. Now. Before is too late."

I reluctantly slid into the leather chair, my agile brain thinking way ahead of my clumsy feet.

Too late for what? Or for whom?

SIXTEEN

I PERCHED ON THE EDGE OF THE CHAIR, prepared to make a quick exit if the hulking bear of a dancer made any sudden moves.

The studio owner leaned back in his oversized chair with his bear-paw-sized hands crossed over his abdomen. Based on the photos plastered on his walls, he had let his formerly hard-as-a-rock six-pack of nicely muscled abs turn into a six-pack of slushies.

"Your friend, Liz, she is not so happy with your progress. She is worried that…" He paused as he tried to find the right expression.

I jumped in feet first. "Liz is worried about what?"

"She say you be da bomb."

I beamed at my best friend's compliment. "She thinks I'm the bomb?"

He pursed his lips and shook his head. "No, I say it wrong. She worry you make dance bomb." He grinned and banged his hand on the desk. "Yes, that is what she say."

My confidence burst faster than an overinflated balloon. Admittedly, Liz is an anal obsessive perfectionist, but it was her wedding, after all. I didn't need to be included in her overly long list of concerns.

"So I come up with idea." He smiled widely and pointed at his broad chest. "I, Boris will teach you. Is good, no?"

Is good? No, no, no. Is *not* good. If I could barely keep

up with the slender and highly patient Bobby, how on earth could I follow this dancing giant?

I tried to think of a polite way to turn down his offer.

"Gee, Boris, I would hate for you to waste your valuable time teaching me to dance. It could take hours and hours to train me."

"It would please me so much to dance with you. Liz, she tell me you are single woman." He winked. "I, too, am single. Very eligible bachelor."

Be still my heart. Which thudded at the rate of a super fast cha-cha. Although the pounding was due to anxiety, not a romantic interest in the "very eligible bachelor" sitting across from me.

"That's so sweet of you," I floundered, trying to direct the conversation away from our mutual singleness and his proposition to tutor me.

"Running this studio must keep you very busy, especially now that Dimitry is gone," I said.

At the mention of the dancer's name, Boris's face darkened like a thundercloud about to burst over the Sierras. He sneered and smacked the top of the scratched oak desk with his palm. "That Bolshevik SOB."

I jumped. My comment must have touched a nerve. "There's a rumor that Dimitry wanted to open his own studio and some of the teachers and their students were going with him. Is that true?"

Boris glowered at me. "Who tell you this? Bobby?"

I shook my head. The last thing I wanted to do was get my teacher in trouble. "No, I'm not sure who I heard it from."

"Dimitry was ungrateful traitor," Boris roared. "I help him come to this country, set him up in beautiful studio, spend much money advertising to bring in students so he have good living. And still have opportunities to compete.

Then what happen? He get big fat head and think he too good to work for me."

"I can understand that. Everyone wants to be their own boss."

"But I was his friend. A very good friend. And what he do for me?" Boris looked at me questioningly.

I shrugged.

"Nothing. I bring in the students and he want to take them away."

"Did you try to stop him?"

"I try to talk but he does not listen. I flatter him. I threaten him, then I…" His voice faltered as our gazes met. "I…"

"Killed him?"

SEVENTEEN

SOMETIMES MY BRAIN AND LIPS lack a noticeable degree of coordination. Occasionally, when a thought is randomly passing through my head, I say it aloud without even realizing it. An example of which had occurred seconds earlier.

"Killed him?" Boris rose from behind the desk, towering over me. "You think I kill Dimitry?"

I shook my head as the not so gentle giant fumed above me. "No, that's not what I meant. But you admit you threatened him."

Boris glared at me, a fleck of spittle resting on his fleshy upper lip. "It was not like that. I did not threaten to kill him. The threat, it was about something else."

I leaned forward, anxious to learn about the "something else."

"Is not your concern. It was private, between Dimitry and me. Has nothing to do with his being killed."

"How can you be sure? Maybe your private business led to Dimitry's murder. Did you tell the detectives about any of this?"

"Why you ask so many questions? This is not your business. Your business is to learn wedding dance." He glanced at his watch. "Is time for my advanced technique class. If you do not learn choreography by end of week, I will make time to squeeze you in."

His thick lips turned up into one of his ferocious smiles. "We will look good together. I like *zaftig* women."

Zaftig? That was a new one. I would have to look it up, but I had a feeling the definition wasn't tall and slender.

Boris picked up his phone, indicating an end to our conversation. I slid my chair back and exited the office. I would have liked to eavesdrop but in the words of the studio owner, "I had much practice to do."

And as far as I was concerned, much detecting to do.

The main ballroom hummed with activity. Students of every age warmed up, either by dancing with a partner, performing knee bends or executing stretches against a wall. Now there was a concept. Perhaps I should try one of those options rather than my normal method of warming up by exercising my lips.

Stan had disappeared, but I recognized a familiar face and walked across the room to join her. "Hi, Paula," I said to the brunette who watched Gregor perform the hustle with a silver-haired female old enough to have danced it back in the disco days.

She smiled at me and pointed at the chair next to her. "Are you still working on the wedding choreography?"

I slumped into the chair. "Bobby is attempting to teach me, and I am attempting to learn, but there's a fairly wide chasm between the two. I don't think I'll ever be able to follow him."

"You'll get the hang of it eventually. At first, it seems impossible to follow the rhythm and feel the musicality. And women automatically want to lead. It's a natural instinct for us."

I chuckled. "So it's not just me being a total control freak."

She grinned back. "Nope, you're normal. Trust me. One day it will suddenly click and before you know it, following will be the easiest thing in the world. It's an amazing high when everything comes together."

I gazed down at the enemy—my two left feet. "At the rate I'm going, Liz will be celebrating her tenth anniversary before anything clicks for me. She complained to Boris about my lack of progress and now he's hounding Bobby."

"Don't worry. Boris is more bark than bite."

"Or flirt than bark. He not only offered to teach me himself, he made some offhand comment about how he's attracted to *zaftig* women, whatever the heck that means."

Paula placed her palm over her mouth, attempting but not succeeding in stifling a giggle. "Boris is an excellent teacher, although he can be intimidating. Yuri said he would consider taking me on, but his plate is full trying to squeeze in so many of Dimitry's former students. There are only four male dance instructors now—Gregor, Yuri, Boris, and Bobby."

I glanced across the room at Yuri. He was laughing and chatting with Tatiana and Wendy, two of the female instructors.

I turned to Paula. "Were you going to follow Dimitry to his new studio?"

She looked surprised. "You heard about that?"

I nodded.

"Dimitry and I competed in dance competitions all over the country this past year. I did so well, we decided I should go ahead and advance to the gold scholarship level." She stared at her feet encased in rhinestone-studded bronze satin dance shoes. "He was such a brilliant dancer and teacher I would have followed him wherever he went."

"When was the studio supposed to open?"

"The official opening was scheduled for mid-February. Dimitry was positive he'd pull in some big prizes at the New Year's Holiday Ball. He also hoped to entice a couple of the premier Bay Area instructors to join him at the new studio."

"He thought he could get some big-name professionals to move out here to the sticks?"

"With the lower cost of living and housing, the foothills are quite a draw. And there are fewer studios competing for students here than in the Bay Area. I think he had several good candidates who wanted to join him."

"I'll bet that ticked Boris off," I said. "Did you know he was aware of Dimitry's defection?"

"He probably threw a fit when he found out." Paula's hazel eyes widened as she contemplated my announcement. "You don't think Boris would have been angry enough to kill Dimitry, do you?"

"That's what I wondered. Do you have any idea which students were following Dimitry to the new studio?"

"Samantha Fielding said she would go. And Dana Chandler, of course. She couldn't bear to be parted from her teacher." The expression on her face signaled more to the story.

"Why do you say that?"

Paula blushed. "Hey, I'm not one to start rumors, especially about the dead, but the two of them were together a lot. And not only on the dance floor. My husband and I were at the Bistro Restaurant last Wednesday night. Dana and Dimitry were there, alone, looking very chummy."

"Maybe he was explaining dance steps to her," I said.

We exchanged glances. Discussing dance steps over dinner?

It was time to have a talk with the prime suspect.

EIGHTEEN

By Friday, I was more than ready for the weekend. Between work and an extra dance lesson Thursday night, I'd barely completed any of my Christmas shopping for my family. By 4:55 my last file was underwritten and approved—I tend to be more lenient on a Friday afternoon. Determined to be out of the bank no later than five o'clock, my purse was clasped in my hand when my phone rang. I looked to see if it was an interoffice call or anyone important.

Mr. Chandler's extension. There was no doubt which category the president would put himself.

I lifted the receiver. "Laurel speaking."

"Tomorrow. My house. Ten a.m."

At the end of a long week, my neurons aren't necessarily operating at peak capacity. "Huh? What? When?"

"Dana would like you to come to our house tomorrow morning." I imagined the digits of my Christmas bonus dropping as his sigh resonated over the phone. "She's nervous about going out in public and would prefer if you came here tomorrow to discuss her situation. We would both appreciate it."

It had to be difficult going from Queen Bee of the local society pages to Queen Suspect.

"If my daughter can babysit, I should be able to make it there by ten."

The conversation ended with the dial tone buzzing in my ear. Evidently, the meeting at the boss's house wasn't optional. I buttoned my black leather coat and slung my purse over my shoulder. The phone rang once again.

I slumped back in my chair and grabbed the receiver. "Yes?" I said with all the enthusiasm of someone still at the office at 5:10 on a Friday afternoon.

"Laurel, what are you doing tomorrow?"

"Hi, Mother. Running errands, Christmas shopping, interviewing murder suspects."

"What?"

"Nothing. What's going on?"

"I want your opinion on something. Can you meet me for breakfast at ten?"

"I'm busy at ten. How about lunch instead? Old Town Grill?"

"What are you doing at ten in the morning?"

Trying to keep my job. "I'll tell you about it tomorrow at lunch."

That seemed to satisfy my mother. Now if I could only satisfy my boss.

JENNA AGREED TO BABYSIT HER brother on Saturday, astutely guessing that one of my errands included chasing down the items on her Christmas wish list, which consisted of gadgets starting with the letter *I,* as in iPhone and iPad. I definitely needed that bonus if my children were going to remain technologically compatible with their peers.

The temperature had dropped the night before and it wasn't uncommon to find patches of black ice hidden in the shadowy recesses of Green Valley Road, especially near the one-lane bridge over Weber Creek. I drove carefully, deciding that I'd rather be late for the meeting than have my car perform wheelies on the slick ice.

The Chandlers resided in a Victorian mansion built by one of the gold rush magnates. The men who supplied the

Forty-niners with food and equipment had become wealthy merchants while the poor prospectors drank and gambled away the bags of gold dust they labored so hard to discover.

The Prius and I arrived at the Chandlers' house only one minute late. The pale yellow mansion with dark green trim sparkled in the bright sunlight. Frost, icing the expansive front lawn, shimmered like tiny diamonds in the emerald-green grass. I drove up the long paved driveway and parked off to the side next to a sporty navy blue BMW convertible.

High-heeled boots and black ice are not a good combination so I stepped carefully, watching out for slick patches of ice on the long brick walkway. No doorbell was immediately evident so I finally banged on the leonine brass knocker, which adorned the oversized oak-paneled doors. The door was flung open in the middle of my pounding.

Bristling black brows and narrowed green eyes couldn't disguise the fact that this kid was handsome, in an ominous *Twilight* fashion. My first thought was that Jenna would *so* love to be introduced to him. My second thought was that was *so* not going to happen. I knew teenage trouble when I saw it.

I introduced myself, but the surly young man ignored my proffered hand. He stepped to the side of the entry, motioning for me to enter. I hesitantly walked into the large foyer, worried my heeled boots would mar the mahogany planks polished to a glossy shine.

"The folks are waiting for you in the sunroom." All six feet of his tense body vibrated with anger. "Maybe you'll be able to talk some sense into my old man."

This must be Rob Chandler, their youngest son. As I recalled, he was a junior at Stanford, probably home on winter break, and most likely the owner of the Beemer parked outside. He was supposedly smart and had inherited Dana's dark good looks. It was obvious he was not happy with his parents.

I followed Rob down a long hallway, peeking into the beautifully furnished rooms on both sides. When he turned to see why I lagged behind, I sped up my pace. Maybe Dana would give me a tour later. From what I could tell, someone had spent a fortune decorating and this might be my only opportunity to ogle.

The murmur of angry voices greeted us as we approached the sunroom, but they abruptly stopped when we appeared in the doorway.

Rob flung himself into a white wicker chair, the nineteenth-century rose-patterned cushions at odds with the twenty-first-century young adult dressed in designer jeans and flip flops, standard attire for California teens in every social strata.

The air simmered with undercurrents. Dana sat in a wicker settee, her fingers destroying the tissue she held into tiny shreds. Mr. Chandler paced in front of the windows that overlooked the back garden, his complexion matching the color of the roses decorating the cushions.

Dana pointed to the seat next to her. I reluctantly walked over, feeling like an unwilling guest in the third act of a Tennessee Williams play. I sat on the loveseat next to Dana, not sure what to do to comfort her. She grabbed my right hand in hers, squeezing so hard my knuckles whimpered.

"Thank you for coming," she murmured in a voice barely louder than a whisper. Her brown eyes were huge and imploring; her face, devoid of make-up, was all angles in the harsh light of the morning sun.

Mr. Chandler stopped his pacing and nodded at me. "Yes, thank you, Ms. McKay, for agreeing to help us with this, um, situation."

"Situation?" Rob practically screamed the word at his

parents. "My mother could be arrested any minute now for murdering her lover and you think we have a situation."

Mr. Chandler froze midpace. "Go to your room. Now. This does not concern you."

Rob jumped out of his chair. "You bet your ass it does." His emerald eyes glittered as he pointed at his mother, who shrank back into the cushions. "Some mother you are."

He delivered one last parting shot before he stomped out of the room. "At least your boyfriend was finally taken care of."

NINETEEN

DANA BURST INTO TEARS. Mr. Chandler threw his arms in the air then slumped into the chair vacated by his angry son. I patted Dana's hand, musing that the lives of wealthy bank presidents aren't necessarily better than those of their lowly mortgage staff.

Dana rubbed her eyes, which only served to make them redder than before. "I'm so embarrassed. Robbie arrived home last night for winter break. His finals were held last week. We couldn't bear to disrupt his studies, so we kept Dimitry's murder and my involvement a secret. Needless to say, he became a little distraught at the news."

Evidently, her definition of distraught and mine were miles apart.

Dana straightened her back and addressed her husband. "Gordon, I'd like to talk to Laurel by myself. Would you mind leaving us alone?"

His son's outburst had aged the bank president at least ten years. As he pulled himself out of his chair, he refused to meet his wife's gaze. His steps were slow and uncertain as he closed the glass door to the sunroom behind him.

With her husband out of the room, Dana recovered some of her natural grace and hospitality. "I apologize for my family, and especially Robbie. Would you like some tea or coffee?" The perfect homemaker was once again in charge.

I shook my head, uncomfortable participating in the Chandler family soap opera. "I'm not certain how I can help."

Dana twisted the wet and mangled tissue in her hand. "I thought since you were accused of murder barely a few months ago that you could relate and maybe give me some advice. Despite Gordon's somewhat gruff demeanor, he has frequently referred to you as Hangtown Bank's own version of Nancy Drew."

Me? Nancy Drew? Cool.

Dana managed a weak smile. "I imagine there are rumors circulating around the dance studio, but I want to make something perfectly clear. Despite Robbie's remarks and what Gordon may or may not think, Dimitry and I never slept together. I have never been nor would I ever be unfaithful to my husband. You must believe me."

No reason not to believe her, except…

"Not that I didn't think of it, or daydream about Dimitry. I mean, who wouldn't?"

She was right. Probably every woman in the studio fleetingly thought of spending time with that primal hunk of man.

Even Stan had desired him from afar.

"Dimitry was an outrageous flirt, and if I'd shown any interest, he would have had no compunction about bedding me. But I would never cheat on Gordon. I love my husband, all two hundred-plus pounds of him."

Okay, got it. She didn't make whoopee with Dimitry.

"But I did do something terrible." Her chin rested on her folded palms as she stared downcast at the floor. "And far worse."

What was worse than stepping out on your husband?

Uh-oh. Was she talking about murder?

TWENTY

MY EXPRESSION MUST have revealed my thoughts.

"Not murder." She gave her head a hard shake. After a second, she added, "But I stole money."

My mouth opened so wide you could fit one of her gold-rimmed teacups into it. "You stole money? From the bank?"

"Of course not. Well, technically I didn't steal it." She traced her finger around the rim of her Spode cup. "Gordon insisted we have an equity line on this house. Back when you could get huge lines of credit with a minimal loan application. You never know when you'll need cash for an emergency. This house is worth a lot and we were approved for a $300,000 line of credit."

Big loan. I wondered if Hangtown Bank funded it.

"Gordon is a busy executive, so I handle all the household chores, which includes paying our bills. Our income is excellent and despite the fact that I love to purchase nice things, I'm fairly prudent in my spending. In twenty-five years of marriage, Gordon has never had reason to doubt any of my financial decisions."

Try supporting two children on an underwriter's salary. I could teach her a few things about prudent.

"When Rob went off to college, I didn't have enough activities to keep me busy. My charities and fundraising events were fulfilling, but there was still an empty hole in my life. I tried confiding in Gordon, but men don't get that empty nest stuff."

"Isn't that why you took up dancing?" I said. "To fill the void."

"Dancing distracted me for a while. Dimitry and I competed at a few local competitions and I looked forward to competing in the Holiday Ball. Buying exotic costumes was fun at first, but eventually, there wasn't enough fringe or sequins to keep me entertained. I needed a challenge that stimulated me mentally, not just physically." She sipped her tea. "One day Dimitry came to me with a proposition."

I raised my eyebrows and she smiled.

"No, not that kind of proposition. A financial one. He wanted to open his own studio, but he didn't have any money. He asked if I would lend it to him. Dimitry and I were close, but I didn't feel comfortable loaning him the money. Then I had a brainstorm and told him I would do it if I could be a silent owner. When he agreed, I was in dance studio owner's heaven. I've chaired numerous fundraisers over the years and the thought of planning glamorous dance showcases and world-class competitions thrilled me. It was the perfect solution to my doldrums."

"What did Mr. Chandler think of the idea?"

The way her face shut down told me the answer.

"He said no way were we going to invest his hard-earned money in some silly dance studio start-up. Gordon didn't like Dimitry. I think he was jealous, but he couldn't figure out a way to stop me from dancing without looking like a possessive spouse.

"We argued over investing in the studio, but Gordon was adamant. And so was I. With Dimitry's dance acumen and my event planning experience and network of friends, I felt the studio would be a huge success. In my mind, I imagined that Gordon would be so proud of what I accomplished that he wouldn't even notice…" Dana paused, a wistful expression crossing her face.

"Notice what?" I asked.

"Notice that I withdrew all the money out of our equity line."

"Three hundred thousand dollars?" I yelped.

She held up three fingers, waggled them at me and nodded.

"Are you—" I almost said *nuts* but that didn't seem the most appropriate comment to make to my boss's wife.

She must have read my mind. "Am I crazy? It sounds like it, doesn't it? I feel like a spoiled wife who has no concept of money."

"Do the detectives know about this? What kind of evidence do they have?"

"They went through Dimitry's bank statements and found large deposits of $25,000 every few weeks. Dimitry needed rent money and a deposit for the new studio. He claimed he had rented space in those beautiful offices in Town Square in El Dorado Hills. Then a couple of weeks later he needed money for the tenant improvements. Those fancy wood dance floors don't come cheap, especially if you want the spring-loaded ones that are much easier on the feet. As far as Dimitry was concerned, our studio must have nothing but the best. He seemed to think I had unlimited funds and treated me like *his* personal bank."

I stared at Dana, appalled that this woman, a respected and admired community leader, possessed such a lack of judgment.

She shook her head and met my gaze. "I know, in retrospect, it sounds absolutely idiotic. Dimitry kept coming up with more and more grandiose concepts. First the high-cost floor then one of those large glitter balls for our special events. He even ordered special mirrors that make everyone look slender."

Mirrors that make you look skinny? Now *that* was a brilliant concept. I needed to find out where you could buy one of those.

"The last check I gave him was supposed to be used for signing bonuses for the big name teachers from the Bay Area. One of the professionals who occasionally performed on *Dancing with the Stars* agreed to be a guest instructor. How could I refuse?"

She couldn't. I would mortgage my house to dance with one of those guys.

"I'm still not sure why your business arrangement with Dimitry automatically makes you a suspect. Didn't you show the detectives your partnership agreement?"

"I was afraid to put anything in writing in case Gordon found out. It seemed better to stick to a verbal agreement. I've been dancing with Dimitry for almost three years and I felt like we had a special relationship. I trusted him."

Amazing how good looks and biceps could transform a banker's wife into a silly teenager.

"Okay, what else do they have?"

"The sheriff is positive Dimitry was my lover since I gave him so much money. They insinuated I killed him in a jealous rage."

"The money aspect is somewhat suspicious, but why do they assume you were angry with Dimitry?"

She stared down at her hands then raised her eyes to me. "Someone overheard us arguing at the studio earlier that afternoon. Someone who heard me threatening that I would…" Her voice broke off.

"Threatening that you would tell someone he stole your money?"

Her eyes locked with mine. "Threatening to kill him."

TWENTY-ONE

JUST WHEN YOU THINK YOU'VE heard everything.

"Pretty strong words," I commented.

"I was upset and it was merely a figure of speech but…" She held her palms up and looked at me apologetically.

"So who overheard your conversation?"

"Anya." She mumbled something under her breath that rhymed with *witch*. "She's the one who informed the police about our argument. I'm certain she and Dimitry were lovers, and I bet she suspected he and I were fooling around. A couple of times my dance shoes disappeared and I noticed her snickering as I combed the studio for them."

I remembered the sultry manner in which Anya and Yuri danced in the studio the other day. "Are you certain Dimitry and Anya were lovers? She and Yuri seem joined at the hip, thighs and most of their movable body parts."

Dana tilted her head to the side. "As far as I can tell, Anya is only interested in one thing…and that's Anya."

I looked at her curiously.

"Whatever it takes for Anya to advance her career she'll do, whether it's sleeping with the other teachers, married or single, or her clients, married or single. Even Boris." Dana chuckled. "Okay, maybe not Boris. She has some standards."

Ouch. So the only man Anya *wouldn't* sleep with was the studio owner who thought he and I would make a great couple. My love life sucked.

I contemplated Dana's remarks. "When did you and Dimitry argue?"

"Around lunchtime. I was so furious with him that I stormed out of the studio and drove home. For weeks, I'd been asking him to bring me copies of the leases, the invoices and the employment contracts with the Bay Area teachers. He assured me the money was well spent, but he could never produce anything definitive. I have no idea where all the money went."

"Maybe he tucked it away in a bank account," I offered.

"Yeah, right. The Bank of Dimitry," she snorted, but in a ladylike banker's wife manner. "I was done with his lame excuses. All I could think about was that the money was gone and there was no studio. No big-name dancers." She cradled her head in her hands. "And no more dream."

"Does Mr. Chandler know what you did?" It was bad enough that her husband suspected his wife was fooling around with the dance instructor. I had a feeling financial hanky-panky would really hit him in his banker's gut as well as his wallet.

She nodded sheepishly and began twisting the tissue again. "Gordon came home for lunch that day as he often does. I was so riled up from the argument I told him everything, that the money was gone and I had nothing to show for it. Gordon was absolutely silent. He didn't even get red-faced like he usually does when he's mad. He stood up from the kitchen table and left. No kiss. No hug. No comment. He got in his car and drove back to the bank."

I was starting to feel much more empathetic toward my boss. My life seemed relatively calm in comparison to what he recently suffered. I still couldn't decide whether or not to believe Dana's claim that her relationship with Dimitry was completely innocent. In the best case scenario, she had stolen money from her husband. Worst case, she had stolen money *and* committed adultery.

"So why did you go back to the studio Thursday night?"

"I had calmed down and hoped somehow I could force Dimitry into telling me what he really did with the funds. He just laughed at me earlier when I threatened to kill him. Said it wasn't the first time someone threatened him."

"You must have been stunned when you heard he was dead."

She stared at me in horror. "Honestly, I couldn't believe it."

I peeked at my watch. We had to wrap this up soon. "It still doesn't seem like they have enough evidence pointing to you. Do you have any suspects in mind? What about those death threats Dimitry said he received?"

"I've racked my brain but, honestly, Dimitry was so unpopular with the male instructors, any one of them could have sent those notes. Boris would have been furious about Dimitry starting his own studio. I'm sure Irina, his wife, suspected he might have been fooling around with Anya, or even with me. As for Anya?" Dana's lips curved in a slight smile. "She's number one on my list but I don't have any proof other than she's a conniving bitch and I'm not sure that's enough for the sheriff."

I edged up from the wicker loveseat. "I need to leave, Dana. I'm not sure what I can do to help."

Dana grasped my forearm so tightly I thought my bones might shatter. "The detectives are still investigating other suspects but you can see it doesn't look good. You're friendly with Detective Hunter so I thought maybe you could put in a good word on my behalf. The D.A. hates Gordon so he probably can't wait to put together a case and prosecute me."

Her frightened eyes implored me. "Please. You're my only hope."

Could I refuse her plea? Possibly.

Would I? Probably not.

I said goodbye, slipped out the front door, started the car and drove the two blocks back into town. Driving past the Bell Tower, I caught up to Doc Wisner's black-and-red nineteenth-century stagecoach. His team of sturdy black horses clip-clopped down Main Street, carrying a boisterous group of boys and their exhausted parents. I followed in their wake on the lookout for a parking spot, which would be at a premium on the last Saturday before Christmas.

A left blinker flashed and a dirty beige SUV scooted in front of the stagecoach, leaving a choice spot directly in front of the Old Town Grill.

Bells jingled as I pushed open the frosted glass door to the Grill. Mother sat in a corner table, tapping away on her BlackBerry, her gigantic diamond blinding me with its beams of light. I hoped she was so preoccupied with her messages, she wouldn't notice I was over ten minutes late.

"Hello, dear," she intoned, not looking up, her thumbs working in tandem. For a sixty-two-year-old woman, her reflexes were excellent. "Late as usual."

"Sorry." My stomach rumbled as I grabbed one of the glossy menus resting on the oak-topped tables. If she was going to ignore me, I might as well distract myself by ogling the photos. I was so hungry I briefly considered ordering a cheeseburger with garlic fries, chocolate shake, and a stack of pancakes. And maybe an apple pie chaser.

Mother punched a button then set her device on the table. Even on a Saturday morning she was dressed to kill in a belted green tweed jacket, complementary forest-green pleated skirt and matching suede pumps, one of which was nudging my ankle. "So what were you doing this morning? You were so mysterious on the phone."

"A special project for the bank."

Our server appeared to take our orders. Mother chose her usual Cobb salad with dressing on the side and I followed suit, wistfully hoping a few stray French fries might leap off the fryer and accidentally land on top of my leafy greens.

"I'm glad the bank finally appreciates your talents. Have you heard the rumors that Dana Chandler was having an affair with that dancer who was killed?" Her powdered nose wrinkled in dismay.

"How well do you know Dana?" I asked.

"We've worked together on several fundraisers. And we're both on the Holiday Can Drive committee." She peered at me over her rose-colored reading glasses. "By the way, we need more volunteers to transport some of the items."

I can take a hint. The Holiday Can Drive would be added to my increasingly lengthy to-do list.

"Dana is such a classy woman," I commented. "I can't imagine her having an affair, much less murdering someone."

Mother took off her reading glasses and sighed. "She certainly doesn't appear capable of murder, but I'm probably not the best judge of character."

Considering she had been known to fraternize with a killer, I agreed with her assessment.

"Do you know Dana from bank functions?" she asked.

I nodded. "They also invited me to their house this morning. Supposedly, Dana is the number one suspect in Dimitry's death. They thought I could help."

My mother's eyes widened. "Honey, I know Mr. Chandler is your boss, but I don't think you should get involved in another murder investigation. Especially one involving a Russian dancer. It wouldn't surprise me if the Russian Mafia was involved."

"Mom, you've been reading too many spy novels." I chuckled at the thought of muscle-bound men sporting black leather jackets running around killing dance instructors attired in see-through mesh shirts.

She shook a manicured index finger at me. "There is a large Russian community living in the foothills and in Sacramento. Many of them have purchased houses through me. Most are very sweet, but you never know what kind of ties they could have to criminals here and abroad."

I pondered her statement. Was there some truth in what she said? Could Dimitry have been involved in a scheme involving the Russian mafia? What happened to all the money Dana had given him? My mind whirled with possibilities—black market vodka, caviar.

Yum. Caviar.

Our server appeared with our entrees. No caviar but a tasty assortment of chicken, bacon and veggies rested atop the crisp greens.

"I suppose you'll investigate whether I want you to or not," Mother said as she took a bite of salad. "It would be terrible if Dana was arrested if she's not guilty. She does a lot of good in this community with all of her charity work. And the bank provides more loans to local residents than any other lending institution. So where would you start?"

My fork hovered over chunks of avocado as I contemplated my approach. "According to several people, Dimitry was not the most popular instructor in the studio, at least among the guys. Plus there could be some jealous females. But I don't know where I can find the time to interview all the instructors."

"I may have a solution for you. Robert and I want to take ballroom lessons."

Tall, Bald and Homely on the dance floor? With my elegant mother?

She really was in love.

"You're not planning a dance routine for *your* wedding, are you?" The bite of egg I'd swallowed turned to cement as I realized how committed my mother was to marrying her new fiancé. Despite her announcement last week, I'd pushed her impending marriage to the farthest recesses of my mind, figuring that eventually she would come to her senses.

I wanted to be happy for my mother. I really did. She'd been glowing like a freshly-facialed starlet since the two of them had begun dating. And even though the woman sitting across from me, dressed in pearls, tweed and high heels drove me crazy most of the time, she had been my lifeline for all of my thirty-nine years. Marriage to Bradford would change our mother/daughter dynamic and I wasn't sure I was ready to share her with anyone else just yet.

She chuckled. "We're in love but we're not as loony as Liz. Robert already admitted he has two sized thirteen left feet, so the best I can hope for is one brief dance at our wedding that won't embarrass us too much."

Yeah, well, good luck with that.

"With Robert's background, he could probably ferret out more information than you can," she said.

My mind recalled Detective Bradford's interrogative technique when he investigated me. Not the most subtle approach, but it couldn't hurt for him to do a little detecting at the dance studio.

And dancing together might be the perfect way to break them up. I felt kind of guilty at such a devious thought, but my only concern was my mother's well-being. And I sincerely doubted Bradford was the man to make her happy for the rest of her life. Their dance lessons could actually serve a dual purpose.

"I can't believe I'm saying this but that sounds like an excellent plan."

Her eyes sparkled. "Detecting while dancing. It certainly can't hurt, can it?"

TWENTY-TWO

MONDAY MORNING FOUND ME singing lustily to "I'm a Single Lady" while I inhaled the scent of a new coconut-lime shampoo Liz guaranteed would make my hair bounce when I walked. Personally, I thought enough of my body parts bounced when I moved, but I wasn't averse to adding shine to my hair.

The phone on my nightstand rang the second I lathered the magical concoction into my reddish-brown curls. I threw open the shower door, grabbed a towel, and picked up the cordless phone.

"Hello," I said, attempting to wrap one cumbersome towel around my shivering frame, and the other over my dripping locks, which made it impossible to hear the response on the other end. The squawking that resonated over the line sounded faintly imperious so I had a fairly good idea who had chosen to interrupt my morning shower.

"Laurel, what the blazes are you doing? It sounds like you're in a tussle with someone." She giggled. "Did I interrupt some morning nookie?"

I poked a finger in my ear trying to decide if it was plugged with water. Did Liz ask if I had my morning cookie?

She forged ahead without waiting for a response. "I have wonderful news. Boris said everyone can get together to practice the wedding routine tonight. Isn't that brilliant?"

Brilliant remained to be seen. I had no idea how well the other members of the wedding party were doing with their lessons, but presumably they were progressing faster than me, since I wasn't progressing at all. At least it would provide an opportunity to squeeze in a little more investigating.

With my morning routine delayed by Liz's call, I blow-dried my hair, slapped on my makeup and dressed in less than half an hour. I threw water and quick-cook Irish oatmeal into a pan and brought it to a boil. Then I stirred in cumin and cinnamon and turned the burner down to simmer.

Ben arrived first at the table. He slid into the spindle-backed chair and threw a three-page document into my hand.

"What's this?"

"It's an addendum to my Christmas list." He grinned at me, the empty space where his two front teeth had fallen out visual proof that despite his improving vocabulary, he truly was only seven years old.

"An addendum?" What kind of spelling words were they giving second graders these days?

He frowned at me. "Mom, don't you know what an addendum is? It's an addition to my Christmas list. I missed a few things in the first one."

I perused the forty-seven new items on the three-page document. My son was an eternal optimist.

Steam erupted from the pot on the stove. I shut off the gas burner before the oatmeal could stiffen into glue. I spooned some of the cereal into a chipped blue enamel bowl, poured in some milk, threw in a handful of golden raisins, and placed the concoction in front of my son. He began shoveling it into his mouth.

"Ben, slow down."

"Yeah, Ben, you sound disgusting," complained his

sister, who had entered the kitchen and was now dishing her own oatmeal into a bowl.

Her brother blinked long-lashed green eyes at her and gave her an owlish look. "Yeah, well, you look…"

She thrust her chin at him. "I look what?"

"You look pretty." He grinned, knowing a compliment from her little brother would be totally unexpected.

I scrutinized my daughter's appearance: tight black jeans, trendy long-sleeved top and more makeup than usual. Jenna rarely wore any cosmetics beyond cherry lip gloss. What was the deal?

"You look nice, honey. Is there something special going on at school today?"

"The winter concert for the jazz band is tonight," she replied. "A bunch of the kids from chorus are going together. I told you about it last week."

Of course she did. I hoped my forgetfulness was only a sign of how overbooked I was and not a sign that an approaching birthday was bringing diminished mental capacity.

I grimaced. "Sorry, I did forget and someone has to watch Ben tonight. Liz issued an ultimatum. Everyone needs to be at the studio at eight."

Jenna placed her hands on her hips and scowled. "Looks like Ben will be visiting the dance studio with you, doesn't it?"

I didn't appreciate Jenna's tone, but my eldest rarely complained when I asked her to babysit. It wouldn't be a huge issue to take Ben along with me.

I looked at Ben and he shrugged. "No biggie."

Okay, that was easy. If I gave Ben a pen and pad of paper, he could add another addendum to his ever-expanding Christmas list. That should keep him out of trouble.

Twelve hours later, Ben and I entered the dance studio. I settled him into one of the white molded plastic chairs next to a round matching table on the side of the large ballroom. Between his Happy Meal treat and a spelling assignment, Ben should be able to entertain himself while I availed myself of the opportunity to talk to some of the teachers.

At least twenty couples of varying sizes, ages and nationalities moved around the ballroom, participants in the newcomer waltz class. Ballroom etiquette mandates that couples dance in a counterclockwise direction, but ballroom technique, as I'd quickly come to realize, cannot be learned overnight.

I chuckled as two pairs of dancers collided. At least I wasn't the only "klutzky" on the floor. Both couples appeared to be in good spirits and they laughed as they ventured back into the circle formation their instructor had demonstrated.

At the far end of the room another couple narrowly missed mowing down several pairs of dancers. The male dancer whirled his partner with force and determination, totally oblivious to the three beats of a waltz melody.

Gregor, dressed in a tight black T-shirt and even tighter designer jeans, his dark hair pulled back in his standard ponytail, was teaching the newcomer class. Or at least attempting to teach them. The Russian instructor stomped to the CD player and the music abruptly stopped. He clapped his hands bringing the dancers to a halt.

"People, please, you must pay attention. Hear the rhythm. Feel the music. Do not rush through it. This is not a race."

The students chuckled and nodded. Gregor's smile looked practiced and insincere. Teaching beginner students had to be one of the less appealing aspects of his job. "Okay, we start again. You two, come closer to me." He pointed to the couple that had been careening recklessly around the floor. They stared back at him with puzzled looks on their faces. "Yes, you, please come here. It will be safer for the class."

Gregor chuckled and the other students laughed along with him. The couple reluctantly moved to the center of the dance floor. Their expressions revealed they weren't happy to be singled out.

I tried not to giggle myself when I recognized the troublemakers. Detective Bradford and my mother. She must be mortified that the teacher had chastised them in front of the other patrons. This dance class could be just the thing to tear them apart.

Ben yanked on the sleeve of my sweater. "Mom, that looks like Grandmother and Detective Bradford."

I nodded at him, intent on watching Gregor demonstrate a basic box pattern.

The shrill cry of a seven-year-old boy echoed across the cavernous room. "Hey, Detective Bradford, are you here to catch the killer?"

Gregor stumbled in the midst of demonstrating the rise and fall of the waltz. My mother paled. My own face burned as twenty pairs of eyes turned to my son. I was *so* not going to get the Mother of the Year award.

As for Bradford, once again the big man startled me. Instead of the anger I anticipated, his face lit up with that smile I only saw when he was in the company of my mother. He loped to the side of the room and scooped up Ben with little effort. My seven-year-old squealed in delight. Whatever connection the two of them had, it was obviously a positive relationship for both.

Bradford whispered in Ben's ear, set him back in his chair then returned to his place by my mother's side. Gregor walked over to talk to Yuri, his frenzied hand movements and somber expression indicative of his distress attempting to keep the class under control. It was difficult enough teaching forty newcomers, much less having the class interrupted by a disruptive child.

I hoped Yuri had some advice for the other instructor that did not entail sending a seven-year-old boy home with his mother.

Yuri shook his head and walked away. Gregor punched a button on the CD player and music filled the room once again. The dance teacher addressed the students. "For now, practice what I have taught you. Try not to crush anyone, please."

He nodded to the class then rushed across the room toward the back of the studio where Yuri had disappeared.

The front door to the studio burst open with a bang. Liz propelled herself toward me, dropping her purse and assorted bags into one chair and herself into another. Her beautiful porcelain complexion, pampered on a daily basis, normally made my friend look ten years younger than the forty she had turned three months earlier. But tonight she looked bedraggled.

"Is anything wrong?" I asked.

Liz's shoulders sagged as she slumped in her chair. "That bozo D.A. is making Brian's life hell, which is making my life equally hideous."

"What's going on?"

She ran her fingers through her highlighted bronzed curls, which oddly enough made her hair look even more stylish than before. How did she do that?

"The D.A. wants someone arrested who we both know, but who I can't say anything about because it's confidential. Brian says there isn't enough evidence to arrest her yet."

"So Brian's in the doghouse."

"More like the outhouse since his boss is such a piece of…" She glanced at Ben who hung on her every word. "I swear that D.A. is so full of himself I don't know how Brian stands it. It's like this every election year."

I murmured a comforting response. The door to the studio banged open once again. Nanette, the dancing nurse, and her friend, Samantha, wandered in, followed by Paula lugging in a huge garment bag.

The three women settled into the vacant chairs alongside ours. Paula noticed my curious expression as she struggled with the oversized vinyl bag. "I'm practicing with Boris tonight and I need to ensure that the length of my competition gown is okay. The seamstress was supposed to hem it so it would fall right at my ankle, but it seems lower than that. If it catches on the heel of my shoe, I could trip."

Ballroom dancing was the most masochistic hobby. Despite years of lessons, there were so many ways you could make a fool of yourself. I couldn't understand why someone would spend thousands of dollars on ball gowns and private lessons if there was a chance that one tiny misstep might land them on their sequined butt.

I didn't have the money, time or the ability to ever worry about competing, but that didn't keep me from watching Paula unzip her garment bag.

"Wow, your gown is gorgeous," Samantha said. The lights from the mirrored ball in the studio transformed the Swarovski crystals on the royal-blue silk dress into miniature diamond stars.

"I love the cut of the skirt." Liz smoothed the fabric between her fingertips. "Who's your seamstress? Do you think it's too late to alter my wedding dress?"

Too late? Yes, my dear Bridezilla, it is much too late to redesign your wedding dress.

"Bet that cost you a bunch of moolah." Nanette voiced the thoughts going through several of our heads.

Paula nodded. "Four thousand dollars. And it's not even new."

I couldn't tell whose jaw dropped the lowest.

"Are you kidding?" You could hear the exclamation marks in the tone of Liz's voice.

"I know it seems nuts," Paula admitted. "But at the gold level I don't have a choice. The judges basically decide who will win first place the second they lay eyes on you. I could be the best dancer out there, but if I don't look and dress the part, I'll place near the bottom. With anywhere from six to ten couples on the floor at the same time, they have less than ten seconds to watch each couple dance. Your dress, and even the way your hair is styled, can determine the outcome."

"It's a good thing I'm only competing in the Newcomer level. I can get by with that hot pink $99 fringed special I bought on eBay." Samantha elbowed her friend. "C'mon, Nanette. Time for our group salsa lesson."

Nanette stood and rocked to the left before she righted herself on her heels. Even wearing three-inch stilettos she barely reached five feet. "I'm ready. Let's go find us some hard bodies." She leered at us then teetered down the dance floor toward the smaller studio in the back.

Paula, Liz and I burst out laughing. I couldn't imagine prowling for hard bodies in my seventies. Not that I was all that successful at half her age.

Paula was still chuckling as she grabbed her garment bag and headed to the ladies' dressing room to change. Mother and Bradford were evidently done terrorizing the other couples on the dance floor and they joined us.

"I can't wait to see your wedding routine, Liz," Mother

said. "Laurel was so excited about learning the fox-trot that Robert and I decided to take a few lessons ourselves."

Liz gave me a self-satisfied "I told you so" smile. I tried to remember if I had ever used the words *excited* and *fox-trot* in the same sentence.

"Honey, why don't we take Ben to your house? We can stay until Jenna comes home."

In less than five seconds, Ben had thrown the last vestiges of his Happy Meal in the garbage can and crammed his homework into his backpack.

We exchanged kisses and said goodbye. It would be far easier concentrating on the dance choreography if I didn't have to worry about Ben searching for killers hiding in the studio. My poor children would probably need years of therapy.

I waved as the three of them exited the studio then turned to Liz. "Where's the rest of the bridal party?"

"They should be here any second. Bobby said he'd be a few minutes late joining us. Boris called a brief meeting of all the instructors between classes. Something about some upcoming competition everyone is involved in."

That must be the reason why Gregor had raced to the back of the studio before the waltz class ended. As if on cue, the door blew open again, bringing in a group of chatting men and women.

"Hi, beautiful." Brian bent over his fiancée and kissed her, transforming her once again into his sparkling bride-to-be. Re-energized by her Prince Charming, Liz sprang into action, directing us to our spots with the efficiency of a drill sergeant on speed.

Bobby had choreographed the routine so all three bridesmaids entered from the left and the groomsmen came in from the right. We would simultaneously perform the grapevine step. Even I could manage that. We were also supposed to gracefully lift our arms but that seemed far too complicated for me. Recently, I'd overheard Bobby muttering something about my Frankenstein arms.

Once we joined the groomsmen, we would dance the fox-trot including some turns and promenades around the room, then fan out for the bride and groom to perform their solo. The best man, a nice guy named Chuck, was my partner. He was remarkably agile for a former football player turned high school math teacher. His grapevine was perfect although he had a tendency to speed through the steps like he must have done in football practice twenty years earlier.

My attention wandered as I watched Anya and Gregor practice a movement that required her to slither down his body then slide between his legs. She was so flexible it was like watching Gumby with breasts.

Yuri wandered into the studio sipping his habitual energy drink. If I had to dance from nine to ten hours a day, a twelve-pack of energy drinks would be a requirement.

Strains of "It Had to Be You" emanated from the sound system so I followed the other bridesmaids onto the floor. I wasn't positive if the reason I walked in last had to do with my official position as matron of honor, or clever choreography. I was grateful the other bridesmaids, masseuses in Liz's spa, seemed to know what they were doing.

Chuck led me for three full steps before I abruptly halted.

"What the heck?" he yelled, as I grabbed his polo shirt in an attempt to stay upright.

"Laurel, what is the matter with you?" Liz said.

"Sorry, I was distracted."

"Hey, I realize it's hard to stay focused when you're surrounded by so many gorgeous men, but you need to pay attention."

"It's not the guys who distracted me." I pointed across the room to where the number one murder suspect and her husband stood.

"What the bloody hell is *she* doing here?" Brian asked, his face livid. He was one angry assistant District Attorney.

I shrugged. Dana might be a murder suspect, but I assumed she was free to do anything she wanted other than leave the area. Brian marched over to the Chandlers.

Dana looked horrified from all the attention. Mr. Chandler thrust his pudgy jaw out, looking like he was prepared to do battle to defend his wife's honor. I darted over but before I could eke out a greeting, Brian turned to me, his palm practically touching the tip of my nose. "Laurel, stay out of this."

Like that would stop me.

"Dana, are you here for a lesson?" I asked, dodging Brian's hand.

She looked happy to explain her presence. "Yes, I'm supposed to, um… Yuri and I…" She stumbled as she attempted to regain her composure. "I need to practice for the Holiday Ball. Yuri offered to take Dimitry's place and compete with me. We have a lesson at nine."

She turned to Brian. "I didn't realize it would be a problem coming to the studio. Is it out of bounds for me?"

Brian blew out a breath. "Technically, no, although I've never run across a situation where a person suspected of murder willingly returned to the scene of a crime, unless they had an ulterior motive in doing so."

"My wife did not kill that piece of slime!" Mr. Chandler shook his fist mere inches from Brian's nose. I'd never seen the bank president lose his composure before. This was so out of character for him.

Dana grabbed her husband's wayward fist and clasped it in her hands. "Let me repeat. My goal is to compete in the New Year's Holiday Ball. I apologize if my presence at the studio is considered unacceptable, but I certainly hope my motivation is understandable."

Liz joined us. With a brief hello to the Chandlers, she coaxed both Brian and me back onto the dance floor.

"Brian, leave that poor woman alone." She slipped her arm around his waist. "I don't think you should be talking to her without her attorney present, anyway."

That thought had also crossed *my* mind as Brian chastised Dana and evidently he realized it, as well. He pulled Liz tight, nuzzled her cheek and whispered in her ear. She giggled and pinched his rear.

I rolled my eyes. Get a room.

I looked over my shoulder. Dana introduced her husband to Yuri. They shook hands, and Yuri led the couple to a table and chairs alongside the dance floor. Dana and her new partner immediately began talking while Mr. Chandler sat glowering in silence. I wondered why he had chosen to accompany Dana. Did he come to support his wife? Or was he merely a jealous husband intent on keeping an eye on his spouse?

Yuri was as attentive to Dana as he should be toward a client, who despite being a murder suspect still had plenty of bucks to spend on dance lessons. Or did she? After spending all that money funding Dimitry's studio, the Chandlers could be in a sticky financial situation.

A vision in midnight-blue strolled onto the floor. Paula's evening gown fit her like a dream. If I ever had the money to compete, I'd need enough Spanx to cover me from my neck down to my ankles.

Paula was followed by Boris. They joined Yuri and the Chandlers at their table. After a few minutes, the studio owner stood and led Paula onto the floor. I wondered how they could dance when our group hogged the CD player, but evidently at the gold level, you could practice your steps without music. Now *that* took skill.

Bobby stopped briefly at their table to chat with Yuri before he walked over to the CD player. Seconds later, the sound of "It Had to Be You," which had shot to number one on my top ten most despised songs list, filtered through the room. The wedding party which had been chatting instead of dancing quickly resumed our positions. On our sixth attempt, the routine went perfectly.

Thunderous applause from the sidelines surprised me. I looked over to check out our rooting section. Salsa class must have ended because Samantha and Nanette cheered alongside Boris.

The studio owner's beady eyes zeroed in on one member of the wedding party. "Ah, Laurel, so light on your feet now, yes?" He shot me a wolfish grin "With more lessons you could be competing with these other beautiful ladies."

Take lessons with Boris? Over my *zaftig* dead body.

Paula joined the two bridesmaids who were heading in the direction of the changing room so her lesson must have ended also. Yuri tossed his energy drink into the wastebasket with a shot that would have made Michael Jordan proud. He stopped to talk to Bobby who indicated our group was finished for the night. Bobby looked like he was finished, as well.

Liz and Brian walked off nuzzling each other. It was kind of nauseating but I was happy that Queen Elizabeth was in a good mood after our practice session. Since I had yet to see Dana and Yuri dance together, I decided to stick around and watch from the sidelines. I sat next to Samantha and Nanette. Mr. Chandler watched from the opposite side of the studio.

"Your group looked good out there," Samantha said.

"Thanks. Maybe once I master the fox-trot I can join you in your salsa class. Is it hard?"

"Not hard enough." Nanette tittered at her double entendre and Samantha punched her on the forearm. Paula said goodbye and exited the studio behind Liz and Brian. The sound of "Just Dance," one of my favorite Lady Gaga tracks, pulsated through the room as Dana and Yuri took to the floor.

I tapped my foot along with the music and watched the couple perform the elaborate eight-count cha cha. Dana swiveled, pivoted, and thrust her hips back and forth at lightning speed. She was at least ten years older than me, but in far better shape. I couldn't blame her for not wanting to miss out on the Holiday Ball competition. She was amazing.

I wondered if Mr. Chandler had ever seen his wife in action before. Seeing her face glow as she danced with the good-looking instructor, I doubted this was the best method for maintaining a successful marriage.

On the other hand, maybe letting your spouse indulge in their favorite hobby was the perfect prescription for creating a healthy, enduring relationship. If I ever had a spouse again, I'd keep that in mind.

Yuri's high cheekbones shimmered with perspiration as the couple performed some type of complicated step that left even me breathless. And I was merely watching.

The song ended and Yuri bent over, his chest rising and falling more rapidly than the frenetic music. They conferred briefly then started again, this time side by side, their legs kicking out with amazing speed and dexterity. Watching them jive was like watching *Dancing with the Stars,* but better, because I had a front-row seat.

Dana splayed her hands on Yuri's rock-hard abdomen and he thrust her up in the air. Her long legs, covered in black leggings, whirled around and around while remaining at Yuri's waist level. Their performance was mesmerizing.

Yuri suddenly bellowed a sound reminiscent of the roar of a wounded elephant. Dana flew out of his arms and slid across the varnished floor. She landed in a sprawl, her face dark with anger that quickly changed to horror.

Yuri clutched his chest, his face as white as a bridal gown. He staggered a few steps then crashed to the floor.

TWENTY-THREE

THERE WAS A BRIEF LULL WHEN nothing and no one moved, including Yuri. Then everyone leaped into action. Dana scrambled to her feet and within seconds she was bent over Yuri's prone body. Boris and Bobby were right behind her and I arrived right behind them.

Dana's dark head rested on Yuri's chest. "He's still breathing. Thank God. I don't understand. What happened?"

Yuri's eyes were closed, his mouth twisted in a gargoylesque grimace. Spittle dribbled out of the corner of his lower lip.

"I called 9-1-1," Nanette announced. "They should be here soon."

Boris made an attempt to lift Yuri into a sitting position but Nanette stopped him. "Don't move him," ordered the nurse. "See if you can find something to put under his head so he doesn't choke."

Bobby ran to the lobby and removed a pillow from the sofa. He returned with Anya hot on his heels.

"Let me through!" Anya propelled herself past the group, falling to her knees before the prone body. She grabbed one of Yuri's hands and drilled Dana with a look so cold it could have turned the Amazon jungle into the Siberian tundra. "What have you done? Have you killed our Yuri, too?"

Dana's dark doe eyes were huge in her pale face. "I

didn't do anything. Yuri and I were practicing for the competition. He collapsed right in the middle of our jive solo."

Anya shook her finger at Dana "Why are you not in jail?"

Dana shrank back against her husband, who had now joined the group gathered around the dancer.

"Anya, please stop." Boris stood, towering over all of us. "We do not know what happened here. I'm sure Yuri, he will be okay." He clasped his hands together and raised his eyes to the ceiling as if praying that his statement would become the truth.

"Yeah, you know Yuri downs those energy drinks like they're soda pop," interjected Bobby. "Maybe he has caffeine overload."

Anya sniffed but she remained quiet, stroking Yuri's motionless hand.

"Where are rescue people?" Boris's voice thundered through the studio. No sooner had he uttered the words than the entry doors were flung open and once again El Dorado County rescue personnel hurried through. The two men in navy blue uniforms told us to clear away as they began ministering to Yuri, who despite the noise and verbal accusations, remained unconscious.

Within minutes, they had Yuri loaded on a gurney headed for Mercy Hospital, the closest hospital to the El Dorado Hills dance studio. He still hadn't regained consciousness and left with an oxygen mask over his nose and an IV hooked to his muscular forearm.

Once Yuri was taken away, Dana and Mr. Chandler slipped out the door. I didn't blame them. If this event had occurred one hundred fifty years earlier, the crowd would have tied Dana up and taken her to Placerville for an old fashioned lynching. That big old Hangin' Tree might have claimed one more victim.

Fortunately, this was the twenty-first century.

With Yuri out of commission that left only two male instructors besides Boris. Did someone have it in for the male dance instructors? And soon there'd be none?

I shook my head. Bobby probably had it right. There was nothing wrong with Yuri other than imbibing way too many energy drinks.

The diet cola I'd drunk earlier had reached its final destination, so a pit stop seemed like a good idea before I left the studio and drove home. I exited the ladies' room and collided with Anya. Coal-black streaks of mascara formed a wobbly trail from her red-rimmed eyes down her colorless cheeks.

And she still looked good!

"Anya, are you okay?"

"No, I am not." She walked into the main ballroom, collapsing into one of the chairs. The lights had been dimmed and we were the only occupants of the vast room.

"You must be upset about Yuri." I dropped into the chair next to hers. "But I'm sure he'll be all right."

"It was so strange," she said, her expression both sad and puzzled. "One minute he is fine then the next minute there he is, lying on the floor, so pale and still."

She placed her palms over her face and started to cry. "What will I do if he is gone?"

"Are you and Yuri, um—" I pondered the best way to ask if she and Yuri were getting it on "—romantically involved?"

Her whole body shook and she continued to sob. "It's complicated."

Yeah, well, what wasn't these days? Since this was my first opportunity to be alone with Anya, I decided to try another tack. "Do you have any idea who could have murdered Dimitry?"

She lifted her head and narrowed her eyes. "That woman, she killed him. I heard her threaten him."

"Just because they argued that day doesn't mean she killed him. Did Dimitry ever say anything to you about receiving death threats from someone?"

With the lights dimmed, it was at first difficult to discern, but something flickered in her dark eyes. "Anya, did you write those letters?"

"I cannot talk." Anya stood up, her posture perfect as always. "I must go to work now."

"You have another job?" I looked at my watch. Almost ten. Not that many employment opportunities at this time of night. "Are you a waitress?"

Her eyes darted to the left and right before she responded. "Yes. Sure. Goodbye." She whirled out the front door before I could ask where she was employed.

I stood up and headed in the direction of the door before I realized I still wore my suede-soled dance shoes, the shoes Liz had lent me until I could buy another pair. The odds of my silver pair dancing out of the evidence room and back into my closet were zilch at this point.

The studio seemed cavernous in the dim light. And spooky. I expected Dimitry's ghostly apparition to waltz across the floor any second.

The sooner I exited this death trap the better. I picked up my pace, noticing that the door to Boris's office was closed. Light shone from under the door so he was either working or talking to someone privately. I walked past his office into the cloakroom and flicked on the light switch. I sat on a bench and removed Liz's black canvas practice shoes. With their one-inch heels and soft expandable fabric, they felt as comfortable as dancing in my slippers.

I slipped on my boots, zipped them up and stood. Before I could stuff Liz's shoes in her tote bag, a loud crash startled me and both shoes dropped to the floor. I bent over to retrieve them and the door slammed shut.

The room went black.

TWENTY-FOUR

IF THE STUDIO SEEMED SCARY earlier, it was downright terrifying now. With no windows to provide exterior light, the room was blacker than the inside of my mascara tube. Was I alone in a pitch-black room with a killer?

I listened for the sound of someone breathing, but my heart beat so loudly, I wouldn't hear a bass drum if it was playing right next to me. I moved my palms along the wall, feeling my way toward the entrance. Had Boris closed the studio, not realizing that someone was still inside? I couldn't be locked in here. I had two kids to go home to.

My left knee bumped into the bench and the sudden jolt made my stomach revolt from both pain and fear. My breaths were quick and shallow, making me feel light-headed and woozy. I felt my way along the wall, finally locating the door. When I tried turning the knob, nothing happened.

A wave of panic threatened to take over as my claustrophobia kicked in.

Calm down, Laurel.

I wiped my damp palms on my slacks and took a couple of deep breaths. Presence of mind was needed if I was going to escape my prison. I grabbed hold of the knob again and gave it another try. It turned easily. Relief flooded through me. I took a calming breath and pushed. The door exploded open with a bang. A menacing presence loomed over me.

I shrieked and landed a kick worthy of David Beckham.

The impact of my round-toed boot against something solid sent a streak of pain up my right calf. The man bent over and swore something unintelligible. I darted past him and bolted out of my jail. I raced into the main room, heading for the exit. Moments later, I realized my car keys were in my purse. And my purse was back in the room I had just escaped.

Lights suddenly blazed throughout the studio. I was prepared to run out the door but since the studio was located in a commercial park in El Dorado Hills, there would be miles to go before I found a safe haven. After a ninety-minute dance lesson and pain radiating from my shin, I could barely outrun a snail, much less a murderer.

"Who's out there?" boomed a familiar voice. Boris? I hoped I hadn't injured him, although it served him right for scaring me like that.

"It's me, Laurel."

Boris limped into the studio, followed by Gregor. They looked puzzled to see me.

"Why are you still here?" Gregor frowned at me. "The studio is closed."

"I forgot my shoes in the back room and then the door slammed shut and I couldn't get out." I smiled apologetically at Boris. "Sorry about kicking you. You scared me."

The two men exchanged glances.

"You better to go now," Boris said. "Is late for mother of small children to be out at night."

"Stay here. I'll get your things." Gregor disappeared into the back, quickly returning with my purse and my tote bag. I grabbed both items from him.

"You guys sure work late," I said, wondering what was going on.

They stood, arms folded, impassive expression on both their faces. Okay, got it. Time to go. I walked to the entrance door with Boris following close behind me. The minute I stepped outside, the lock clicked.

Weird behavior, but this whole night had been strange from start to finish.

I unlocked my car, buckled my seat belt, popped in my Bluetooth and hit a familiar name on my contact list.

"Hi, luv, what's up?" Liz giggled. "Did Boris try to play footsie with you after we left?"

Considering how hard I walloped Boris, it was more like I had played footsie with his shin, but that wasn't the big news of the night.

"Yuri collapsed right in the middle of practicing the jive with Dana."

"Omigod. Is he okay?"

"I hope so. He was alive but unconscious when the paramedics drove him to the hospital."

"What do you think happened?"

"I don't know. Bobby thinks Yuri drank too many energy drinks. Anya accused Dana of trying to murder him. The Chandlers slipped out right after the ambulance took off for the hospital."

"If Yuri dies they'll close the studio again," she said. "Balls. I can't believe this is happening to me."

Bridezilla had returned.

She sighed. "Sorry. I don't know what I'm saying these days. What happened to Yuri is terrible. You don't think Dana could possibly have anything to do with it, do you? Wait a second. Brian needs to know about this."

Liz put me on hold. I began to think the call was lost when she returned.

"So what did Brian say?"

"He called the D.A. at home. I pretended to load the dishwasher but I overheard part of the conversation."

"Anything worth sharing?"

"Let's just say that by New Year's Eve, Dana is more likely to be dancing in an orange jumpsuit than a rhinestone-covered ball gown."

TWENTY-FIVE

AFTER A RESTLESS NIGHT SPENT dreaming of Dana waltzing in an orange jumpsuit, my sleep-deprived face resembled the toaster waffles in our freezer. I pawed through the clutter in my bathroom vanity in search of the no-name super-secret moisturizer Liz had given me a few weeks before. She never explained why it was super secret or why it remained unnamed so I was a tad concerned sprouts might start growing out of my face. When my pillowcase wrinkles disappeared in less than a minute, I was hooked. It was definitely preferable to *be* tired than look tired.

Jenna flounced into the kitchen slamming cabinet doors and muttering under her breath. I contemplated dumping some of the miracle cream into her blueberry smoothie to see if her crabbiness would disappear as fast as my wrinkles. I managed to deposit both kids at their respective schools and arrive at the bank parking lot a few minutes early.

Tires squealed as a white car with gold letters on the side and that ominous row of lights on the roof zoomed into the lot and parked next to my slot. Two men stepped out of the sedan. One of the men was a deputy I recognized from a previous encounter. The man accompanying him was also no stranger.

What were Tom Hunter and the young deputy up to? The bank didn't officially open until nine. Based on Tom's dour expression, he wasn't here to make a deposit. Fortunately I didn't have anything to worry about. At least I didn't think I did.

I quickly slid out of my car and caught up to them. "Are you here on official bank business?" I asked, trying to keep up with the long strides of the two men.

"More like bad business," he muttered as we walked through the parking lot. He abruptly halted in front of a spotless navy four-door sedan. The personalized license plate on the rear bumper read *1 BANK.

He pointed at the vehicle. "Is that Chandler's car?"

I nodded. Everyone who worked for the bank recognized Mr. Chandler's car. It was the big, expensive Mercedes parked in the space marked Bank President that bore the not-so-subtle license plate.

"Kind of obvious, isn't it?" Tom remarked.

His question threw me. "Mr. Chandler's the *President!* Modesty isn't one of the adjectives I'd use to describe him. He has no reason to cover up his success."

He yanked on my elbow and motioned for the deputy to go ahead. "I wonder what else your boss covered up. You were at Golden Hills Studio last night, right?"

"Uh-huh. Did you hear about Yuri? Do you know how he's doing?"

"He's still at Mercy Hospital. In a coma."

I sucked in my breath. This was worse than I had imagined. "Do they know what happened?"

"We're investigating. From all accounts, the studio was packed last night."

"They held a group salsa class, plus the members from Liz and Brian's wedding party were all there. Even my mother and Bradford. It was a real zoo."

Tom looked at me in disbelief. "Bradford is taking ballroom lessons? That man must be head over heels in love with your mother."

What kind of remark was that?

I glared at him. "Of course he is. He adores her. And like any sensible man, he wants to please her." This detective had no idea how to be sensitive to a woman's needs. Maybe it was a good thing Tom had broken up with me before I discovered what an insensitive clod he truly was.

A pained expression crossed his face. "Laurel, I know you're upset about what happened between us."

"Don't flatter yourself, Detective." As I brushed past him, he grabbed my hand and my entire body ignited. I hated that every time he touched me, my insides turned to molten mush.

"Look, I need to talk to you about what happened at the studio last night," he said. "I understand both the Chandlers were there."

I nodded. "Dana wanted to practice with Yuri and Mr. Chandler came with her because—" I stopped because I wasn't totally clear why my boss chose to escort his wife to the studio the previous evening.

"Dana and Yuri were dancing together when he suddenly screamed and collapsed on the floor." I shuddered as I recalled Yuri's pale face and still form. "Everyone went nuts. Anya accused Dana of killing him. Bobby insisted Yuri must have overdosed on caffeine."

Tom stopped for a minute and pulled his notepad out of his jacket pocket. I stood there, shivering from the brisk morning air, while he scribbled some notes, punctuating them with multiple question marks.

The detective finally looked up from his notepad. "You're freezing. Let's get inside. Since you were at the studio, I'd like to know what you observed. Can we talk about that later?"

His fingertips grazed my chin as his eyes met mine. "And once this case is solved, can we talk about us?"

I brushed his hand away. "There is no us, but feel free to make an appointment if you want to discuss the recent events at the dance studio."

Tom opened the door for me then followed me into the bank lobby. He stopped at the front desk to speak with Vivian. One smile from the hunky detective was enough to turn the normally cranky receptionist into a drooling ditz. I meandered through the maze that led to my cubicle, wondering about the early-morning visit. If Tom didn't come to the bank to interrogate me, why was he there?

Stan hovered at my desk, a legal-sized manila file in his hand. Ostensibly it looked like he wanted to discuss a loan, but I knew better. Despite his attempt to disguise himself as a harried underwriter, he was hunting for dance dirt.

He flung himself into the gray tweed chair reserved for hardworking staff. "I can't believe I missed out on all of the excitement. I knew I should have booked my lesson for last night."

"What lesson?"

Stan thrust his left shoulder forward and attempted to give me a smoldering look, which with Stan's gray eyes and weak chin, made him resemble a Dilbert character.

"T.A.N.G.O, kiddo," he chanted. "Remember that lesson I took the other day when I was spying at the studio? Anya said I'm a natural."

I cocked my head and reflected back on Stan's performance. He had been surprisingly good.

"It was so much fun I decided to take more lessons. Anya said we could compete some time."

"Wow. That could mean a ton of money and time."

"Yeah, but think how much fun it could be. Maybe you and I should compete together."

Since the odds of me competing with Stan were as high

as the cow not only jumping over the moon *but* supplying me with a glass of chocolate milk, I simply nodded.

Stan grabbed his file and headed down the hallway. In less than five seconds he was back, waving his hand and urging me to follow him.

Now what? I stood and followed him into the open area of the bank where the assembled staff watched aghast as our fearless leader was led out of the bank, metal cuffs restraining his hands behind his back.

Mr. Chandler's face was redder than Ben's fake Rudolph nose. At his side, Tom Hunter urged him along, but kindly, not with force. The young deputy followed both of them, one side of his face turning an interesting hue of purple and blue.

Stan nudged me with his elbow. "Do something."

"Me? Do you think I have some kind of magical powers to remove handcuffs from our boss?" It was getting more and more difficult lately to determine what tasks were included in my job description. Did Mr. Chandler need a detective, a lawyer or a locksmith?

Belle raced into the room. The executive assistant normally exuded a practical and peaceful demeanor. Today the right collar of her tailored white blouse was tucked into her navy suit while the left stuck straight up, the starched pointed end aimed at the ceiling. Her black curls, which were usually restrained by a barrette, formed a fluffy black halo around her pale frightened face.

Her frantic eyes scanned the room and zeroed in on us. She zoomed over. "They arrested Mr. Chandler."

"What happened?"

"I was sitting at my desk when the big guy, you know, the really good-looking one?" She looked at me for confirmation.

Yeah, yeah, big good-looking detective.

"He asked if he could speak to the president, so I went into the boss's office and told him some men from the sheriff's department were here to see him. Mr. Chandler came out and they all shook hands then went inside and closed the door. I couldn't hear much other than muffled voices but then Mr. Chandler's voice grew louder. I pretended to be typing, but I could see through the glass window of his office that he was getting all worked up. His face was red and he was waving his arms around. I was really worried. He's on high-blood-pressure meds, you know."

I shook my head. So far, I wasn't privy to the Chandler family's medical history, but at the rate we were bonding, I would probably soon know the president's cholesterol count *and* his prostate levels.

"I thought I should keep an eye on him just in case, and the next thing I knew, he tried to punch that young deputy in the eye." She smacked her fist into her palm for emphasis. "Mr. Chandler missed, but the deputy jumped away so fast, he whacked his cheek against the door."

Stan and I exchanged looks. The deputy must have said something that upset our fearless leader. Belle pushed me toward the front of the bank. "C'mon, Laurel, talk to the detectives. They can't truss Mr. Chandler up like a turkey."

Stan chuckled. "Well, he is kind of a stuffed shirt."

Belle skewered him with a look of disdain.

"What do you expect me to do?" I protested.

She threw her hands up in the air. "I don't know. You're the one who's supposed to be the brilliant detective. Mr. Chandler thinks you're amazing so go do something amazing."

He does? Okay then. There was one thing I knew for certain and that was if Mr. Chandler ended up in jail, there definitely wouldn't be anyone signing our Christmas bonus checks.

TWENTY-SIX

I RACED OUT OF THE OFFICE IN such a hurry I forgot my coat. The brisk December wind blowing through my thin rose pink cotton sweater transformed me into a raspberry popsicle. I trotted down the sidewalk, hoping to catch the officers and their presidential prisoner before they drove out of the parking lot.

Mr. Chandler stepped into the back of the patrol car, his lips curled in displeasure. As I recalled from my one and only backseat ride in a squad car, the interior of the cars were as aromatic as the Hangtown Bakery, but not in a good way.

"Tom!" I waved my hands to get his attention.

He leaned in, spoke with the deputy then walked over to meet me. "Laurel, we have to get going. And you're obviously freezing." His gaze dropped momentarily from my face to my chest. My nipples were happily saluting my former boyfriend, either because they were too cold to know better or because they were hoping he would heat them up.

I crossed my arms over my disobedient breasts and tilted my head to meet his wary eyes. "Is Mr. Chandler under arrest?"

"I can't share that with you," he said firmly.

"Are you kidding? How do you think the bank can function if the president is in jail? What about our customers?"

I was so annoyed I began poking him in the chest with my index finger. "We could have a run on the bank. That wouldn't be good for the bank, or this town."

He pulled on his earlobe, a little habit that meant he
wasn't absolutely certain what to do in this situation. It was
nice to know I could read one of his tells. Maybe it wasn't
so terrible to have a daughter addicted to Texas Hold 'Em.
Some of the poker-playing skills she had shared with me
could come in handy if I ever turned my amateur sleuthing into a full-time job.

"Look, your boss tried to punch a deputy. We can't
ignore something like that in order to keep your bank customers happy."

"Yeah, but Mr. Chandler missed, so technically he
didn't assault him." Did a missed attempt count? "Your
deputy must have provoked him."

"Deputy Mengelkoch may have been a little out of line
with one of his remarks."

"What did he say to set Mr. Chandler off?"

Tom stuffed his hands in his pockets and rocked back
and forth as he pondered how much to share. "That's none
of your concern. I have to get out of here, but we need to
talk. Are you home tonight?"

Four days until Christmas Eve. Ten days until Liz and
Brian's New Year's Eve wedding. Home was the last place
I should be tonight, but it was time the detective and I had
a tête-a-tête, whether it was about the murder or about the
two of us.

"Call me, I'll be around."

He put his hand on the small of my back and gave me a
little push in the direction of Main Street. "Go warm up. I
don't want to see you shivering when I show up tonight."

Like that was going to happen. My internal temperature
gauge always went awry when he was in the vicinity. As
I headed back to the bank, the patrol car pulled up next
to me. Tom rolled down his window and I heard our boss
bellowing from the back.

"Laurel, tell Belle to call my lawyer."

I gave Mr. Chandler a thumbs-up and threw him an encouraging smile, letting him know I was on it. I raced down the street, threw open the lobby door, and stomped down the hallway to my cubicle, hoping my activity would eventually generate some heat to my frosty tootsies.

It was after nine and the bank was officially open. Several Main Street store owners were already on the scene, milling around the bank lobby and conversing with one another. The branch manager and tellers assured the customers it was business as usual. Based on the worried looks on some of the merchants' faces, not many of them were buying it.

I scurried down to my cubicle before any of the staff could quiz me. Stan perched on the corner of my desk, contemplating his manicured nails, his polished Cordovan loafer swinging back and forth.

"So, what's the scoop?" His eyes gleamed bright behind his wire rims.

It wasn't up to me to confide the information Tom had shared about the altercation between Mr. Chandler and the deputy.

"I think it was all a misunderstanding," I said.

"Did they let the Prez go?"

"Nope."

"Did they take him to the jail?"

I shrugged.

"I wonder if the jail has his and her cells," he said.

"What are you talking about?"

"With Yuri collapsing last night, don't you think Dana will be arrested?"

Nuts. It seemed like everywhere I turned, there was a member of the Chandler family in trouble with the law.

Poor Robbie. Knowing what my daughter suffered when

I was a murder suspect, I could sympathize with the young man. What a way to spend his Christmas break.

"Go back to your cube. I need to talk to Belle." I shooed Stan away and he actually took my not-so-subtle hint and disappeared. I dialed her extension and relayed Mr. Chandler's request. The executive assistant sounded much calmer, especially now that she had a directive from her boss. Belle was as competent as they come, so Mr. Chandler's attorney might arrive at the jail before he did.

After all the morning commotion, it was impossible to concentrate on my loan files. If Mr. Chandler wasn't released soon, local bank customers might close out their checking and savings accounts. Hangtown Bank's business model was based on trust and reputation. Once word spread that the president had been arrested, who knew what would transpire?

I yanked out a yellow legal pad, drew a large circle in the middle of the page and filled in Dimitry's name. I added spokes for the different parties involved with the victim. So far there were Boris, the studio owner, Anya, Tatiana, and Wendy, the female instructors, and Yuri, Gregor, and Bobby, the male teachers. Since Yuri was in a coma it was yet to be seen if his current condition was tied to Dimitry's murder. He could suffer from some type of physical ailment that had been exacerbated by his frenetic lifestyle.

Then there were Dimitry's students, some of whom I still had not met.

Plus Irina, his wife.

Hmmm. I rubbed my Bic against my lower lip. There had been no sightings of the widow since she'd gone into labor in the studio. It had been almost two weeks since Dimitry's death. It couldn't be easy taking care of a newborn by herself. Perhaps she'd welcome a visit and a baby gift for her little girl.

Aww, a little girl. It brought back memories of the night my eldest was born. That night had been hell. Twenty-two hours of labor and three hours of pushing. Irina had no idea how easy she'd had it with her forty-five-minute delivery.

Now who would have her address?

Stan plopped into the chair again. "Perfect timing, Watson," I said.

"I figured by now you'd have a plan of attack. The lobby is a circus. We need to do something. Soon."

I shoved my chart toward him. "This is a list of everyone I can think of who is associated with Dimitry. But there are students I haven't met and folks we may not even know exist. The sensible thing is to start at home base."

Stan looked confused, which wasn't surprising.

"Dimitry's widow. As far as I know, Irina hasn't been to the studio since their little girl was born. Surely she has some idea who might have wanted her husband dead."

"How do you know she isn't the murderer?"

I screwed up my face as I mulled it over. "I guess it's possible. But she's really short so it would have been difficult for her to whack him on the head. Unless he was bent over."

"Or sitting," Stan suggested.

Hmmm. Not bad, Watson.

"So how do you propose talking to her? Does she even know who you are?"

"We met in the studio a couple of times. The poor thing is probably overwhelmed with the baby, and devastated by her husband's death. I thought a baby gift might cheer her up." I smiled at Stan. "And maybe something chocolate for the new mama to nibble on."

"Do you know where she lives?"

"Nope. That's where you come in. Didn't you say you scheduled a lesson with Anya tonight?"

"Ah, yes, the lovely Anya. That woman doesn't even have to swivel to sizzle."

I threw him a quizzical look. "Forgetting something, Stanley?"

He looked puzzled.

"Um, like you're gay?"

He snorted. "I may be gay but I'm not dead."

"Whatever. But be careful. Do you think Anya will give you the address if you ask?"

He blew on his fingertips. "Are you kidding? Women love to share stuff with me. I'm like everyone's GBFF. I'll charm her address book right off of her."

"Yeah, fine, but please be discreet. And if she doesn't have it, maybe you can get it from Boris."

Stan shuddered. "Now that guy makes me quake in my Cuban-heeled dance shoes. If you want my opinion, he's your murderer."

"Just because he's big, scary-looking and named Boris doesn't make him a killer. He's probably a teddy bear trapped in a grizzly bear's body."

"Sounds like you've got the hots for the big boy." He smirked.

I rolled my eyes, but Stan wasn't totally wrong. I did have the hots for a big boy, but it wasn't Boris. I peeked at my watch. In a few hours, my favorite big guy would be knocking on my front door and I hoped this time he'd be in a cuddly mood.

TWENTY-SEVEN

WITH THE DETECTIVE PAYING A house call that could be personal as well as professional, my nerves were stretched thinner than the vermicelli I served the kids for dinner.

"Mommy, there are only four days left until Christmas," announced Ben as he sat at the table shuffling his soggy peas around on his plate. I kept a watchful eye on those peas since our kitten had an affinity for greens. More than one string bean or pea had been slipped under the table to our weird vegetarian cat, with disastrous consequences to my beige carpet.

"Everything is under control, honey."

"You've been working so hard. Do you need me to help with any chores?" He smiled at me, his freckled face and missing two front teeth aimed straight at my heart.

"Flattery will get you nowhere, Ben." Jenna stood up and ruffled her brother's shaggy mane. "We're on a strict budget so don't expect Mom to get you everything on your list. And if you don't treat me nicer, Santa will leave a lump of coal in your stocking."

"You're a meanie," Ben cried, knocking over his plate and scattering a multitude of miniature green spheres across the tile floor.

"And you're a munchkin," proclaimed Jenna. "A very messy munchkin. That's okay, Mom, I'll pick them up."

The doorbell chose that auspicious moment to ring. Oh, well, the detective wasn't dating me for my culinary ability or domestic skills. On second thought, he wasn't dating me at all.

I ran to the front door, leaving my children to deal with the great pea debacle. A blast of frigid air greeted me, as did Detective Tom Hunter. He wore his soft chestnut crushed leather bomber jacket, the one that made him look like a Top Gun pilot.

I'm such a sucker for men in leather.

He entered the foyer and total silence enveloped the house. Not even the muted strains of two skirmishing siblings pierced the quiet. They had better not be eavesdropping.

"Um, hi, Tom. Can I get you something to drink? Glass of wine?"

Plateful of peas?

He shook his head then paused. "Well, I am heading straight home after this. Maybe a glass of wine to warm me up. It's cold enough to snow tonight."

If Tom wanted to be warmed up, I would be more than happy to personally accommodate him. But I'd bring out the wine for starters.

"Have a seat in the family room and I'll be right back."

My meager wine collection was stored in one of my kitchen cabinets. Liz had recently given me an award-winning bottle of Grenache from the David Girard winery in Coloma. El Dorado County was dotted with successful wineries that year after year put out gold-medal winners. Our beautiful hills not only produce solid gold nuggets, but also liquid gold in the form of fine wines.

The bottle rested next to a supersecret stash of dark chocolate truffles, a gift from a coworker. They were so supersecret that even I'd forgotten they were hidden there. The chocolate goodies would be the perfect accompaniment to the ruby-red wine.

I walked into the family room with a tray bearing the truffles in a crystal bowl plus two glasses of the aromatic wine. Much to my surprise, both kids were engaged in conversation with the detective.

"Hey, Mom, did you know Kristy gets to go to Tahoe for Christmas?" Ben's lower lip stuck out an inch as he aimed a perfected pout in my direction. "They're gonna snowboard and sled and snowmobile. How come we never get to do cool stuff like that?"

Ben punched Jenna in the arm. "Get it? Cool like snow." He rolled on the floor laughing at his second-grade wit.

"Tahoe for Christmas. That's nice," I remarked.

"My folks rented a place for two weeks. Technically I was supposed to have those weeks off, assuming there were no murder investigations…" Tom's voice trailed off as he noticed Ben's ears perk up at the word *murder*.

"Did you know my mom tripped over a body at the dance studio?" Ben asked the detective.

Tom and I exchanged glances. I was such a bad role model for my children.

"Ben, it's time for bed. Jenna, please make sure he brushes his teeth."

The kids said good-night to the detective then disappeared upstairs. I placed the tray on my glass-topped coffee table then went over to the CD player. Soon the soothing sounds of Michael Bublé singing big band oldies filled the room. It almost made me want to break into a fox-trot.

Almost.

I joined Tom on my comfy but outdated flowered sofa, picked up my wineglass and took a sip. Yummy. The blend of raspberry and spices in the Grenache was perfect for a romantic winter evening.

Tom rested his head against the back of the sofa. He stretched his long legs, encased in beige cords, under the table. "Ahhh, this is the first chance I've had to relax all day." He sipped his wine, set the glass on a coaster and turned to me. "Any chance I can lure you down to my end of the couch?"

How easy did he think I was?

In less than two seconds, I was cuddled against Tom's chest, my head resting against his rock-hard pecs like I belonged there. His fingers stroked the fine strands of my hair. For a big man, he was amazingly gentle. His tender touch moved down my body and any annoyance I had felt toward him melted away as if those lost weeks had never occurred.

"I've missed you," he said, his breath warm against my ear. My insides felt like one of those chocolate molten lava cakes. Steamy, sweet, and ready to erupt.

I turned to respond and his hungry lips met mine. All the feelings I'd tried to forget came roaring back like a category five hurricane. I kissed him as eagerly as he kissed me. We clung together until the phone rang, interrupting an embrace that could have led to trouble.

We broke apart with a start. I jumped up and smoothed down my skirt, which had ridden up my thighs during our prolonged kiss. I raced into the kitchen to answer the unwelcome call.

"What?" I muttered ungraciously after seeing that my caller was only Stan.

"Hey, what's the matter?" he said. "Did I interrupt a romantic interlude?" He hooted knowing that 99.9% of the time he would have been right in surmising the answer was a resounding *no*.

"Yes. No. I mean, what do you want?"

"I thought you were all hot to get Irina's address." Stan sounded frustrated and I didn't blame him. A mere four hours ago, the widow's address was my top priority. It was amazing how one sizzling kiss could distract me from my sleuthing. Heaven only knows where my overheated hormones might have taken us if we hadn't been interrupted by my pal.

"Sorry. I have a lot going on right now. Did you have a difficult time getting it from Anya?"

"Anya said she didn't have it with her so I asked Boris."

"I'm not sure it was a good idea to tell him I wanted Irina's address. Did he look suspicious?"

"Boris always looks suspicious. Are you *sure* he's not ex-KGB?"

"No, I'm not. Hopefully, Boris won't be suspicious of…" My voice trailed off as I realized Tom was leaning against the doorway, a frown darkening his face.

Stan babbled on about his success. "Anyway, Paula was in the office talking to Boris when I stopped by. She found Dimitry's address and phone number in her BlackBerry. I told them you were dropping off a baby gift tomorrow night and that seemed to satisfy the big guy."

I wrote the address on a notepad, said goodbye then turned to Tom. I pointed to the bottle of red. "More wine?"

Tom eyed the bottle then shook his head. "Nope, I need to keep a clear head, especially when I'm talking to you. Now, why do you need Irina's address?"

"I have a baby gift for her. She's been through so much with her husband's murder and the birth of their child. It's the least I can do."

He threw one of his practiced "I don't believe a word you're saying" looks at me. "Why do I think you have an ulterior motive for this visit?"

"You know I think Dana is innocent. Someone needs to help her. Her husband's arrest in the office today could only have compounded her distress."

"She has plenty of stuff to worry about. In fact, they both do."

"So what's going on with Mr. Chandler? You haven't mentioned him all night. I hope you weren't kissing me to distract me from asking questions." I laughed then stopped when I realized he wasn't joining in.

Instead, he stood silent in the doorway, his face reflective. I couldn't tell if he was thinking about our brief moment of passion or if he was back in official mode contemplating how much he could share with me.

"You already know we hauled off your boss because of his attempted assault on a police officer."

"Yes, but he didn't actually hit the deputy," I felt obligated to point out. "How long are you planning on keeping him in jail, or did his attorney get him out already?"

"It's not easy to get bail if you're arrested on a homicide charge."

"*Homicide?* What are you talking about?"

"We have witnesses who placed him at the scene of Dimitry's murder."

I froze. "Gordon Chandler, the president of the bank, was at the dance studio the night Dimitry was killed?"

"Yes, he was. Funny how he failed to mention that to the authorities."

Funny how he'd failed to mention it to me.

TWENTY-EIGHT

TOM'S REVELATION STUNNED ME. Mr. Chandler had encouraged me to play detective when he'd actually been at the scene of the crime.

"Why on earth would he kill Dimitry?" I asked. "He's the president of the bank. CEOs don't commit murder." As soon as the words left my lips I realized how naive it sounded, but I still couldn't imagine my boss doing anything that would ruin his reputation.

A murder rap would sure do that!

"Anyone can commit murder with the proper motivation," Tom replied.

"So how did you find out he was on the premises?"

"That elderly nurse, Nanette?" Tom looked at me for confirmation and I nodded my head. "She noticed the license plate on his car when she left the studio after Yuri collapsed. On the night Dimitry was killed, the parking lot was full so she had to park on the street, right behind a Mercedes with a license plate boasting *1 BANK. Talk about stupid criminals."

"My boss is not a *stupid* criminal. He's a very smart criminal." My face reddened when I realized my defense needed a little work. "I mean, he's not a criminal at all. Just because he happened to be at the scene of the crime isn't sufficient evidence to arrest him for murder. Did the D.A. put you up to this? You know he doesn't like Mr. Chandler."

Tom's jaw tightened. "Are you accusing me of conjuring up evidence in a murder case?"

"Um, no, of course not." I gulped. "But what else do you have?"

"That is none of your business. I've already told you far too much. Trust me, hon, we know what we're doing."

I bristled. What did he mean it was none of my business? Of course it was my— Wait a minute. Did he call me *hon?*

Focus, Laurel.

I rested my back against the counter. "I thought the reason you stopped by tonight was that you wanted my insight into Dimitry's murder."

"Oh, that was simply an excuse to talk to you." His face colored a little. "I wanted to discuss why I broke it off after Thanksgiving. I felt I owed you an explanation about what was going on in my head."

My heart rate ratcheted up to a billion beats per minute as I waited for his explanation.

Tom approached as I stood frozen in place. Part of me was anxious. The other dreaded his revelation. He wrapped his arms around me. I resisted for all of two seconds then relaxed in the warmth and strength of his embrace. Despite the one-foot height difference it still felt like we belonged together. Why *had* he broken up with me after a brief two-week relationship?

I tried to remain silent, waiting for his explanation, but the urge to know why he'd suddenly disappeared out of my life was too strong and I pushed him away.

"Only a few weeks ago, we were sitting in there." I pointed in the direction of the living room. "Locked in each other's arms. You got a call, left for an investigation and never returned. Never even called to tell me why."

He started tracing patterns on my countertop with his index finger. "I was scared. That's basically the reason."

That was not the answer I was expecting. "Scared?"

"Frightened of being in a relationship. Falling for someone so hard that if something happened to them it would tear my heart and life apart. Again."

It was barely two years since Tom's wife died so I could understand his concern.

"But we only saw each other a few times," I protested.

"Yes, but I was…falling for you. After all hell broke loose with that last investigation, I didn't know if I would ever see you alive again. I wondered if I could handle that kind of emotional involvement. Maybe someday, but I don't know if I'm ready for it yet. Especially given my chosen profession."

He rubbed a hand over his five o'clock shadow and gave a mirthless laugh. "Although for some reason my profession has me running into you in the most unexpected places. Now why is that?"

In the words of the bank president, I have a knack.

Tom grabbed my hand in his. "This case seems to be wrapping up—" he held up his palm as I started to interrupt "—even if you don't quite see it the way we do. We have info you don't, Laurel." The look in his eyes grew soft. "Maybe we can spend some time together up in Tahoe. We'll both be there for Liz's wedding."

"How come you're not in the wedding party?"

"Brian has several good friends. And my schedule is too unreliable, especially given your propensity for tripping over dead bodies."

He reached for me, but we were interrupted by the raucous sound of Tom's cell playing "Jingle Bells." He noticed my amusement and mumbled "Kristy's idea," before walking away to carry on a conversation with the other party.

He listened, frowning. "I have to go." He slapped his phone shut.

"Everything okay?"

"No. Definitely not okay." A perplexed expression crossed his face. "Yuri's tox results came back."

"Tox results?"

"We ran a toxicology screen on Yuri. The lab results indicate traces of something that would have been highly unusual for him to have imbibed normally."

My eyes widened at the implication. I had assumed like everyone else that Yuri had overdone the caffeine with his multitude of energy drinks. Or that he had an undisclosed heart condition that caused his collapse.

"Do you think he was poisoned?"

He nodded. "Most likely at the dance studio. Interesting that Dana was there for the first time since Dimitry was killed. And her husband happened to accompany her that night, as well. Too much of a coincidence for me."

I slumped against the counter. Despite the fact that Mr. Chandler had withheld some damaging information from me and the detectives, I still couldn't believe he was involved with Dimitry's murder or Yuri's poisoning.

"Did Yuri wake up from his coma? Maybe he ate something that accidentally poisoned him. You can't assume the Chandlers had anything to do with it," I protested.

"We aren't assuming anything, but unless Yuri normally added antifreeze to his energy drinks, there's a strong possibility your boss committed both murders."

My eyes widened to the size of the dinner plates sitting in my sink. "Both murders," I squeaked.

"There was another piece of bad news." Tom drew me closer in preparation for his announcement. "Yuri died a few minutes ago."

TWENTY-NINE

THE NEXT MORNING I WAS MORE determined than ever to visit Irina. I still couldn't believe that two male dance instructors from the same studio had been killed. There had to be some correlation despite the fact they were murdered using different methods.

Or were there two different killers?

A frisson of fear shot through my body. That was too horrible to contemplate. But equally tragic was the thought of our bank president imprisoned in a jail cell.

My children were now officially out of school and on winter break. Since I wouldn't be home until late, I told Jenna to warm up the previous night's leftover spaghetti for their dinner. I warned my son if there was any evidence of him hiding vegetables in the house or in the kitten's stomach, that he definitely would receive only a lump of coal for Christmas. Ben's face whitened but he could tell I was serious. I had no idea how I would discipline him after the holidays were over, but at least for the next three days, I held the upper hand.

The atmosphere at work was total doom and gloom as employees congregated throughout the office, debating the future of the bank. Those reflections eventually led to the staff wondering about their own continued employment. Fortunately, with only two days until Christmas Eve, most of the local shopkeepers were too busy minding their own stores to worry about closing their bank accounts.

At lunchtime, I ran out to get a sausage sandwich at

Hot Dog Haven. The proprietor of the tiny bistro asked for my financial advice. "So what's the deal with Chandler?" Marty asked, slathering my bratwurst with half a bottle of mustard. "Do I need to find another bank?"

The guy standing in line behind me interjected, "The rumor is your president is up Hangtown Creek without a paddle."

I rolled my eyes and turned around to address the guy. Based on the size of his gut, he must be a regular at the Haven. The woman standing behind him, the owner of a downtown nail salon, chimed in. "I heard the bank was shutting down and we need to get our money out fast."

"The bank is fine. Your deposits are insured, so they are fine. And Mr. Chandler *will* be fine." That last comment was spoken with my hopes high and my fingers crossed. My nerves were stretched so thin, the screech of Marty tearing paper made me jump. He wrapped my sandwich then tucked it into a carryout bag festooned with his "hot doggy" logo, a golden retriever licking his lips. I opened my wallet and handed him a five-dollar bill.

"Well, I don't cotton to murder," said the guy behind me, "but if Chandler killed that dancer fella 'cause he was humping his wife, you can't honestly blame him."

"Men," muttered the salon owner.

"Mr. Chandler did not murder anyone," I said with gritted teeth. "And Mrs. Chandler did not fool around with the two dead dancers."

"She was screwing two of them dancers?" He shook his head in amazement. "Now don't that beat all?"

I grabbed my paper bag from Marty and headed back to work before I could wreak further damage to the Chandlers' reputations. That conversation reinforced my desire to do whatever I could to help the president.

With my mission to save my boss and therefore the bank

on my agenda for tonight, I left the office at five sharp and drove over to our local big-box store. Based on the number of cars circling the lot in search of a parking space, the local Budget Mart was not struggling for business. I hovered for a full five minutes as one family packed up their two double strollers and buckled four children and a load of parcels into the backseats of their van. If I thought my life as a single mom was hectic, what would it be like to have four toddlers at home, plus a husband?

After snaring their parking spot, which I almost lost to an overzealous SUV driver who attempted to sneak in while the family slowly backed out, I entered the overdecorated, overstocked and overly noisy store.

Wild-eyed parents pushed shopping carts filled with boxes of all shapes and sizes as well as screaming children of all shapes and sizes. I dashed over to the children's apparel, which in this superstore was located at least a half-mile from the entrance. The infant-sized sleeper in red-and-white stripes with a matching stocking cap should put Irina in a festive mood. The two-pound box of deluxe chocolates definitely would do the trick.

The toy section seemed a football field away from the baby department. I selected two of the Nintendo games on Ben's list. That meant two gifts down and forty to go, if he had his way. Which of course, wasn't going to happen. As his elder sister said, we were on a budget this year.

My own budget could dwindle to the size of Ben's allowance if Mr. Chandler's arrest had a huge impact on the bank. Our customers had plenty of banking options to choose from at local branches of nationwide banks. If we lost deposits, it would diminish our ability to make new loans, leading to reductions in staff.

My shoulders slumped as I stood in line waiting to make my purchases. It felt like not only my family's welfare, but the well-being of the entire bank rested on my ability to solve the murders. My spirits flagged as my line moved forward a mere two inches while the cashier installed a new roll of paper tape into her register. At the rate we were going, it would be Christmas by the time I reached Irina's house.

The store manager must have been equally anxious to ring up more purchases and get the customers out of the store, because three more registers opened up. I zipped over to the express cashier, grabbed a foil-wrapped marsh-mallow Santa Claus for energy, and was back in my car a few minutes after six. I tucked the baby outfit and candy into a holiday gift bag and stuffed in a few sheets of red tissue. I consider gift bags to be one of the greatest inventions of the century, almost on a par with my DVR.

It seemed rude to show up at Irina's doorstep without any warning, so I stuck my Bluetooth on my ear and dialed her number. The squalling of an infant confirmed that I'd reached her home phone.

"Allo?"

"Irina, this is Laurel McKay from the dance studio. Liz Kendall and I bought a baby gift for you and I wondered if I could drop it off tonight. I'm not too far away from your house."

The baby's cries diminished to a distant murmur, which made it easier to hear Irina's response.

"Da, I suppose you can come by to the house although I have company here. Hold on." The sound of the phone clattering on a hard surface assaulted my ear. "Yes, is okay, my company is leaving. You know where we live?"

"I found directions on the computer. You're a few miles down Black Horse Road, right?"

"Da, number 1571. On the left side. The driveway she goes way up to the house."

The dial tone buzzed in my ear before I could say good-bye, but at least Irina was amenable to me stopping by. I'd hoped to converse with her in private, but as a new mother and recent widow, she probably had frequent visitors.

Black Horse Road was only five or six miles from the Budget Mart but in the opposite direction from my house. Still, if I only stayed at Irina's for a half hour or so, I could be home by half past seven.

I drove down North Shingle Road looking for the sign for Black Horse Road. Headlights blasting from oncoming cars made the search far more difficult. According to Mapquest, I should be almost… There it was.

The narrow two-lane road was paved but rutted and not in the best shape. I worried about driving into potholes bigger than the Prius. Headlights shone from the top of the hill as a vehicle slowly wound down the steep, twisty road in my direction. I drove into a pullout on the side of the road and waited for the SUV to pass.

I was surprised Dimitry and Irina lived in such a remote area. So far I'd only passed two other houses. Maybe the tall pines and solitude reminded them of the Russian countryside.

My little car complained about the uphill climb but eventually I spotted a driveway on the left with Irina's address scrawled on a piece of wood. Not the most ornate entrance but at least it was legible. The driveway was even narrower than the road, half gravel and half dirt ruts. Obviously Dimitry had not poured any of the money he borrowed from Dana into any outside improvements.

The long winding driveway finally ended in a flat patch of gravel in front of a rustic log house. The porch was stocked to the roof with several piles of firewood. Irina would have an entire winter's supply to keep her and the baby warm.

I parked next to a dirty white Chevy Silverado. The truck seemed too big for the petite woman to drive, so her company must still be visiting. I stepped out of my car into the frigid night air. The scent of wood smoke combined with the sweet smell of cedar pines made the air smell like Christmas. I grabbed my purse and the gifts from the front seat.

The front steps creaked as I climbed up to the porch. The drapes to the front window were open, exposing a fire burning in a massive stone fireplace in the living room, but the room appeared to be empty.

Before I could grab the bronze door knocker, the door flew open.

Irina stood in the doorway next to the most massive person I had ever seen outside of the World Wide Wrestling Championships. He was at least six foot nine, and could probably knock down the Incredible Hulk with one swat of his huge hairy paw.

He frowned at me and muttered something under his breath. When he stuck his right hand into the pocket of his Big and Tall black leather coat, I sensed danger. I backed down the porch steps, mentally berating myself for getting involved in a situation that involved the Russian mafia.

Why hadn't I heeded my mother's advice?

I had almost reached the safety of my car when my heel slipped on a piece of gravel. My purse went flying in one direction. The baby gift flew over my head, landing in an evergreen shrub. The sound of two pounds of candy bouncing on the hood of my car made me cringe.

I was too big to bounce, so I merely landed flat on my back, doing an ungainly version of a snow angel. Unfortunately, the pebbles I landed on were far less comfortable than the soft cushy snow I used to play in.

The beak-nosed bald-headed giant loomed over me. He took his hand out of his pocket and aimed a long slender object in my direction.

THIRTY

THE THREATENING OBJECT IN HIS right hand rattled as he lowered his left hand to lift me off the ground. My overactive imagination had visualized the big man toting a gun. Not a soft pink rattle.

Someone needed a lesson in diversity training.

"You okay?" the man squeaked in a high-pitched voice. This was definitely a day for eliminating stereotypical assumptions. The combination of the Minnie Mouse voice with the Mr. Clean physique caused me to lose it. I sat up, giggling uncontrollably.

"Vladimir, you are scaring her," Irina scolded the gentle giant as she approached us. The widow had thrown an embroidered ivory shawl over her shoulders. The baby was nestled against her chest and wrapped so snugly she resembled a baby burrito.

I latched on to Vladimir's gargantuan hand and he lifted me off the ground with ease and an unexpected gentleness.

"Thanks, um, *spasiba?*" I used the only Russian word I knew besides *vodka*.

"No problemo," he responded with a thick accent. He murmured something to Irina. She nodded and replied in her native tongue. They exchanged kisses on both cheeks and he plodded to his truck and climbed in. The engine roared and the truck barreled down the drive, sending a farewell plume of dust in our direction.

Irina waved at me to follow her into the house. I retrieved my purse, the baby gift and the box of candy that had landed on the hood of my car unscathed. I was relieved to see we hadn't lost a single piece of chocolate. I bustled after my hostess, anxious to get inside to the warmth of her cheery cabin.

Irina led me down a dark, narrow hallway into the living room. The walls were paneled in knotty pine and decorated with several Russian icons. The color and detail work of Russian art has always fascinated me. I walked over to examine one of the more ornate pieces but Irina nudged me toward her sofa. I plumped down on the slightly soiled olive-green cushions, resting against the green-black-and-cream-striped afghan that covered the back.

Irina sat in a sturdy maple rocking chair decorated with pastel flowers stenciled on the back and arms. The baby remained asleep as Irina rocked back and forth in silence. I placed the baby gift and the box of candy next to a sewing basket resting on the solid maple coffee table. The temperature shift from the frigid winter air to the torpid heat in the living room caused perspiration to drip down my face, so I unbuttoned my leather coat and shrugged it off.

Irina finally broke the silence. "Thank you for baby gift. It is very nice of you to come visit us."

I breathed out a sigh of relief that Irina was okay with my unscheduled visit. I thrust the red velvet box of Russell Stover's finest at my hostess. "Would you care for some candy?"

She grinned, displaying a tiny gap between her two front teeth. Irina wasn't an exotic dark-haired beauty like Anya, but she possessed a gaminelike charm, which was particularly enchanting when she finally smiled.

"No, but you are most kind. Would you like hot tea?" She pointed toward a burnished brass samovar resting on a side table next to a couple of delicate china cups in a gold-edged dark-blue-and-white pattern. The tea would have been welcome if I hadn't been sweltering in the ninety-degree heat of the living room.

A shaker full of chilled vodka sounded far more appealing.

"Sorry, I can't stay long. I need to get home to my children."

Her face lit up at my comment. "Ah, you are mother, too?"

I nodded. "My kids are much older. My daughter is sixteen and my son, Ben, is seven. I'm a single mother like you."

Irina looked at me with sympathy. "Your husband he was also killed?"

Not exactly, although I did recall *wanting* to kill him when he announced he was leaving me for another woman. But Hank was still alive and annoying me whenever he had the opportunity.

I wasn't sure how to explain my complicated relationship with my ex, so I merely shook my head. Her question provided an excellent segue into the topic of Dimitry's murder.

"Irina, I'm very sorry for your loss, but have you thought about who might have wanted to harm your husband?"

She raised her eyes to the ceiling as she rocked back and forth occasionally patting the baby nestled in her arms. "I not quite sure how to say this. My Dimitry, he was very popular with the ladies. I love my husband but he has wandering ways." Her face darkened and the chair began to rock faster. "When I become pregnant, it create problems and we cannot have the sex. Dimitry, he need the sex to feel like a man."

I smiled at her, empathizing with her predicament. "You're a better person than I am. When my husband left me for another woman, I *did* want to kill him. Didn't you get mad at Dimitry?"

She shrugged. "I could yell and I could cry, but Dimitry…he would do what he wanted to do."

"What about the other male dance instructors? Were they jealous of him?"

"Dimitry, he could be very charming one day. Then next day he more like a…" She paused and tried to compose her thoughts. "He be more like lying bastard scum."

Alrighty then. Irina's grasp of English was far better than I expected and she definitely wasn't as naive as I originally thought. She was realistic about the man she had loved and married.

"Right before little Katya was born I decided to prepare for my trip to hospital. I open suitcase and what do I find?" Her eyes flashed with anger. "I find beautiful ballroom gown."

"A present for you?"

"No! Not for me. It was for tall woman. For his whore. So I took my scissors and cut it in tiny pieces. Then I throw it away."

Wow. Little Irina had a big temper.

"What did he say when you told him what you did?"

"He was very upset. He say he going to start costume business and that I spoil everything for him. I never know what to believe from Dimitry, so I tell him next time I find him hiding something from me, I cut off his…" She mimicked a body part that undoubtedly meant a great deal to Dimitry.

I eyed the sharp blades of the scissors sticking out of her sewing basket and decided I'd better be careful how I phrased my questions.

"You've spoken with the detectives, haven't you?"

"*Da,* several times, I speak with Detective Hunter. He

ask if Dimitry is involved with any criminals before we come to this country. In Russia, is not safe to talk to police so all I tell him is that Dimitry want to be huge pie maker."

Huh? What did baking pies have to do with ballroom dance?

Irina noticed my confused look. "Let me see, it is American expression. Very strange, I think. Dimitry, he keep fingers in many pies."

My stomach growled as I pictured a chocolate pie topped with swirls of fluffy white whipped cream. Next time I did some detecting I'd better eat something more filling than a marshmallow Santa.

"Are you saying Dimitry was involved in other things besides opening his new dance studio?"

Her head nodded, keeping rhythm with her patting motion on little Katya's back. "He tell me he has big idea and soon we will be rich Americans and can move to villa on a hill.

"Dimitry has told me this story so many times before. But this time…" She closed her eyes for a few seconds then opened them wide.

"This time I think maybe he mean it."

THIRTY-ONE

THE BABY WOKE, STARTLING BOTH of us. Her rosebud mouth opened and closed rapidly, a sign that someone else was hungry. I decided I'd bothered the bereft widow long enough so I grabbed my purse and stood up. "Thanks, Irina. Please let me know if I can help you in any way. It must be tough living alone this far out in the country."

"*Spasiba*. I am grateful for your kindness. Maybe if you hear something from the big detective, you will let me know? Detective Hunter reminds me of Russian black bear. He look cuddly, but better to be careful what you do and say around him. He is scaring me a little."

I smiled. Sometimes the detective scared me a little, too. I said goodbye and jumped in my car, my heart going out to the little girl who would grow up without her father. My own father had died in a car accident when I was ten. Thirty years later, I still missed his presence. No matter what pie-making scheme Dimitry had cooked up, no one deserved to have their life end in such a vicious manner.

A light rain was falling, and I needed to concentrate on driving, not detecting. If the temperature dropped a few more degrees, it could turn into snow. My eyes remained glued to the road as the windshield wipers flicked back and forth, their soft clicking reminding me how late it was getting and how careful I had to be driving on the dark, twisty road. Deer, raccoons and the occasional mountain lion lived in these woods. I sure didn't want to run over Bambi and his mother.

I negotiated the last hairpin turn on the slick road. The sharp crack that punctuated the air shattered my front windshield, leaving a tiny hole to the right of my face. I slammed my foot on the brake and the Prius slid sideways toward a fifty-foot drop into a tree-filled canyon.

Branches laden with pine needles brushed against the windows as the car careened toward the precipice. I jerked the wheel in the opposite direction and began spinning out of control. My heart lodged in my throat as the faces of my children flashed through my mind.

The car revolved almost 360 degrees before slowing. It skidded another twenty feet, sliding into the muddy ruts along the left side of the road but opposite the dark canyon on the other side. The car finally stopped, one of the back tires gasping out a last breath as the vehicle listed to the left.

I briefly rested my head on the steering wheel, shivering from the chilly air blowing through the shattered windshield. One of my tires must have hit a rock or something. I shivered again, but this time from realizing what a close call I'd had. Only a few feet separated my tiny car from the steep drop of the canyon.

The Prius had landed so close to a huge tree trunk that I was unable to squeeze out of the driver's-side door. As I climbed over the console, I vowed to eschew all candy until New Year's Day. I opened the passenger door and stepped out. My heels sank into the squishy red foothill mud, an expensive reminder to never wear suede shoes when investigating a murder.

An immense snowflake pattern was etched across the cracked windshield. The safety glass had kept it from disintegrating into a million pieces, but visibility would be zero. The left back tire slouched haphazardly in the muck.

My stomach churned in dismay as I contemplated the damage to my car.

A roar of a motor starting up in the distance provided a momentary hope that someone would drive up and rescue me, but as the noise of the engine grew fainter, I realized there was no alternative but to trudge back to Irina's house.

The wind whistling through the trees and the light drizzle seeping down my neck did nothing to improve my mood. My cell phone provided a tiny beam of light. It also displayed the fact there was no cell reception, at least where I was currently standing. In this area, the phone service could bounce from no bars to five bars within seconds.

I was glad my mother wasn't there, because she would certainly have dispensed a lecture on the many reasons why you should always carry a flashlight in your car.

I hate when she's right.

During the day, the few residences along the road undoubtedly possessed a beautiful view of the snow-capped Sierra Mountains, but my vista consisted of scary black trees silhouetted against an almost starless midnight-blue sky.

The distance to Irina's house was less than a half mile, but as I trudged uphill it felt far longer. My two-inch heels didn't help my progress although I was able to proceed without any rest stops. Maybe those dance lessons were finally having a positive impact.

Lights blazing from the windows of Irina's cabin perked up my flagging spirits. I sprinted up the steps to her front porch and tapped lightly, not wanting to wake the baby in case she had settled down for the night. Irina opened the door a crack and peered over the chain latch.

Her eyes widened in surprise. "Laurel, is something gone wrong?"

My mind briefly flitted with the thought that it was odd Irina assumed something was wrong, but I pushed it away. I explained about my accident and she ushered me into the house. I removed my muddy shoes and followed her into the kitchen, which was decorated with bright blue tile counters, yellow walls, and red stoneware. The scent of fresh baked bread permeated the small room. My stomach gurgled at the smell and sight of the golden loaf resting on a braided towel.

Irina giggled and pointed at my noisy abdomen. "Come sit. You make the call and I will cut you piece of bread. It just come from oven."

My stomach growled a thank-you as I accepted the cordless phone from my hostess. I pulled my AAA card from my wallet and dialed the toll-free number on the back. The body shop that owned the tow truck was located in Placerville, so they assured me the truck would arrive in less than twenty minutes. We arranged for the driver to come to Irina's house so I wouldn't have to wait in my cold, dark car.

I would need transportation home, but I couldn't decide whether to call my mother, who would undoubtedly chastise me all the way to my house, or Liz, who was unlikely to approve of my investigating when I was supposed to be one hundred percent devoted to her bridal functions.

My brain would function better once it was fed some fiber-filled carbohydrates. I decided to hold off phoning anyone for a ride until after I savored some of Irina's homemade bread. She placed a thick slice on the table along with a glass of milk.

"Mmm," I mumbled, my mouth crammed full of the flavorful bread that had been slathered in butter. Even the butter tasted better than normal.

She smiled. "Is good, no?"

"Is good, yes." I wiped my crumb-covered lips with a soft red damask napkin and glanced around the cheerful room, my eyes landing on a colorful teddy bear cookie jar. The ceramic lid, which was the head of the bear, was off kilter. It looked like Irina had recently refilled it. Could fresh baked cookies be in my future? My taste buds grew anxious savoring yet another treat.

Irina noticed the direction of my gaze. She stood and hastily cleared my plate from the table. It landed in the sink with a clatter. "The truck he will be here soon. We should wait in the front room."

Okay, I can take a hint.

Little Katya was asleep, lying on her stomach in a tiny maple wood cradle. Irina settled back in her rocking chair and closed her eyes. I sat on the sofa feeling ill at ease. I had intruded on the poor widow not once, but twice in one evening.

My bladder suddenly announced it was full and needed to make a pit stop. Irina rocked quietly and snored loudly, her lower lip blowing out with each sonorous snort.

I recalled two open doors near the rear of the kitchen. Perhaps there was a half bath at that end of the house. I entered the kitchen once again and was pleased to discover that my deductions were correct. One door led to a small laundry room and the other to a bathroom.

After I finished my task, I washed my hands then discovered there were no towels in the bathroom. My hands dripped on the wooden kitchen floor so I grabbed a towel lying on the counter next to the cookie jar. I'm not usually obsessive compulsive but something about the jar with its lopsided teddy bear head hit me wrong. I started to slide the lid shut when the shrill blast of a vehicle horn startled me.

The lid leapt out of my hand and skidded across the blue

tiles. I snatched at it, hoping the lid hadn't been chipped by my clumsiness. When I looked down, the gaping hole of the teddy bear jar grinned malevolently at me.

I stared in astonishment at a cookie jar that was totally devoid of any mouth watering fresh baked cookies. Someone had chosen to store something much colder in the cookie receptacle.

Something cold, silver, metallic and…

Deadly.

THIRTY-TWO

ANOTHER SHRIEK OF THE TRUCK horn interrupted my thoughts, which were basically to get as far as possible from a house where they stored weapons with their cookies. I ran into the living room and grabbed my purse and coat, mouthing my thanks to my hostess. Katya was screaming, her tiny two-week-old lungs producing at an operatic level. Irina looked puzzled at my hasty exit, but she busied herself attempting to soothe her infant daughter.

I slipped into my heels, opened the front door and hopped down the steps. I yanked on the heavy tow truck door and heaved myself into the cracked black leather seat, which squeaked out a well-worn welcome.

"Let's go," I yelled to the driver.

His grizzled face looked puzzled but he merely shifted gears and headed the massive yellow truck in the direction of my car. The driver was probably used to dealing with frantic females, although I doubted any of his previous passengers had recently discovered a gun in a cookie jar.

My ragged breathing subsided as we neared my car. There was no reason to panic because the teddy bear cookie jar housed a weapon. Since they lived so far out in the woods, Dimitry probably felt they needed protection. Owning a gun in the countryside was as natural as owning a dog. Or a pickup truck.

The AAA driver parked his vehicle in front of my Prius. The driver, who introduced himself as Harley, grabbed an oversized flashlight that would have received my mother's gold seal of approval. His jaw worked from side to side as he directed the beam across my windshield. Harley leaned forward and scrutinized the round hole in the middle of the glass. A million tiny cracks spiraled out from the tiny hole.

"Can you unlock the car?" he asked. "I'd like to check somethin' out."

I delved deep into my purse, located my keys and beeped the car open. Harley slid into the passenger seat and rummaged around the carpet. Five seconds later he exited the car. "Open your hands," he said.

My cheeks flushed with embarrassment. Harley was going to lecture me about the multitude of empty Kit Kat candy wrappers that had burrowed under my seats. I waited for the sticky pieces of paper to fall into my palms. Instead, I felt something hard and metal.

No bigger than a…bullet.

I screamed and the small metal object flew into the air. It landed on the asphalt, bounced on the pavement once, then twice, before it careened into the canyon on the other side of the road. Harley looked at me like I was crazy. I was beginning to think someone certainly was.

"That wasn't a bullet, was it?" I asked.

"Sure was. Although now I won't be able to tell what kind of gun it come from. Did you hear a shot when you was driving?"

I shook my head. "Not that I noticed. The windows were closed, the radio was on, and I was concentrating on watching the road. The windshield shattered—" I snapped my fingers "—just like that."

Harley pushed his navy baseball cap back on his thick gray-streaked hair and shoved his gnarled hands into his jean pockets. He rocked back and forth mulling over the ramifications of a stray gunshot hitting my windshield.

"Well, it coulda been a hunter, I s'pose."

"This late at night?" Unless they needed some venison or a rabbit for dinner, that seemed like a long shot to me.

He shrugged. "There's all kinds a fools out there toting guns when they hadn't ought to. Would've been interesting to see if that bullet come from a rifle."

I couldn't imagine someone hiding behind a tree and deliberately shooting at me. Of course there was that mysterious gun in Irina's cookie jar. My evening was starting to feel like a B-grade movie.

"I gotta report this to the sheriff's department," Harley said. "Since someone shot at you." He walked to his truck and called back over his shoulder. "I'll call the office and they'll arrange for a patrol car to meet us."

I reached into my purse and pulled out my cell phone as I trotted along behind him. This time all five bars were lined up. That great big satellite in the sky was finally smiling down at me.

"Don't worry," I said to Harley, as I speed dialed my own personal contact in the sheriff's department. "I have it covered."

THIRTY-THREE

Tom did not disappoint. He arrived with red lights flashing, sirens blaring and tires squealing. The official display was probably unnecessary, but he was at my side in less than ten minutes and I was grateful to have him there.

Harley and Tom consulted while I remained in the tow truck attempting to stay warm despite the truck's sputtering heater. Another patrol car arrived with two officers, one female deputy and a guy who looked vaguely familiar. When he tromped past the bright headlights of the truck, I recognized Deputy Katzenbach, AKA, Buzz Cut, last seen at the Golden Hills Dance Studio the night Dimitry was murdered.

After much discussion, the tow truck driver handed his flashlight to Buzz Cut. He glanced at me as he walked past the truck and I mustered a weak smile, which was met with a distinct frown. With a frustrated look on his face, the deputy shone the light down into the canyon.

Were they looking for the missing bullet? The next time someone dropped a small metal object in my hand, I would look before I threw. Deep in thought, I started when someone rapped on the window. The heavy door opened with a groan and Tom's worried eyes met mine. "How are you holding up?"

I tried to reply, but the magnitude of the incident, and the realization that I could have been killed finally hit home. My shoulders heaved as I gulped back sobs.

Grown women don't cry just because someone tries to shoot them.

Tom gently lifted me from my high perch in the cab of the truck until we were standing inches apart. His comforting arms encircled me as he stroked my back, letting the warmth of his body conduct its way into mine. I could have stayed locked in that position forever, hip to hip, thigh to thigh.

I raised my head from his broad chest and a tremor quickened my heartbeat as our glances met. It was almost worth getting shot at to realize Tom had feelings for me.

Almost.

A shrill whistle pierced the silence and we jumped apart. Deputy Buzz Cut motioned for us to join him. Tom's long legs made it to the side of the canyon in three strides. I trotted after him.

"Did you find it?" Tom asked.

The beam of the flashlight was centered on a spot about fifteen feet down the ravine. I inched forward to get a better look and inadvertently jostled the deputy's arm. The flashlight fell out of his hand and landed with a thud on the wet soil. All three officers frowned at the clumsy culprit.

"Sorry," I mumbled.

Fortunately, the flashlight still worked and after a few minutes they were able to locate the spot the deputy had previously identified. Trying to decide who would climb down the slippery slope to retrieve the bullet was another matter.

Buzz Cut vehemently shook his head back and forth. "Look, I've got two bad knees. I'm not screwing them up just to get a bullet your girlfriend stupidly threw away."

I was about to chastise Buzz Cut for calling me stupid when I realized he had referred to me as Tom's girlfriend.

I could live with that.

"I'll go," offered the female deputy. Before Tom could protest, she slithered down the muddy slope. She prodded and poked at some of the overgrown bushes on the hill. After a few minutes she shouted in triumph, the expression on her face exultant, at least via the limited light from the flashlight. The deputy stuffed something in her forest-green jacket pocket then zipped back up the hill. She was as nimble as a mountain climber. And as pretty as a movie star.

The young deputy's cheeks and clothing were streaked with mud, but I could tell she was elated by her success. Tom flashed a huge grin at her as she handed over her prize. She returned the smile and winked.

What did that mean? And when did the sheriff's department start hiring cover girls as deputies?

Tom deposited the bullet into a plastic baggie, which made me wonder if he restocked his supply of evidence bags whenever he knew he'd be meeting with me.

Tom conversed briefly with Harley. The tow truck driver approached me, his shoulders hunched, hands deep in his pockets. "They said I can haul your car to the shop. Now that they got that bullet it will be okay to fix the windshield and tire."

We both turned and stared at my sad little car. Harley must have noticed my forlorn expression. "It'll look like new by tomorrow afternoon," he reassured me. Great. But in the meantime what's a working mother to do?

The crunch of tires and the beam of headlights brought my answer. The Toyota Land Cruiser didn't even come to a full stop before the female passenger burst out of the car.

I guess a daughter is never too old to worry her mother.

"Honey, are you okay?" My mother's short platinum hair stood up in silvery spikes. Although her navy wool coat was buttoned, the brass buttons weren't lined up.

Bradford stood in the background shuffling his feet, looking a little disheveled himself.

"What are the two of you doing here?" I asked them.

"Tom called Robert and we immediately jumped out of…" She hesitated and amended her statement. "Did someone really shoot at you?"

I nodded, and she threw her arms around me. She finally released her hold and stepped back, scrutinizing me. "You're sure you're okay?"

"I'm fine. It was probably a hunter," I said. "Why would anyone want to shoot at me?"

Four questioning faces turned in my direction.

"Yes, Laurel, why *would* anyone want to shoot at you?" asked Tom.

No reason I could think of other than I was butting my head and my butt into the wrong person's business. Both my body and brain felt drained so I followed my mother and Bradford in the direction of his muddy SUV. Tom placed his hand on my arm and stopped me.

"We're almost done here. I'll drive you home."

"It's okay, I can ride with them."

His brow furrowed in response. "No, we need to talk. Give me a minute."

I exhaled and waved goodbye to my mother and Bradford. She took a few steps, paused then rushed back to my side.

"Please stay out of trouble." She gave me one more squeeze. I hugged her back, hoping trouble would stop finding me.

Tom gave the deputies some final instructions then gently guided me toward his official vehicle. I slid into the passenger-side front seat, my nostrils quivering as the smell of his musky men's cologne mixed with the scent of male sweat from the car's previous occupants.

Tom maneuvered the vehicle past the tow truck and patrol car then turned left and proceeded in the direction of Green Valley Road. The clock on the dashboard said it was almost nine.

I called Jenna and told her I'd been delayed. She responded that she hoped the reason for the delay was because I'd been out Christmas shopping for my devoted children who had dusted and vacuumed the entire house while I was gone.

I thanked my darling daughter and calculated there were two and half more days of housekeeping help from my industrious elves before packages were opened and they morphed back into normal chore-averse children.

I glanced at Tom but his eyes were on the road, his knuckles tight as he squeezed the steering wheel. Since he was the one who suggested driving me home I would leave it to him to initiate our conversation. Otherwise, the odds were high I would stick both muddy heels into my mouth.

After a brief drive spent in silence, we arrived at my house. Tom parked in the driveway and turned the ignition off, but kept the heater running. He reached for my left hand and turned to face me. Despite the dark, I could read the concern on his face. When he finally spoke, his voice cracked with emotion. "Laurel, if that bullet had been a few inches closer we wouldn't be sitting here right now."

My stomach tightened as I squeezed his hand, fully aware of the deadly truth of his words.

"Did something happen while you were at Irina's that could have precipitated an attack on you?"

I chewed on my lip, gnawing off my remaining lip gloss, as I tried to recall anything that might be pertinent. "An SUV passed me as I was driving up the road to Irina's place but that could have been a neighbor. Irina introduced me to some big guy named Vladimir who looked like Howie Mandel on steroids. She didn't mention whether he was a friend or a relative. He drove off right after I arrived at her house.

"Oh, and I meant to tell you. I found a gun in Irina's cookie jar."

His hand tightened on mine. "You neglected to mention a gun stored in a cookie jar?"

I glared at him. "Sorry, it's been a busy evening, what with the shooting and everything."

He rubbed his left hand over the stubble on his chin. "Okay, I'm going back out there tomorrow morning to see if we can retrieve additional evidence in the daylight. I'll talk to Irina then."

"It could have been a kid fooling around," I offered since that was the option I personally preferred.

"It's a possibility. But kind of a slim one since it was dark." Tom still looked worried. "We do have to consider you've been sticking your nose…"

I slid across the seat and stuck my celebrated nose right next to his. "All I'm trying to do is help an innocent man."

A frustrated look crossed Tom's face as he struggled to bite back a retort. "Laurel, listen to me. We have more than enough evidence to arrest your boss on homicide charges. You've been running all over the county asking questions and stirring things up that may have nothing to do with the murders."

"Fine." I yanked my hand from his.

We sat in silence until Tom reached out for me again. "Laurel, when I saw how close that bullet came…"

His voice broke and I slid closer. My arms wrapped around his neck as he drew me towards him. Although the center console kept our hips from touching, it did not stop our lips from meeting. A lightning bolt shot through my body as his lips pressed against mine. A slight noise distracted me and I pulled back momentarily. As a face pressed itself against the window I did what any mother would do.

I screamed.

THIRTY-FOUR

THE WHITE FACE BOBBING OUTSIDE the driver's-side window definitely cooled the heat wave that had threatened to steam up the car. Tom hit the power button and his window rolled down. I leaned across him so I could converse with the little intruder.

"Ben, what are you doing out here? And why aren't you wearing your parka?"

Ben jumped up and down, either from excitement or the cold. "Mommy, Santa was here early! I heard his sleigh and reindeer dashing across the roof."

"Honey, you know Christmas isn't for another three days. Maybe you heard some squirrels chasing after acorns." The clatter on our roof tiles was occasionally so loud I swore the fluffy-tailed tree rats had built a bowling alley in our attic.

"Nope, it was Santa. I heard his jingle bells ringing." Ben's face switched from ecstatic to crestfallen. "But he didn't leave any presents."

Tom and I exchanged glances. We were out of the car and at Ben's side in seconds. I shooed Ben back in the house then Tom and I both walked the perimeter. It was too dark to ascertain if there were any footprints on the hard ground. Tom checked the windows but all the latches were locked. As was the back door.

We examined every inch of the interior but other than a few embarrassing dust elephants, everything seemed in order. Jenna had been upstairs studying in her room. She heard nothing that sounded like Santa and his reindeer or even a gang of rowdy squirrels.

Tom and I stood on the front porch, puzzled by the lack of evidence that a prowler had paid a visit. "Do you think Ben could have imagined the noises?" Tom asked.

"It's hard to say. He does have a vivid imagination."

Tom smiled and drew me closer. "Sounds like he might have inherited that from his mother."

"Hey, I just like to think outside of your investigative box."

He opened his mouth but evidently thought better of responding. Then he said, "Do you want me to arrange for a patrol car to periodically drive by your house tonight? I don't feel comfortable with you being alone with your kids. I'd stay here myself if I didn't have to get home to Kristy. Our neighbor's daughter is babysitting her and I'm already late."

"No, I'll make sure to set the alarm. It probably was some type of animal. After all, Jenna didn't hear anything unusual." I placed my palm over my mouth as I felt a yawn coming on. It was past everyone's bedtime.

Tom still looked worried. "Call me if you hear anything unusual. Anything at all. Please don't be a hero."

He kissed me goodbye and once he was out the door, I promptly slammed it behind him and double locked it. I set the house alarm, something I'd never felt was necessary living in this peaceful community. But if someone evil knew where we lived, I wasn't taking a single chance.

With no car on the premises, I needed a way to get to work the next morning. Even though there was no proof of Ben's imaginary Santa Claus or a hostile intruder, I decided it would be better if the kids spent the day with their grandmother. Mother picked up all three of us. We stopped at her house first to drop off the kids. Bradford sat at the table reading the newspaper and nursing a cup of coffee, obviously quite at home in her kitchen. Were these senior citizens cohabiting?

I pushed those unwelcome thoughts aside. Despite my feelings about Bradford and his relationship with my mother, for today, I was grateful that a former police officer was there to protect my children from harm. My mother dropped me off at the bank then headed down to the Centurion real-estate office in Cameron Park.

The atmosphere in the bank was somber, far from the chaotic morning we had encountered two days earlier. Tomas Novi, the chief financial officer, had temporarily assumed Mr. Chandler's executive responsibilities.

A few minutes before noon, John Regan, the bank's attorney, arrived at our office. He met with Mr. Novi for over an hour then they both left the bank. The chief financial officer, whose youthful face was at odds with his mane of white hair, looked like he'd added a few more wrinkles in the last few hours.

Since Christmas Eve fell on a Saturday, the bank would be closed on Friday so our annual employee gift exchange was scheduled for three in the afternoon. Normally the "dirty Santa" version of exchanging presents produced good-natured giggles and a few snarls when someone decided they'd rather confiscate a gift that had already been opened, rather than select an unknown wrapped present.

Today the staff was subdued as we gathered by the fourteen-foot Christmas tree. Whenever a number was called, that person would quietly walk to the stack of wrapped parcels, choose an item and open it.

Vivian unwrapped her gift—a gingerbread man cookie jar—which led to oohs and aahs from some of the female employees. As far as I was concerned, nothing says Christmas more than a gingerbread man cookie jar, but the gift was an unpleasant reminder of Irina's teddy bear jar with its dangerous contents.

Did the new widow have any other deadly items hidden in her house? Such as antifreeze? Useful not only as a coolant for a car engine but also as poison?

Stan and I left work a few minutes early. We arrived at the body shop just before they closed at five. My auto insurance covered the windshield replacement and my roadside service plan covered the rest which meant I still had a little room on my plastic for Christmas gifts. I drove back into town and parked in one of the town lots. My head swirled with thoughts of murder and murderers, making it difficult to concentrate on my shopping.

As I strolled down Main Street, my somber mood lifted. I peeked into the festive window display of Placerville News Company. The store, founded in 1856, was crowded with other holiday shoppers also buying last-minute gift items. Scents of cinnamon, pine and cloves bombarded me with nostalgic memories of my youth, of walking along the sidewalk, hand in hand with my father. My portly pop would never have been able to resist the dancing Santa in front of the Candy Strike Emporium. The candy-filled mecca almost lured me into its chocolate clutches, but I resisted.

For now. I was fairly certain there was a piece of tawny port fudge with my name on it that would require a stop before I returned home.

Placerville Hardware, the oldest hardware store west of the Mississippi, was crammed from its ceiling to its wooden plank floor with every tool imaginable, as well as more culinary items than I could ever dream of using. My mother had mentioned she needed a new cast-iron skillet and this store had the biggest selection in the area. They also had the largest selection of cookie jars I'd ever seen.

My hands began to tremble so I averted my eyes from the colorful display, pushing past other customers in my haste to forget the previous evening's events. By the time I reached the cashier, my hands had stopped shaking enough for me to throw in a few pieces of homemade caramel logs, which were conveniently displayed next to the register.

The skillet felt like it weighed at least twenty pounds, so I decided to drop it off at my car rather than drag it all over town while I finished my errands. As I trudged down the sidewalk a large man dressed in a camouflage hunting jacket, tan cap with ear flaps and tall laced-up boots burst out of the door of the camping supply store, nearly colliding with me.

"Laurel, fate has brought us together once again."

I summoned up a nervous half smile. "Hi, Boris, are you off on a hunting expedition?" Since my hands have the tendency to move when I talk, I narrowly missed flattening an important part of Boris's anatomy with the shopping bag containing my cast-iron gift. Fortunately, the agile dancer scooted back in time to ward off a numbing blow from the frying pan.

"Please, let me help." Whether out of self-defense or old fashioned politeness, Boris reached out to grab the heavy bag. Since my arm ached from lugging the skillet down Main Street, I acquiesced.

"Thanks." I directed my eyes to the forest-green canvas satchel he carried in his other hand. "Are you taking time off from the studio?"

He nodded. "Yes. The studio, I close her from Christmas Eve to New Year's. The newspaper reporter from the *Mountain Democrat,* he is very persistent. First he calls about Dimitry and now he is calling about poor Yuri, so I think it better to disappear. In Russia, is not good idea to talk to newspaper peoples."

With the studio closed there would be no opportunity to rehearse the wedding dance, a thought that caused me to break out in a wide smile. Boris looked startled but he responded with a grin of his own, displaying a set of canines that outmatched Count Dracula.

"I go to Tahoe. It will give me nice break to spend time in the mountains. I have a little cabin on west shore not too far from the lake. Lots of snow for cross-country skiing. You are skier, Laurel? Downhill, perhaps?"

That depended on your definition of "skier." I owned a parka and insulated pants, ski mittens, hat, and matching scarf in a beautiful turquoise-and-pink knit. I also had skis, poles, and boots. Given the choice of donning all that gear and schussing down the slopes or nursing hot-buttered rum in front of a roaring fireplace, it wasn't too hard to guess where you could find this skier.

I shrugged in response.

"Ah, perhaps someday we ski together." The right corner of his bristly black moustache lifted as he winked at me. "Night skiing is very romantic, especially when there is full moon shimmering on snow-covered slopes that no one has yet traversed."

Ah, yes, nothing like the frigid night air of the mountains to unleash a woman's passion.

We reached my little car. I beeped both locks open and threw my purse in the front seat as Boris stowed the package in the back of the Prius.

"So, Laurel, have a good Christmas. I hope you get all things you deserve."

"Umm, thanks. Have fun in the mountains."

"I shall. You try stay out of trouble, no?" His bushy dark brows melded together resembling a pregnant caterpillar. Then his gaze turned to my recently repaired car.

Knowing me, "no" was probably the correct answer.

But his comment made me wonder if he knew about my
recent problems. I climbed into the car, turned on the ignition and waited for Boris to walk away. He stood still,
his gaze contemplative, as I backed my car out of the parking space then shifted gears into Drive. When I looked in
the rearview mirror, he was talking on his cell phone, his
expression troubled.

THIRTY-FIVE

A STACK OF MAIL GREETED ME when I arrived home, including two parcels sitting on the wrought-iron table on the front porch. Goody. Christmas gifts. I love presents.

I picked up a large battered box that looked like it had come via a slow freighter all the way from Kona where my brother currently resided. Hopefully it was stuffed with more of that deliciously addicting 100% Kona coffee from the big island of Hawaii. And maybe some macadamia nuts. Better yet, chocolate-covered macadamia nuts.

The other package had no return address but it was postmarked from Sacramento, so it could be from my godmother, a sweet eighty-year-old named Betty who loved to bake. And since I loved to eat, her presents were always a delightful surprise.

I dumped the mail and parcels on the kitchen table, anxious to discover what tasty treats were hidden inside the boxes. Pumpkin jumped on the table and pawed at the unmarked parcel. I was about to remove our playful pet when she howled, the fur on her back bristling like an outraged porcupine. She batted the box off the table then ran off.

I picked the package off the floor and examined it. It didn't appear damaged. I grabbed the scissors out of one of the kitchen drawers and with one swift motion ripped through the tape that sealed the carton from my inquisitive eyes.

Snow, in the form of those peanut-sized particles shippers use to annoy package recipients, poured down on the table, floating to the floor. Pumpkin reappeared and grabbed a few pieces with her front paws. They stuck to her nails as she tried to claw her way through them. With a puddle of white stuff pooling by my feet, I lifted another box out of the carton. It measured about one foot long and eight inches wide. Also wrapped in brown paper and sealed.

Headlights blazing up the driveway interrupted me so I went to greet the kids and my mother. They tromped into the house carrying a stack of shiny foil-wrapped packages. The time spent with their grandparent appeared to have been productive, at least from the standpoint of their wonderful mother who hoped to be on the receiving end of some of the gifts.

I returned to the kitchen and slit open the tape on the mystery package. The box revealed an unexpected surprise.

"Oh, look, Mom, it's one of those Russian nesting dolls," Jenna said. "You know where each doll gets smaller and smaller."

"Oh, yes. They're called *matruska* dolls or something like that."

Jenna grabbed the wooden doll. The painted face smiled at us, blue eyes unblinking, the wood decorated in all three primary colors. Jenna twisted it open and as she had predicted, a tinier version was nestled inside.

Ben grabbed the little doll from Jenna and ripped it apart. Another matching pint size version was inside. I took it out of Ben's hands and screwed opened the head to find an even tinier doll. Almost identical to the first three painted wooden dolls yet with one slight difference—this one had a slash of red drawn right where a heart should be.

Was that red paint? Or blood?

A gift or a threat?

Never one to be interested in dolls, Ben disappeared upstairs. My mother and Jenna stared at the dolls then at me.

"Who do you think could have sent this?" Mother asked.

"I have no idea." I examined the inside of the box for a clue to the identity of the sender.

"Is someone trying to scare us?" Jenna asked in a tremulous voice.

I shook my head, refusing to allow such a negative thought. "It's a traditional Russian present. It's probably from Irina to thank me, although..." I checked the parcel; the postmark was dated prior to my visit to her house.

My mother frowned but remained silent. Neither of us wanted to upset Jenna any further.

Jenna's cell rang, saving me from an explanation. Hard to believe her teenage boyfriend had come to *my* rescue. She raced upstairs to continue their conversation in private.

"I warned you investigating these murders could be dangerous." My mother examined the base of the largest doll then set it back on the table. "Someone must be worried you're getting close to figuring out who the killer is."

"Don't you think they would have left something more frightening than a set of dolls?" I countered. "Besides, the police are still holding Mr. Chandler in jail for the murders." I gazed at the miniature doll with the bright red splotch. My hand shook as I placed it on the table. "So does this confirm someone else is the killer, and they don't want me nosing around?"

"I don't know." My mother picked up the tiny doll and rolled it around in her hand. "I think Robert and I should spend the night here. What do you think?"

I was a tough woman; I didn't need anyone to play bodyguard, did I?

My voice quivered as I bravely responded, "Sure, I'd love that."

THIRTY-SIX

AFTER WEEKS OF HOLIDAY shopping, baking and wrapping presents, I never cease to be amazed that Christmas itself feels as if it lasts all of ten seconds. It was kind of weird having my mother and Bradford staying at the house for the three-day weekend, but the kids enjoyed all of the attention and presents. And I liked having extra elves to help with kitchen duty.

Since I had no clue what to get Bradford for Christmas, Mother had mentioned he enjoyed reading historical novels. Books n' Bears recommended local author Naida West, and Bradford was thrilled with my gift of her Gold Country trilogy. I was thrilled no more unidentified packages arrived on my doorstep.

Before I knew it, the day after Christmas arrived. Based on the stacks of multicolored ads falling out of my daily newspaper, this day was being marketed with more fervor than the main event, the birth of Jesus.

But who was I to complain? I'd leafed through the glossy ads in the morning paper even before my first cup of coffee. With Christmas falling on a Sunday, the bank was closed on the twenty-sixth. I piled the kids in the car and spent the day dragging them from one post-Christmas sale to another.

My first bargain coup was a pair of fluffy emerald-green Grinch slippers marked down to $3.99. How could I possibly pass them up? Jenna decided she could live without a matching pair of Grinch slippers. She chose a tunic top in a shade of rust that matched her hair. Ben was willing to settle for Spider-Man pajamas and a chunk of discounted peppermint bark to munch on while we finished our shopping.

The three of us entered Folsom Fabulous Footwear to check out their two-for-one shoe sale. Several feet of new snow had fallen in Tahoe and I needed a new pair of boots before we drove up to the mountains for the wedding. As I rounded the corner of one of the aisles in the boot section, I ran into a dance student from the Golden Hills Studio.

"Hi, Laurel," Paula said as she zipped up a tall black stiletto-heeled boot. "Did you have a nice Christmas?"

"It was great. Say, those are attractive," I remarked, admiring the etched design at the top of the boot. She stood and paced up and down the aisle, her smile reversing into a frown by the time she returned to her chair.

"They look great but they don't feel great." She slid the leather boot off and flexed her left foot in my direction. "It's difficult finding anything wide enough for my bunions. One of the hazards of ballroom dancing. They keep growing larger."

So now I had that to look forward to. Bigger bunions. It was a good thing my career in ballroom dancing would be over in less than five days.

"Are you still performing in the Holiday Ball?" I asked.

She nodded. "Boris and I are dancing together but as soon as this competition is over, I'm switching to another studio. I don't feel safe there."

"I saw Boris in Placerville the other day, shopping for camping gear. He said he was spending a few days at his cabin in Tahoe. He even invited me to go skiing with him."

Paula burst out laughing at my expression, which must have reflected how thrilled I was with the studio owner's invitation.

"Boris is quite an accomplished skier. Did you know that years ago he won an Olympic medal for the winter biathlon?"

"What on earth is that? Dancing while skiing?"

She chuckled. "Now that would be some event. No, the biathlon incorporates downhill skiing with rifle shooting."

I shuddered. Had the studio owner invited me for a little night skiing in order to get rid of me? Permanently? Or was my imagination careening out of control?

Paula opened the lid of another box and lifted a suede boot out of the tissue. "How's the wedding dance coming? Do you need to find a place to rehearse?"

"Once Liz found out Yuri was poisoned, she decided it wasn't safe for us at the studio. Her exact words were—" I made two air quotes above my head "—'What if someone in the bridal party is poisoned? It would bloody well screw up my wedding.'"

Paula chuckled. "Sounds like the bride is focused on one thing only."

"You've got that right. I can't wait for Brian to slide that gold band around her ring finger so they can sail off into the sunset."

Paula lifted an inquiring brow. "Sail? This time of year?"

"Their honeymoon is a Hawaiian cruise."

"That sounds lovely. Richard and I spent our honeymoon on a Mediterranean cruise. In fact, our anniversary is coming up next month. Five blissful years. Speaking of my husband…"

A tall, handsome, silver-haired man approached. His blue eyes twinkled as he gave me a hearty handshake.

"Nice to meet you, Laurel. Will you be performing at the Holiday Ball, as well?" When I shook my head, he inquired whether I was going to watch any of the events.

"Anyone can watch the competition," Paula explained

when I looked confused. "You can buy tickets to view different events. The evening performances are kind of pricey, but that's because the pros are performing. On New Year's Eve, Bobby and Tatania are dancing in the Rising Star event and Anya and Gregor will be competing against some world-famous professional couples." Paula reached into her oversized designer purse, pulled out a bright pink flyer and handed it to me.

"I much prefer watching ballroom to dancing it myself but the wedding is that evening," I glanced at the flyer. "Hey, the competition is at the Royal Tahoe Resort. That's where Liz is getting married. In fact, I'll be driving up on the thirtieth for the rehearsal."

"How perfect. My scholarship event is that afternoon," she said. "Maybe you can stop by for a few minutes. I guess I'm the only amateur from Golden Hills competing this time. Dana was supposed to dance with Yuri, but…" Her voice trailed off.

I sighed. "It's horrible, isn't it? Dana must be beside herself with grief. I still can't imagine our bank president killing anyone, no matter how jealous he was."

"It sounds to me like they've arrested the right person," Richard said. "I was concerned about Paula being at the studio but with that Chandler fellow in jail, I can relax. My wife is too passionate about her dance to worry about her own safety."

Paula smiled fondly at her husband. "Richard has all of these important clients to deal with and how does he spend his time? Worrying about me."

"Are you an attorney?"

Richard made a face at the mention of the legal profession. "No, I own Mason Wealth Management. We're an investment banking firm."

He reached into his pocket and handed me his business card. "You never know when you might need a good financial manager to help you with your portfolio."

"My portfolio is barely large enough to keep my kitty supplied with cat food, but if Hangtown Bank needs to cut back on staff, I may be looking for a job. I'm a mortgage underwriter."

"With your experience analyzing financial statements, you could easily transition into this end of the financial sector. We offer a full range of services to our clients, from stocks and bonds to commodities."

Paula smiled at her husband. "Richard is the consummate salesman."

"The financial markets can be difficult to gauge but we invested wisely in the commodities market and our clients are thrilled with their returns." He put an arm around Paula. "My wife is a huge asset in the business."

He turned to me. "And we're always looking for new talent."

I smiled at Paula. "You'll be happy to hear that my underwriting skills are far superior to my ballroom dancing skills."

She laughed. "Just keep practicing. By this time next year, you could be competing, too."

Richard's gaze was proud as he looked down at Paula. "My wife is totally dedicated to her dance."

She smiled affectionately at him. "And fortunately, Richard is totally dedicated to me."

We said our goodbyes as they headed for the register and I went in search of my kids. It was nice to see a couple who cared so much for each other. Someday, I, too, hoped to gaze fondly at my spouse, assuming a new spouse was in the picture for me. For right now, I would concentrate on gazing fondly at a new pair of boots, a far easier task.

A half hour later I was not only the owner of a pair of

black midcalf boots, but I had also found silver shoes to replace the broken pair still sitting in an evidence locker. They weren't as well crafted and lacked the suede soles of my old dance shoes, but they were considerably cheaper. Since I would be wearing them for less than eight hours during the wedding and reception, the cost was manageable. At least I only had one dance routine to worry about. I couldn't imagine worrying about multiple dance performances through several days of a ballroom competition.

I now knew that ballroom dancing was a stressful, competitive and potentially dangerous sport, particularly at the professional level. Female dancers often risked life and limb during complicated aerial lifts with their partners. Lack of sleep or concentration could result in a critical injury. Stress levels among the studio's professional dancers would be extraordinarily high during this competition.

It could be the perfect opportunity to find out more about the killer, although I had to be ultra careful.

The last thing I wanted was for my new shoes to also end up in an evidence locker.

THIRTY-SEVEN

THE NEXT TWO DAYS WERE A BLUR of activity. Even though Liz still had an occasional Bridezilla meltdown, she was realistic enough to realize that holding a shower, bachelorette party and a wedding during the holidays might be one too many festive events.

On Wednesday night, the two bridesmaids, my mother and I threw Liz a combined shower/bachelorette party at the Snooty Frog, just down the street from Mother's office. Michelle, the owner, whipped up an enormous batch of her smoked salmon tortellini alfredo. Between the to-die-for pasta, gallons of wine and a karaoke machine one of the bridesmaids thought would be a good idea, we had wonderful memories of Liz enjoying her last moments as a single gal.

Despite my protests, someone shoved the mike in my hands and I eked out a rendition of "I Will Survive" that hopefully would *not* survive nor go viral on YouTube. My mother and I stayed behind to clean up after the happy guests and bride-to-be departed.

"I didn't have a chance to tell you the latest news about Dana," she said.

"Oh, no, what happened now?"

"The Board of the Hangtown Women's Guild asked her to step down from her position as president. It's a shame because she's done so much good for our community."

I shoved the paper plates in the garbage bag. "I know life isn't fair, but that totally sucks."

"I agree but there's nothing you can do about it. Just concentrate on enjoying the wedding weekend."

I was planning on enjoying the wedding weekend. Especially once the wedding was over. But in the meantime, I was still concerned about Dana and Mr. Chandler, the bank, and well…me.

SINCE MY PRIUS WAS NOT equipped to haul three people, luggage, skis, and snowboards, Bradford and my mother decided to leave a day early and take the kids up to Tahoe on Thursday. The senior citizens agreed they would not co-habit in front of my kids so Mother would spend the night with Jenna, and Ben could hang out with his oversized pal.

With our fearless leader locked up, our mortgage division was overwhelmed with borrowers wanting to close by year end. Or maybe they wanted to ensure the bank still had the money to fund their loans.

Although the loan department was busy, the tellers spent far more time filing their nails than filing any paperwork. The gossip around the office was that significantly more money was flowing out of the bank than coming in. Numerous local merchants had either withdrawn substantial amounts of money or completely closed out their accounts.

Not only were new deposits absent, but so were our end of the year bonuses. Several employees grumbled, but considering the impact Mr. Chandler's arrest had on the future of the bank, we were lucky we were still employed.

I'd counted on receiving my own bonus by the thirtieth to offset the expenses of Christmas, the wedding, and our stay at the beautiful but not inexpensive Royal Tahoe resort. Liz had offered to pick up the tab for our hotel room but I refused. The hotel expense was the price one paid for friendship. I would do anything for my best friend, as evidenced by my torturous dance lessons.

My phone rang in the middle of checking off underwriter conditions. "Laurel speaking," I said, concentrating on getting the current loan file I was working on off my desk and over to the funding department.

"It's Dana." Her voice caught as if she might break into sobs at any moment.

"How are you holding up?"

"Okay, I guess. Poor Gordon is still in jail. They haven't set bail yet. The boys are furious with me..." At the mention of her sons, a torrent of tears flooded the phone line.

Eventually, she calmed a bit and got down to the reason for the call. "Tomas Novi said the bank is losing a ton of clients. I can't believe I created such a mess. Is there any chance we could meet?"

Since I still believed in Mr. Chandler's innocence I was more than happy to get together with Dana. With the kids at Tahoe my only task this evening was to pack. We agreed to meet at the Pantry as soon as I got off work. With reporters from local newspapers and national gossip magazines camped at her Victorian mansion in the hopes of snaring a story, it seemed safer to meet elsewhere. One rag had published an issue featuring a photo of Mr. Chandler being led into the courthouse for his arraignment. The title still burned my eyeballs: *Banker Bludgeons Bimbo's Boyfriend*.

Dana might be many things, but she definitely wasn't a bimbo.

A little after five, I entered the coffee shop looking for the pretty, short-haired brunette. A platinum blonde with Gwen Stefani curls waved at me from one of the maroon leather-backed booths. Being the astute detective that I was, I headed in her direction.

"Nice, um, disguise," I muttered, taking in the curly

wig and blue-tinted glasses that rested on Dana's nose. With new lines etched alongside her pale lips, the getup made her look more like a faded rock star than a bank president's wife.

"A reporter followed me into town. Fortunately, I'd already stuck this old wig into a bag in case I needed to make a switch. Then I stopped at Placerville Clothing Company and bought this new outfit to fake him out." She stretched her arm toward me. "Don't you love the feel of this natural cotton?"

I rolled my eyes. Dana needed to focus on murder, not fashion.

She patted her artificial curls. "Gordon always loved this wig. Whenever I would put it on he used to…" She blushed and fortunately our server chose that moment to stop at the table and drop off some menus. The young waitress didn't bat an eye at Dana's strange disguise and I was thrilled with the server's interruption. The last thing I wanted to visualize was the portly president and his blonde bewigged wife engaged in some marital role-playing.

We took a few minutes to peruse the menu. With a sleek bridesmaid dress to fit into, my choice was easy—the low-fat, low-calorie, low-taste dinner of grilled fish and veggies. Once we ordered, Dana took off her oversized glasses and rubbed her eyes. "My life has been hell this past week. We've hired Michael Girling for Gordon's criminal defense work, but I had to put up a $250,000 retainer."

The expression on my face must have reflected my thoughts. Ouch!

She nodded. "Right. And that's on top of the $300,000 that I gave to Dimitry, which used up our entire equity line. With property values still in the tank, we have no equity left in our house. We're also upside down on the value of a vacation home we own in Tahoe."

The Chandlers owned a vacation home in Tahoe? I wondered if they ever let family, friends, or favorite employees stay there for free.

"The attorney is trying to get Gordon released on bail,
but it's not easy on a homicide charge. Even if the D.A.
allows it, the bail amount will be a huge sum of money
like two million dollars, and we don't have the collateral
for that."

"Can your family help?"

She lowered her eyes. "No, they're not... Well, let's just
say our relatives are not happy about this situation, nor are
they able to help financially. And I can't see Gordon ap-
proving for me to hold a spaghetti fundraiser at the Elks
Lodge to raise bail money. He has his pride."

One would think that wearing an orange jump suit 24/7
might erase some of those prideful notions, but what did
I know?

"Dana, I wish I could lend you money, but since there
were no Christmas bonuses—" I threw that in because
technically it was her mess that impacted all of the bank
employees "—my balances on my credit cards far exceed
the balances in my bank account."

Her face grew paler than the platinum wig she sported.

"I'm sorry," I said. "That was out of line."

"No, you're absolutely right. My crazy idea to open a
dance studio with Dimitry has led to the murder of my
teacher, the arrest of my husband, and bank employees
possibly losing their jobs. Maybe even the closing of the
bank." She wiped her palm over damp eyes. "Can you
ever forgive me?"

The waitress chose that moment to bring our dinners.
I looked at my diet plate with distaste. This conversation
would be far more palatable if some batter-fried onion

rings were smiling up at me instead of the overcooked veggies.

"There's nothing to forgive, Dana. Let's concentrate on figuring out a way to spring your husband. Do you have any idea what evidence the police have other than him parking his car close to the studio the night Dimitry was killed?"

"The police probably haven't shared everything with me but Gordon evidently called Dimitry a couple of hours before he was killed and left a threatening message on Dimitry's voice mail. They have proof of the call on his cell." She fiddled with her salad, rearranging the greens and ending up with one tiny piece dangling on her fork. "I still can't believe my husband went to the studio to convince Dimitry to end our so-called affair. How could Gordon believe I would be unfaithful after all of these years?"

"Um, well, you did give all that money to your dance instructor without telling your husband." Dana's naïveté amazed me. She needed to get out of her mansion and experience life in the real world. I looked at the slightly askew wig on her head and decided she was already learning about the seedy realities of life.

"Anything else?"

"Not telling the detective he was at the studio is, of course, a huge deal, but I think it's understandable. My husband knew *he* didn't kill Dimitry so he didn't think it was necessary to share."

Typical CEO response.

"Oh, and they went through Gordon's car after they arrested him. You know what a stickler my husband is about making sure all of the bank regulations are strictly followed? He's the same way with his car. He personally makes sure that all maintenance items are done right on schedule. With the first snowstorm of the season predicted, it was no surprise to me what he had stored in the trunk of his Mercedes."

I contemplated my arsenal of winter supplies. "A shovel? Window scraper?"

"Of course. Gordon is prepared for every eventuality," she said. "That's also why he had an open container of antifreeze."

THIRTY-EIGHT

IT WAS LOOKING MORE AND MORE like the only way to get my boss a "get out of jail free" card was to figure out who killed the two dancers. While it didn't surprise me that Mr. Chandler carried a supply of antifreeze in his car for a winter emergency, it sure didn't help *our* case since the odorless and colorless liquid was the ultimate cause of Yuri's death. If the District Attorney and the sheriff were positive they had the culprit, it was going to take the skill set of an underwriter to prove them wrong.

Dana and I parted with hugs. She agreed to keep me informed of any new updates and I promised to continue investigating. With the wedding taking place at the same location as the Holiday Ball, I might be able to ferret out some information.

I returned home just in time for the ten o'clock weather forecast. The weather guy stood next to his electronic map and not alongside the highway freezing his icy butt off, which meant it wasn't snowing yet. Why television news shows think their audience enjoys watching ice crystals form on a reporter's face every time a blizzard blankets the mountains never ceases to amaze me.

According to the forecast, there should be no new snow until the morning of New Year's Eve at the earliest. I had no problem with that. We'd be safe and cozy in our mountain lodge and there was nothing prettier than watching soft snowflakes fall on the cobalt-blue water of Lake Tahoe.

Especially from inside the resort.

The phone rang and my maternal autopilot kicked into gear. I ran into the kitchen to grab it, worried something had happened to the kids. My caller ID revealed there was no need to fret. "Hey, Stan, what's up?"

"I'm so screwed."

"How eloquent. What's wrong?"

"My car won't start and I need a ride."

"Up to Tahoe? Sure. Without the kids and their gear I have room for you. What time will you be ready to leave in the morning?"

He cleared his throat. "Umm, how about now? I'm at the Golden Hills Studio. AAA said it wasn't the battery so they're towing the Beemer to the dealer."

"What are you doing at the studio this late?"

Stan emitted a sound that was a combination of a moan and a wheeze. "Anya talked me into competing in the new-comer tango event at the Holiday Ball. We just finished practicing, but she already took off. Said she had to be somewhere by ten."

"Are you kidding? Why didn't you tell me you're competing?"

He blasted a sigh over the phone line. "I didn't want anyone to find out in case I totally embarrassed myself."

I was stunned Anya had talked Stan into dancing at the New Year's Ball. It was worth the drive to find out how she'd managed to do it. When I arrived at the studio twenty minutes later, Stan catapulted out the door and into my car almost before the vehicle came to a full stop.

"Anya sure has amazing persuasive abilities," I commented. "She should join the legal profession. How come you were able to practice tonight? Boris told me the studio was closed this week."

"The teachers all have keys in case they need to rehearse their routines before an event. I can't believe I'm competing either, but Anya is positive I'll take first place in newcomer tango." Stan shifted in his seat and turned in my direction. "Did you know that the more awards the teachers and their students take in a competition, the better opportunity they have of winning the Top Teacher award for that event?"

"No, I didn't know and I don't particularly care, although…" I mulled over his statement. "So what do they get if they win Top Teacher? A trophy? Money?"

"Anya said this competition is so big the top award is ten thousand dollars."

"Wow. That is a big prize. Would that be significant enough to kill someone?"

My eyes were glued to the road, but Stan's snickering echoed throughout the car.

"Laurel, no one would kill for $10,000."

"Hit men kill for less than that. Plus the prestige of winning Top Teacher could result in additional clients. Those hourly rates add up."

No response. I briefly took my eyes off the road and glanced at Stan. He was stroking his chin with his index finger, always a sign of deep intellectual concentration. Probably adding up all of the money he'd recently spent on his private lessons.

"You could be right," he said at last. "Anya told me if she had enough points from competing in different approved dance events throughout the year, she could win an additional $50,000 grand prize. But I can't imagine Anya eliminating other instructors in order to win the top teacher title. Plus, she needs as many points as possible and that includes dancing in the professional round. With two of the three male teachers from the studio out of the picture, she's forced to dance with Gregor. He's good but

not nearly as accomplished as Dimitry and Yuri were."
Stan chuckled. "Gregor is totally gaga over Anya. But I
don't think it's reciprocal."

"I'd love to see Anya and Gregor dance together in the
competition," I said.

"This might be your last opportunity to watch her perform. She told me tonight she's moving to Miami as soon
as she has enough money."

"That's a big step. Is she relocating because of the murders?"

He shrugged. "Who knows? It's difficult enough un-
derstanding her tango instructions. She keeps muttering
something about how it's too hot for her here."

"Too hot?" The thermometer gauge on my car indicated
the outside temperature was thirty-two degrees. "Anya
thinks Miami will be cooler?"

"Honestly, that woman does not make a lot of sense.
She mumbled something about getting away from the bad
government men who are following her. She's the most
paranoid person I've ever met."

I slowed down when I noticed a black-and-white high-
way patrol car hidden behind a curve on the highway.
"What does she mean by bad government men? Like the
CHP?"

"I thought maybe she was referring to immigration officials. She's in this country on some sort of visa. Boris
sponsored all of the Russian dancers—Anya, Dimitry,
Irina, Gregor, and Yuri."

That was an interesting tidbit of information, although
I couldn't see any relevance to the recent murders.

"Have you asked her if she knows anything about the
deaths at the studio?" I asked.

"I wanted to but she's been too jumpy during my last
couple of lessons. I attributed it to nerves because of the

upcoming competition. It's not easy switching dance partners at the last minute."

"She and I spoke the night Yuri collapsed," I said, "but she was really evasive and all I learned was that she has a part-time job elsewhere. When I see her at the resort I'm going to try talking to her again."

Stan raised his left hand. "Hey, no bugging her until after my dances are over. I don't want Anya wigging out on me. She's more volatile than a Molotov cocktail right now."

The last thing we needed was to make the situation more explosive. I would tread lightly through the ballroom minefield.

THIRTY-NINE

SUNSHINE AND DECEIVING cerulean-blue skies greeted me the next morning. While it looked cheery outside, the temperature in Tahoe would be in the teens and twenties. When Liz first announced her engagement, I envisioned a beautiful summer wedding in a winery or some other picturesque venue in our rolling green foothills. But for some reason, the woman who had waited forty years to tie the knot decided a winter wonderland would be the perfect backdrop for her nuptials. The fur-trimmed wedding gown she discovered in one of her numerous bridal magazines might have played a part in her decision.

Liz's wedding planner had scored a last-minute cancellation on the wedding chapel and small banquet room attached by a covered walkway to the new Royal Tahoe Resort. The imperial theme of the resort fit perfectly with my friend's concept of a regal wedding. The only issue had been arranging everything in less than three months. Armed with wedding magazines and an Excel spread sheet listing every conceivable detail, right down to the pastel sugar-coated almonds, it was amazing what an organized Bridezilla could accomplish.

Although this wedding wouldn't be on the scale of the Prince William/Kate Middleton nuptials, it could be a close second as far as pomp and circumstance. I didn't have a problem with her fur-trimmed sheath-style white velvet wedding dress, but if Liz decided to accessorize with a tiara, her lady-in-waiting would officially crown the bride-to-be herself.

Packing for a winter wedding is not a minimalist venture. Between my bridesmaid gown, several cocktail dresses, shoes and bags in three different colors, ski parka, practical snow boots, my new impractical cute boots, a shovel and bag of salt in my trunk, it was a good thing the kids had gone ahead. Otherwise, I would have had to strap them to the roof of my car.

Right before I left, I refreshed Pumpkin's food and water and admonished her to behave for the pet sitter. I could swear she rolled her almond-shaped eyes at me before she stalked off, tail high, to plan some mischievous revenge in our absence.

I zipped up the hill and arrived at Stan's beautifully restored cream-colored Victorian in ten minutes. Stan was out of his front door the second I pulled into the driveway. His red-and-black ski jacket was at odds with his black dress shirt, tie and pants but he wouldn't have time to change before the competition. We shifted my suitcases around and squeezed in his, plus garment bag and shoe tote.

Stan deposited his water bottle in my cup holder then plopped into the passenger seat. I attempted to reverse out of the driveway, warily watching the cars zipping past on the busy street. I love the pastel clapboard Victorian houses in downtown Placerville, but most of them are located on busy thoroughfares. I waited several frustrating minutes for a break in the traffic.

Once we were on Highway 50 heading east, it was only a seventy-five-mile drive to the west shore of Tahoe. Assuming we didn't hit any black ice or careless drivers, we should arrive at the resort by noon.

"Can you speed up a little?" Stan's fingernails drummed a belligerent solo on the armrest.

"No," I snarled at him. Watching out for those ominous patches of black ice on the road always make me nervous and, admittedly, a tad crabby. Bridezilla would never forgive me if I had an accident. Her spreadsheet did not allow for delays.

"Admire the scenery." I pointed to the churning rapids of the American river rushing past us on our right. "It will calm your nerves."

"I'm not nervous," Stan snapped, but he turned to gaze out the window at the redwoods and cedars towering over the highway, their branches still laden with snow from an earlier storm. I punched in the button for my CD player and soon we were listening to Faith and Tim—my favorite country couple—serenade us as we drove the windy highway.

Other than a white SUV that insisted on tailgating us for a short stretch before I finally pulled off the road and let him pass, the ride was uneventful. We pulled up in front of the massive rock and glass exterior of the Royal Tahoe Resort a few minutes before noon. Although the miniturrets at both ends of the grandiose building made the resort look less like Camelot and more like the Victorian folly in the *Rocky Horror Picture Show,* every aspect of the resort was meant to be impressive, and it was.

Stan jumped out of the passenger side of the car, grabbed his suitcase and garment bag, and was wheeling his way through the revolving door before anyone even noticed my tiny car surrounded by massive SUVs.

I hated to be a pill, but when the valets continued to ignore me, I climbed out of the driver's seat and stopped one of the guys unloading the canary-yellow Hummer behind me. I tapped on the epaulet of his royal blue regalia.

It wasn't your standard Tahoe mountain attire but it did have a certain sense of cache.

"Hi, Tim," I said, assuming the name typed on his badge was his. "Did you miss me?" I pointed to my Prius, whose top half was periwinkle, but whose bottom half was now coated in gray slush from our drive.

He sniffed then extracted a numbered ticket from his pocket. "Sorry, I didn't notice you. Are you here for the competition?"

"No, I'm a member of the Kendall/Daley wedding party."

He jumped back a few inches and practically saluted me. Either the D.A.'s office or my gal pal had some royal pull around here. "Sorry, ma'am. Of course, I'll have your bags taken in immediately. It's too early for check-in, so we'll store everything until your room is ready."

Tim directed me toward the lobby. I stopped at the ornate registration desk and confirmed my room would not be ready until four. I punched my mother's cell number but there was no answer. A call to Jenna's phone went directly into voice mail. It was almost twelve-thirty so they could be dining in one of the many restaurants in the resort. Or using other hotel facilities the desk clerk had spelled out for me, such as the underground grotto, waterfall and swimming pool with swim-up bar.

Darn, I should have packed a swimsuit instead of all that thermal underwear.

I dialed Liz's cell but again went directly to voice mail. There was no point roaming the massive hotel in search of my family or my friend. They would call when they received my messages. The lobby bustled with people attired in fur-trimmed parkas, tight black ski pants and pastel Ugg boots. Interspersed with the skiers were a few snowboarders dressed in loose-fitting jackets and cargo-style pants.

What made this mountain resort even more entertaining were the gaudy stiletto-heeled peacocks stalking through the lobby headed in the direction of the ballroom. I followed a woman attired in violet satin, the slit of her skirt rising almost to her belly button. Her décolletage, on the other hand, plummeted to her waist. She was a wardrobe malfunction just waiting to happen.

Between the elegantly curled, moussed, and sprayed coiffures of the dancers, both men and women, the intensity of their makeup, including false eyelashes and bright red lipstick, and the rainbow-hued costumes, I felt like I'd been transported to a circus. I was grateful to be a bystander and not performing myself. The pressure of competing against other dancers in appearance as well as technique would be overwhelming.

With little else to do until my room was ready for check-in, I followed the stream of dancers to an enormous ballroom. An attendant at the door stopped me and asked for my ticket. Five minutes and twenty dollars later, I entered the room. Rectangular tables with chairs for eight were placed along the perimeter of the glossy wooden floor. Men dressed in tuxedos or shirts, vests, and black trousers wore numbered signs on their back. They whirled and twirled their colorful partners around the floor. How would I locate Stan in this crowd?

"Yoo-hoo. Laurel, over here," yelled a familiar voice. One of the things I like best about Stan is that he never suffers from shyness. A couple of the bystanders frowned, but I was thrilled he'd found me among the crowd.

I squeezed past a couple of female dancers whose waists were as big as mine—when I was ten. The expression of relief on Stan's face reinforced my decision to stop in and support him. "What time are you competing?"

"We're on in four more dances." He looked at his watch. "Which will be in approximately six minutes."

"That's not very long." I was surprised the dances lasted slightly over a minute each. How could the judges ascertain the winners in that short amount of time? It gave them less than ten seconds per couple to mark their scores in at least five different categories.

"Trust me, it's enough time to screw up and not place. But performing poorly is the least of my worries."

I directed a questioning look at my pal. That was when I realized one significant part of his dance equation was missing.

"Where's Anya?"

Stan shrugged, his facial expression bleak. He was obviously upset about his missing partner. Was there a reason to be even more concerned about her absence?

Someone tapped me on my shoulder. I jumped high enough to make a rim shot if a basketball hoop had graced the gigantic ballroom.

"Sorry, Laurel, I didn't mean to startle you," said a beautiful woman attired in a hot-pink rhinestone-covered satin gown.

I examined the unfamiliar face with its thick makeup, inch-long eyelashes and elegant French twist and discovered Paula Mason. "Wow, I almost didn't recognize you," I said, before realizing she might not take my comment as a compliment. "I mean…"

Paula laughed. "It's okay. I can barely see out of this fringe of false lashes but if this is what it takes to come in first then I'll do it. I'm glad you found time to watch the competition."

"Stan's supposed to dance with Anya in a few minutes so I stopped by to support him, but she hasn't shown up."

Stan pointed at his watch. "Two minutes now." His thin

shoulders drooped and I sensed his exhilaration evaporate as his dream of winning a competition also evaporated.

Suddenly a slender bronze arm reached out and grabbed Stan's right hand. He disappeared into the throng of dancers.

Seconds later, Stan and Anya strolled onto the floor as he presented her to the audience. The strains of a familiar tango emanated over the sound system. As the couple swept past us, I was impressed that Stan had mastered the look of a tango dancer in ability and appearance. With his hair slicked back, he resembled the professional male dancers. By my estimate, there had to be at least two gallons of hair gel spinning around the dance floor.

Despite my supportive remarks to Stan, never in a million years had I anticipated that he would actually be a contender in his newcomer tango competition. I watched in shock as my pal maneuvered his way around the wooden floor.

"Your friend is really good," Paula said. "At this level, the women pros usually back lead their amateur partners, but he's leading Anya all by himself. He really has this nailed."

"I'm stunned. Stan's been dancing for less than three weeks."

Paula smiled. "He's either a natural or Anya is an even better teacher than I thought she was. I can't believe she waited until the last moment to appear. That's so unprofessional."

The sight of my buddy sternly and seamlessly executing the tango made my eyes well up with tears. The elation on his face was a memory I would never forget.

The music ended and applause filled the room. Paula and I clapped heartily and awaited the return of the tango king and his partner. As the couple worked their way through the crowd, Stan looked ecstatic, but Anya appeared worried. She glanced in our direction and I waved at both of them, assuming they would join us. Anya said something to Stan then disappeared out the door. He headed in our direction, but his expression was far from elated.

"Stan, way to go," I said, clapping him on his numbered back.

"Thanks. I was so relieved when Anya finally showed up, I didn't even have time to be nervous."

"Why did she wait until the last minute?"

Stan looked to the right and left as if afraid someone would eavesdrop on our conversation. He muttered something, but the raucous sound of samba music drowned his words and I couldn't catch what he was saying.

"Stan, speak up. I can barely hear you."

"She's afraid someone is trying to kill her."

Paula gasped and so did I.

"Why does she think that?" I asked. "Is it those government agents she was telling you about?"

"Government agents?" Paula looked even more confused than I did. "You mean Immigration officials?"

He shook his head. "I don't think it's immigration she's worried about. She's a nervous wreck, but she promised she'd be back for tomorrow's competition."

"You're dancing again? But the wedding is tomorrow."

Stan looked as guilty as if he'd robbed my cookie jar. "Okay, I might be a little late for the wedding. But I'll definitely make it to the reception. Liz won't even notice I'm not there."

I glared at him.

"She won't realize I'm missing unless someone brings it to her attention. You know how Liz is. She'll be completely focused on Brian. And her dress. And her shoes.

But I'll never have another opportunity to win first place with the lovely Anya."

I dug the toe of my boot into the ground. Queen Elizabeth would be royally unhappy if she discovered Stan chose the ballroom competition over her highness.

"You know, Stan, there will be other competitions."

"Yes, but I'll never be paired up with Anya again. The woman is so amazing. And after this weekend, she's disappearing. She said it's not safe for her to stick around. Not only that—" he looked at me, his eyes pop-eyed behind his wire-rimmed designer glasses "—she said it's dangerous for someone else."

"Who?" I leaned forward with anticipation then fell backward into my chair when Stan poked his finger in my chest. The temperature in the room felt like it dropped forty degrees when he answered my question.

"She said it's dangerous for you."

FORTY

THE FANTASY WORLD OF SATIN AND sequins disappeared as a reality check set in.

"Me? Why would Anya think it's dangerous for me?" My mind raced as I counted the reasons why I could be in peril. I didn't have to count beyond one. "Because I'm investigating the studio murders?"

Stan looked fearful. "I barely talked to her. After she grabbed my hand, she lectured me on what steps to lead. We danced and then she said she had to go. When I asked her what was wrong, she said it was too risky for her here. I told her we would protect her and that's when she said you were in danger, too."

"But I barely know Anya. She must be involved with the Russian Mafia. Or the Murderati."

"Murderati?" Paula asked.

Okay, so I got my favorite mystery blog mixed up with my mobs.

I grabbed Stan by his skinny black-shirted shoulders and shook him. "Did Anya specifically mention my name?"

He pursed his lips and I released my hold. "Well, she said my friend. I assumed she meant you."

I tapped my foot while I thought over his comment. "Could she be referring to Paula? She was sitting next to me."

Paula's face turned paler than the wedding gown Liz would be wearing the next day. "You think I'm in danger?"

"I don't know and obviously, neither does Stan. I'll try to get in touch with Tom—I mean, Detective Hunter."

Paula nudged me and pointed toward Boris, who waved his meaty hand from across the room. "Maybe Boris knows what Anya is talking about. I need to practice with him before we go on so I'll see what I can find out. If you two are still around at four, come watch me compete."

"I'm not sure if I'll make it today," I said. "Will you also be dancing tomorrow?"

She crossed the fingers on both hands. "If we make it into the finals today, we'll be competing late in the day tomorrow."

I wished Paula luck then looked down at my cell. Oops. Messages from everyone: Jenna, my mother, and the bride. Stan and I left the ballroom and I listened to my voice mail as we maneuvered our way among the multitude of dancers milling around the long hallway. One of the females bumped into me, leaving a tan imprint on the arm of my bulky white cable-knit sweater.

"Ick. No wonder they all look like they stepped off a plane from Hawaii."

Stan chuckled. "Yeah, Anya said the hotel arranged for the dancers to have a bronzing room in case someone needed a quick tan fix."

Between the artificial tans, makeup, elaborate hairpieces, and occasional pair of factory-made breasts, the only things not fake were the competitors' dance abilities.

I returned my mother's phone call. She and Bradford were at Harrah's playing the slots and the kids were in the video arcade perfecting their hand and eye coordination. Jenna had tried to talk Bradford into joining a poker game, with her acting as his consultant, but he had officially explained why that wasn't going to happen. I was relieved everyone was having fun.

Liz, on the other hand, was not fine. The white calla lilies the florist had special ordered had not arrived. What was I going to do about it?

Never let it be said that Laurel McKay would let a little thing like a death threat interfere with her best friend's wedding plans. I called Liz back and told her I was on it and went off to deal with the unfortunate florist. After an hour of hand wringing from the owner of Floral Perfection, we decided that white poinsettias could replace the calla lilies in the original arrangement. Post Christmas, they might be a bit bedraggled but so was I at that point. If he stuffed enough lilies of the valley and white roses throughout our bouquets, no one would even notice.

By the time I finalized the floral decisions it was almost four. The wedding rehearsal wasn't scheduled until six so I had time to kill and no one to kill it with. Since I'd already paid for admission to the afternoon competition, I decided to go inside and watch Paula. It was the least I could do for a fellow Golden Hills student and should only take a few minutes. I was curious to see how light on his feet the burly Boris would be. I also wanted to see if Anya had returned.

There were more bystanders in the ballroom than earlier probably because this was the highest level that an amateur could compete with her professional partner. Paula stood next to the studio owner who dwarfed the other male instructors in size. Since they were competing in the standard dance category Boris was clad in tails instead of the open-shirted style worn in the Latin dance competitions. A far cry from the survivalist gear he'd worn last week.

I spied an empty seat next to an attractive older man who I belatedly recognized as Paula's husband, Richard. He smiled in recognition. "Hello, Laurel. Did you change your mind about competing?"

I emphatically shook my head. "Nope, this reinforces that I never ever want to compete. But I thought it would be fun to watch Paula. She doesn't appear the least bit nervous."

"My wife has nerves of steel." He chuckled. "Nothing fazes her."

"She mentioned you recently took a Mediterranean cruise for your five-year anniversary."

Richard smiled and nodded. "Did she tell you we met on a cruise ship?"

I leaned closer. "That's so romantic. Tell me more."

"My first wife had passed away two years earlier from cancer. The ordeal was such a strain that I had turned into a recluse. My kids were worried that I wasn't getting out enough so they arranged for the whole family, grand-kids and all to go on a Caribbean cruise for my fifty-fifth birthday."

"You have wonderful children. I hope my kids are still talking to me by the time they're grown up."

"I'm a lucky father and an even luckier husband. One day when the ship was out at sea, I decided to try my hand at skeet shooting. I'd been duck hunting out in the delta but never tried hitting a clay pigeon. It was love at first shot!"

My face must have reflected my "huh?"

"Paula worked on the cruise ship facilitating a lot of the activities and excursions, you know, like shopping activi-ties, bridge, shuffleboard, that kind of thing."

What a sweet story. I guess it proved you never knew when and where you would find a soul mate. In Richard's case, it had apparently happened twice in one lifetime. Would there be a second act for me, as well? My expres-sion must have appeared pensive because he reached over and briefly touched my hand. "Sometimes it takes a while to find that special person."

I nodded back. Liz had Brian, my mother had Bradford, and Paula had the delightful Richard. Would the universe ever decree that a hunky detective should be in my life?

The strains of a Viennese waltz echoed around the room and I was transported into another century where women with elaborately curled hair wore flowing satin gowns and elbow-length matching gloves. The men looked debonair in their tails, crisp white shirts and glossy black shoes. Boris was masterful at leading Paula, even evading what appeared to be a trap set by another couple to lock the studio owner into a corner.

After four dances in a row, I was exhausted from watching the competitors. I couldn't imagine keeping up the pace without a transfusion of Jolt Cola. Especially considering that quickstep was included as one of the required dances. One of these days I would have to look up its history. My guess was that some young maiden was running away from a frisky partner when that one was invented.

Boris and Paula's quickstep was electrifying. They hopped and skipped around the room, their feet barely skimming the floor. I was certain they had nailed first place in all five events when, without any warning, Boris crashed to the floor, taking his partner with him. Two other couples who had been hot on their footsteps tripped over the downed dancers. The music stopped and for a second there was stunned silence.

Then World War III began.

FORTY-ONE

THE THREE COUPLE PILE-UP reminded me of a traffic accident. Tempers flared and obscenities were yelled in a variety of languages. At one point I thought Boris was going
to belt one of the other men. Several of the judges, who
had narrowly missed being crushed by the fallen dancers,
tried to untangle the competitors. I glanced at the entrance
to the ballroom and saw a petite blonde woman rushing
out the door.

What was Irina doing here? Was the new mother competing at this event? And why wasn't she sticking around
to see if Paula or Boris were injured?

Richard ran off to assist his wife, who looked shaken
but not hurt. One of the other female dancers sat on the
floor in a cloud of iridescent pink chiffon, rubbing her left
ankle. Boris flexed his right hand but I couldn't tell if he
was injured or merely anxious to punch someone.

After a lengthy discussion, the six judges decided all
of the couples would advance into the finals the next day.
That way those who were slightly injured would have
twenty-four hours to heal. And time to ingest some potent
anti-inflammatory meds, the staple of the ballroom dance
community.

I decided to wait for Paula's return to tell her how great
she and Boris had looked prior to the crash. Paula's color
was high and two of her curls drooped against her cheek
but other than that she didn't appear to have been hurt. As

she slid into her chair, I noticed a tear in her skirt. "Oh, Paula, you were dancing so beautifully. What happened?"

"That couple from Australia intentionally shoved Boris and the next thing I knew we were all piled on top of each other."

"You must be relieved you didn't injure anything other than your dress."

She followed my gaze and gasped. "I didn't even notice it ripped." Paula abruptly stood up and swished down the aisle with Richard right on her heels, looking as worried as she was. Paula was lucky she had such a sympathetic and devoted spouse.

I'd been so distracted by the fracas I'd lost track of the time. As I stood up, my eyes were drawn to something sparkly under the table. I bent over and picked up the tiny item, a crystal from Paula's dress that must have fallen off and rolled underneath the table.

I stuck the stone in my purse. Hopefully Paula had a few spares in case one of them fell off and needed to be replaced. I left the ballroom, stopped at the front desk to officially check in and arranged for my luggage to be delivered to my room.

I walked to the elevator and as the elevator doors slowly closed, my eyes locked with the somber gray eyes of Vladimir, standing in the lobby holding a dance program in his immense hand. Now why was the Mr. Clean clone at the hotel?

My mind raced with tales of Vlad the Impaler, the famous Romanian leader. Did this Vladimir have any desire to maim or impale anyone? Or had he already done that to the man who had been married to Irina?

By the time the elevator arrived on my floor, I decided the stress of watching ballroom dancing combined with wedding jitters had sent my imagination into overdrive. Tonight I would forget about murder and concentrate on my best friend's wishes.

I shoved my card key into the door, barely glancing at the massive oak furnishings and the lakeside view. I grabbed the phone and dialed my mother's room next door. Supposedly the rooms she and Bradford were assigned had a connecting door so all four could be together.

"Hi, Mom," said Jenna. "What's up?"

"Just checking on you guys. Are you having fun with your grandmother?"

"Yeah, we're having a great time." She lowered her voice to a whisper. "She's way more fun since she's been getting it on with Bradford."

"Jenna! That's no way to talk about your grandmother," I chided her then giggled when I realized she was right. Mother *was* way more fun now that she was getting some.

"Sorry," she apologized. "Grandmother is in the bath-room. Do you want to talk to her?"

"No, that's okay. I need to get ready for the wedding rehearsal. You know we're meeting at the King's Tavern at seven?"

"Yep, Liz already called to confirm we'll be there."

We signed off and I jumped into the shower. Liz had hired a hairstylist and makeup artist for the entire bridal party tomorrow. I couldn't wait to see what kind of miracles she could work on me.

In less than an hour, I was ready, garbed in a navy blue empire waist chiffon dress that flattered my curves. I grabbed my clearance evening bag, checked to make sure I had my room key then took the elevator down to the lobby. On the way down I noticed that the bright orange sale price tag was still attached to my purse, so I stopped at the front desk to ask for directions and also to borrow their scissors. It was one thing to find a bargain. It didn't need to be advertised to the rest of the hotel.

The woman behind the front desk pointed me to a long corridor on the right. I followed the signs to the tunnel walkway, which led to the hotel wedding chapel. Liz stood next to Brian, her arm linked in his, smiling up at her fiancé. I hugged both of them then stepped back to scrutinize the radiant bride.

"You look oddly calm," I said, puzzled by her tranquil demeanor on the night before her nuptials.

"I mixed her a Xanax cocktail," said Brian. "It should last through dinner."

"Isn't he a sweetie?" she chortled as she ran her fingers playfully up and down his forearm. Brian seemed tense so he must have skipped the anti-anxiety meds. His cell rang and he pulled it out of his pocket and walked away. His face was somber as he hung up and joined us.

"We have a minor problem."

"It's okay, just hang loose," Liz said in a singsong lilt, already emulating the laid-back lingo of the islands in preparation for their Hawaiian honeymoon.

I eyed her warily. I was beginning to think I preferred Bridezilla Liz to this chirpy medicated version.

"Chuck went skiing today and a snowboarder crashed into him," Brian said. "He called from the hospital and his leg is broken."

"What a terrible thing to have happen," I said. "Poor Chuck."

"Didn't I instruct the bridal party *no* winter sports activity until after the wedding?" Liz planted her hands on her hips and scowled.

Now that sounded more like my friend.

"We're going to need a replacement." Liz turned to Brian. "Who can we get to be your best man on this short notice?"

Suddenly I felt the presence of a man who was without question the best man for the job. The three of us stared at the new arrival. Liz circled her prey, a calculating look in her hazel eyes as if she was trying to determine if the newcomer could be turned into a dancer in less than twenty-four hours.

Tom was a better detective than I gave him credit for. He took one look at Liz and shook his head. "I have no idea what you're going to ask me, but I can already tell you the answer is no."

Liz hooked her arm over his. "Our best man broke his leg today and can't be in the wedding party. Laurel thought you could take his place, and I know you wouldn't want to disappoint her."

The expression that crossed the detective's face was of relief and maybe something even better.

"Sure, I'd love to be Laurel's escort."

Liz's smile could have lit up the entire ballroom. "Great. We're about to start the rehearsal for the wedding ceremony right now." She stepped into the chapel and threw out her parting gift. "Later tonight Laurel can teach you the dance steps for the reception routine."

The bride and groom disappeared into the chapel and Tom turned to me with a stunned expression.

"Don't stress," I said. "We have bigger things to worry about than our two pairs of left feet partnered together. Do you remember Anya from the dance studio?"

He nodded. "Anya Taranova, the gorgeous brunette with the great…" His voice petered out probably in response to the peeved expression discernible on my face. He concluded with, "one of the female teachers in the studio."

Never let it be said that Laurel McKay was jealous of another woman, even one with two percent body fat. "Yes, the teacher with the fabulous body and the flexibility of a rubber band."

He chuckled. "What about her? Is she in that competition they're holding here at the resort?"

"She's Stan's partner, but she was MIA until a minute before their event. Then she disappeared right after they competed, but not before she told him someone is trying to kill her."

His left eyebrow quirked upward. "Why would someone want to kill her? Chandler is in jail, so this can't be tied to the studio deaths."

"I still say my boss is innocent." I held up my hand as he started to protest. "But I'm not certain Anya was talking about the murders. Stan said she was worried about government agents but he didn't know which government."

"Many of the Russian émigrés are in this country with only a visa. If they get into trouble or are arrested, that's all it would take for them to be sent back to their homeland."

"But why would it be dangerous for me?"

Tom looked startled. "For *you?*"

"Anya implied I was in danger." I nibbled on my lower lip as I mulled over Anya's warning to Stan. "Or at least, I think she did."

"I heard about that melee in the competition this afternoon. She was probably referring to ballroom dancing being too dangerous," he said. "Speaking of which, don't you think this wedding dance will be a disaster if my matching set of clodhoppers is involved?"

I sized him up, my mind digressing from detecting to another direction. One that involved a room beginning with the letter B. And I wasn't thinking of a ballroom.

I sighed. It was best to leave those thoughts buried.
Time to concentrate on three things.
 Surviving the wedding.
 Teaching Tom to dance
 Staying far away from danger.
 How hard could it be?

FORTY-TWO

WE BREEZED THROUGH THE rehearsal in less than an hour. Tom had served as the best man in a prior wedding so he jumped into his new position with ease. I didn't trip or drop anything, including the ribbon-covered paper plates we used in place of the real bouquets. Thanks to her anti-anxiety cocktail, Liz beamed throughout.

The wedding chapel of the resort was the most beautiful chapel I'd ever seen. Beneath the thirty-foot A-line pitch roof, floor-to-ceiling glass windows overlooked century-old pine trees set against the backdrop of the sapphire-blue lake. Any bride would long to be married in such a beautiful setting. Standing next to my best friend brought back memories of my own wedding eighteen years earlier when our positions were reversed and she acted as my maid of honor.

I prayed that Liz and Brian would honor their vows forever. Sometimes a divorce becomes inevitable, but that still doesn't make it any easier. I shook my head clear of those painful memories. My life was moving forward in the right direction. And so was the wedding couple. Liz and Brian were mature, stable and absolutely perfect for each other.

After the rehearsal, the wedding party joined the other invited guests in the banquet room of the King's Tavern restaurant. The kids and I were seated with my mother and Bradford at a round table for eight. Stan approached our table and offered to work with Tom if he required any help learning the wedding dance choreography. Stan had managed to memorize the entire routine by watching us practice it one evening.

"Thanks, we may take you up on that offer," I said. "Any more Anya sightings?"

He shook his head. "I don't know if I should try to compete tomorrow. I'd hate to upset Liz."

I rubbed his shoulder. "I think you should give it a go. You were awesome today and like you said, you may never have this opportunity again. I doubt Liz will even notice you're not in the pews. In fact, she probably won't notice me, and I'll be standing right next to her."

He chuckled. "Our little Brit is all grown-up. She's going to be one beautiful bride."

Ben stopped his attempts to build a fortress constructed of the peas and carrots adorning his plate. "Mommy, do you know who I'm going to marry when I grow up?"

Stan and I both smiled. I was fairly certain the answer was Tom's daughter who was also Ben's best friend. "Oh, let's see, I bet you want to marry Kristy."

He frowned and shook his head. "Nah, she's okay for a bud, but she's too bossy. I'm gonna marry Anya."

The carrots poised on my fork flipped off, landing in my glass of chardonnay. "You want to marry Anya?"

Ben turned to me, his freckled face in earnest. "Well, I'm gonna wait until I grow some more. She's kind of tall for me right now. But she's really hot. Her boobies bounce when she dances."

Talk about hot. My face felt like it was on fire.

"Why were you watching her boobies?"

"Because they were bouncing, of course." Ben seemed puzzled by my lack of comprehension of the male psyche. Despite sixteen years of marriage, I was as confused as ever. Stan almost choked trying not to laugh at Ben and he refused to make eye contact with me.

I decided to ignore Anya's bouncing boobs for now and let my son down gently. Young boys' egos are easily bruised. "Anya may be a little old for you, honey."

"Nah." He shook his head back and forth, his shaggy locks flying. "She told me I was adorable. When I was in the studio. Seriously."

The dance instructor who claimed she was being pursued by killers had been talking to my son? Now that was a problem.

Seriously.

FORTY-THREE

IN THE BEGINNING OF THE twentieth century, lawmen located in large cities spent a considerable amount of time on their feet, which led to the disparaging slang term of "flatfoot." In my lawman's case, it was difficult to discern if he was flat-footed or fat-footed. What was easy to detect was that he didn't possess one dancing gene in his entire body, particularly his *feet*.

We practiced for two hours and at midnight we called it a night.

Tom looked more harassed than I'd ever seen him and that included the evening he confronted a murderer. "Look, Stan, I'm never going to get it. Liz and Brian need to find another best man because it obviously isn't me."

Stan and I exchanged looks. Less than eighteen hours until the ceremony. All of a sudden Stan's face lit up. "Hey, Tom, you have the ceremony nailed, but there's no rule that says just because you're the best man, you have to perform the wedding routine with the matron of honor. I'll be done with the competition by then and Laurel and I can dance it together. If Liz has enough champagne, she won't even notice the substitution."

Since Stan was eight inches shorter and seventy pounds lighter than the burly detective, that was unlikely, but by that time of the evening would anyone care? Definitely not the newly married bride and groom. We agreed it was the perfect solution. I hugged Stan good-night and collected my evening bag. Tom offered to escort me to my room.

We remained silent on the elevator. I half hoped Tom would reach out for me but vaguely remembered that hotel elevators are frequently equipped with video cameras. I didn't need any memories of a brief elevator interlude showing up on YouTube. We strolled down the corridor in the direction of my room. With Bradford, the kids and my mother asleep next door, we kept our voices low. I voiced my concerns regarding Ben's comments about Anya. "Should I be worried about my children's safety?" I asked.

"Laurel, I'm sure there's nothing to worry about. You know how kids are. Anya probably said something kind to Ben and he's blown it out of proportion. All she has to do is crook a finger and men drool. Even pint-sized males."

My eyes narrowed, but the detective's keen analytical skills kicked in as he realized his poor choice of words. Within seconds, his arms were wrapped around my waist and my attention was diverted. His lips were soft and tasted of champagne, but everything else was rock hard. I pressed my body against his and melted into his kiss.

There was a distinct possibility I might have leaped up and wrapped my legs around Tom's waist, but we were interrupted by the clatter of a room service attendant picking up discarded trays outside the guest rooms. He smiled knowingly as he rolled his cart down the hall. We probably weren't the first couple he'd encountered making out in the hallway.

"I better let you get your beauty sleep. Not that you need any," Tom amended. "Tomorrow's a big day."

I reluctantly agreed although I could already tell that the recent stimulus would not assist me in getting a good night's rest.

My dreams that night were turbulent and troubled. Dancers in beautiful gowns wearing conical black witch hats circled Liz, who was dressed in her fur-trimmed wedding gown. Her arms were wrapped around someone small as if she was protecting the person from the cackling brood of hostile dancers. The face of a small boy appeared. Scared.

I woke up screaming just as the sun rose over the Sierras. The image of Ben's terrified face in my dream would not subside. I finally threw on my pink fluffy robe, grabbed my card key and walked out of my room into the hallway. The same room service attendant was delivering a breakfast tray to the room across from mine. He winked at me. Little did he know the only thing that made me scream in bed last night had been a nightmare.

I banged on Bradford's door. The fluffy white shaving cream on his cheeks accentuated the frown on his face. "What's going on? Is something wrong?"

I shoved my hands in the pockets of my robe. "No, um, just missing my kids. Everything okay with you boys?"

He nodded, the froth on his face scattering foamy white droplets on the grass cloth wallpaper. "Sure. Ben's still asleep. Do you want me to wake him?"

"No, sorry, I'll see you guys at breakfast." I waved goodbye and trudged back to my room, feeling like an overprotective mother. I jumped in the shower and tried to scrub away the niggling feeling, but even the soapy lather of the hotel's pine-scented shampoo couldn't erase my unease.

FORTY-FOUR

THE KIDS, MOTHER, BRADFORD, and I were enjoying a late-morning buffet at the hotel when the bride called.

"Laurel," she shrieked. "I forgot my veil. I can't get married without a veil."

Hmmm. Thousands of brides might disagree with her statement. But we were on the home stretch and my job was to keep her calm and not bothered by her latest sticky wicket. "Don't worry. I'll handle it."

Speaking of sticky, I watched Ben dig into a third waffle from the stack on his plate. "Honey, you're going to make yourself sick."

"Yeah, you're gonna be swinging from the chandeliers from all the sugar in the syrup," admonished Jenna.

Ben's eyes opened wide as he turned his syrup-covered face to his sister. "The hotel lets you swing from their chandeliers?"

"No!" we yelled in unison.

I swallowed a last bit of scrambled eggs and pushed my plate aside. "Mother, Liz forgot her veil. With so many wedding chapels in Tahoe there must be some type of bridal apparel shop nearby."

Mother chewed on her bagel, her mental Rolodex going into action. "You know with all the dressmakers here for the dance competition, they may have some white netting they could turn into a veil."

"You're a genius. Do you mind watching the kids for the next couple of hours?"

"Can I play video poker?" Jenna asked. "I devised this equation that will limit the statistical possibilities if you always—"

"No poker for you," I informed Jenna. "And definitely no chandeliers for you, young man."

His frown lasted two seconds before it morphed into a wide grin. "How about snowboarding? It's only noon and the wedding isn't until five."

I shook my head. "Nope, the boss says no more snow activities for anyone in the wedding party, or their relatives."

"Liz is mean," sulked Ben.

"No, she's not. Today is a special day for her and we don't want to do anything to spoil it."

"Why don't we all go see that new *Toy Story* movie," said Mother, coming to the rescue as usual with a wonderful suggestion, wonderful for everyone except me since I still had to locate a substitute bridal veil. I love the *Toy Story* movies.

Bradford insisted on picking up the breakfast tab, and I departed for my matron of honor duties, feeling secure that the kids were in safe hands. My first stop was the area where the dance competition was being held. Costumes and accessories should be situated nearby. When I entered a meeting room located two doors down from the main ballroom, I discovered wall-to-wall, one of-a-kind creations.

Never in my life had I encountered such beautiful fairy-tale dresses. It was like entering Cinderella's walk-in closet, *after* she married Prince Charming. Ball gowns in every hue of the rainbow were painstakingly detailed with embroidery, beading and crystals that glittered in the light from the overhead chandeliers. I'd also never seen such hefty price tags for individual gowns. The dresses ranged from $2,000 to $5,000. Considering how scanty some of the Latin costumes were, that boiled down to $100 per inch for the more revealing outfits.

Several people waited in line in front of the makeshift dressing room. Most ballroom dresses were made of a combination of Lycra and other fabrics. They ranged in size from extra small to extra large. The addition of Lycra allowed for greater stretching power, and I was tempted to try on one of the larger more conservative gowns for fun. But first, I had to find some netting for my bride's improvised veil.

A petite blonde was bent over a table using a small tube of adhesive glue to attach some stones onto the bodice of a striking coral dress. When I tapped her on the shoulder, she raised her eyes then flinched. I jumped back, equally startled.

"Irina. You *are* here."

Duh, good detecting, Laurel.

Her catlike green eyes grew wary. "*Da,* I help Olga Zakarova make costumes for the dancers."

"Wow. I had no idea you could make costumes as well as dance. These are gorgeous."

She relaxed and a small smile flitted across her face. "The dresses, they are very expensive to buy, so many of us are taught to use needle and thread almost as soon as we learn how to dance."

I smiled back at her. "The guys are lucky. All they have to do is put on a tux or shirt and slacks."

She giggled. "Dimitry, he was hopeless. One time he try to put crystal back that fell off one of Paula's dresses. He not happy when he glue his fingers together."

Based on her comments when we spoke at her cabin the other day, Irina should have glued her husband's *zipper* shut.

I looked around and realized her baby daughter was missing. "Who's watching Katya?"

"Uncle Vladimir."

I lifted my arm well above my head. Irina grinned and nodded.

"I didn't realize Vladimir was your uncle. Does he also compete?"

"No, not in the dance. Many years ago when he was still living in Moscow, he compete in different sport."

"He's so enormous. Is he a weightlifter?"

"No, he compete in biathlon in the winter Olympics." I cocked my finger at her and she nodded. "*Da,* is very difficult sport."

"I can barely stand up on my skis without falling down," I said. "I can't imagine hauling a rifle around. How did he do in the Olympics?"

"He won the silver medal. Only lose by one point."

"That must have been tough."

"Yes, he claim the person who won the gold medal cheated," she said with a sigh. "They used to be best friends but Vladimir will no longer speak to Boris. It is sad because Boris is my friend."

My eyes widened. "Boris, the studio owner?"

"Yes, is difficult situation. Vlad was most unhappy when he find out the owner of the studio where we dance was his old enemy."

A couple of dancers walked in and began rummaging through the dresses on her rack. "Excuse me, I should go help them."

"Of course, I almost forgot why I came here. Liz left her veil at home. Do you have any white netting we could use? She's getting married in…" I looked down at my watch. "Four hours."

Irina pursed her lips then told me to wait. She crossed

the room and in less than two minutes was back with a swatch of netting and a plain white satin headband. I watched as her needle zipped in and out of the fabric, faster than a mosquito on the attack.

In what seemed like mere seconds, Irina attached the lightweight fabric to the anchor that would rest on the bride's hair. She grabbed a dozen fake stones, all similarly sized, from a small bowl and used the special adhesive to glue them across the top of the headpiece. The final product was even prettier than the original veil.

"That's beautiful. I can't believe how quickly you put that together."

She shrugged, a wistful expression crossing her pretty face. "It's nothing. I do it all the time. We add stones to the dresses and the shoes. It makes more flash."

"More flash?" I asked, confused.

"Yes, the better the stone quality, the more the sparkle. You must have flash to impress the judges. Like Paula. She is at the gold level so she must have the best crystals on her dresses."

This whole topic of dressing to please the judges was really intriguing. Maybe if I could afford a four-thousand-dollar dress, it wouldn't matter if I bothered to learn the steps.

"Do you make Paula's dresses for her?"

Irina's face darkened and she shook her head. "Paula is so fussy she must have specially designed dresses. When she and Dimitry go to competitions in Vancouver and Toronto she always buy brand-new gown and it always must come from Didier."

"Where's Didier?" I asked.

"No, is not a place. Is person," Irina said. "Didier is famous ball gown designer from Quebec. Paula met him long ago when she worked on cruise ship. He brings his dresses to many of the big shows."

"It's a good thing her husband does so well."

Irina shrugged. "I think it's silly to pay so much for new gowns when I can make them for much less. At first Dimitry agree with me but then he change his mind."

Her eyes welled with tears. "I guess Dimitry think I not good enough for his clients." She reached for a tissue but the box was empty.

I fumbled in my purse for a clean tissue and noticed the stone I'd retrieved from under the table the day before. I pulled it out and showed it to Irina.

"This crystal fell off of Paula's dress yesterday afternoon. Do you think you'll be seeing her and could return it?"

Irina took the crystal and rolled it around her palm. She plucked a similar sized stone from a tiny bag stored in her sewing kit and compared the two. Then she walked over to a window and held them up to the light.

She handed the stone back to me, wearing a puzzled look. "Are you sure this is crystal from Paula's dress? It is much nicer than my stones. No wonder she is so fussy about her dresses. It shines like diamond." Irina's lower lip quivered. "Dimitry, he used to say diamonds are girl's best friend. I'm not sure what he mean. Is another strange American expression."

Since diamonds unfortunately have never been *my* best friend, I agreed it was another peculiar idiom. I glanced at my watch. No more time for chitchatting, even though it was fascinating to learn more about this crazy world of competition dance.

I opened my purse, shoved Paula's crystal inside the side pocket and took some twenties out of my wallet. "Irina, what do I owe you?"

She pushed the money aside. "Is nothing. Tell Liz I very happy for her and hope her marriage last a long time." Her voice broke and I was afraid she was about to burst into tears when her gaze suddenly shifted to the doorway. Her face turned whiter than the netting she held in her hands and her eyes flared into emerald embers of anger.

"I must go." She threw the headpiece into my arms, pushed past the dancers in the doorway and rushed out of the room.

FORTY-FIVE

BY THE TIME I UNTANGLED MY arms from the netting and folded up the veil, Irina had disappeared down the hallway. She was one volatile Russian.

Speaking of volatile, if I didn't deliver the substitute veil to the bride, a volcanic eruption might ignite in Liz's chambers. I scurried into the elevator and seconds later, knocked on the door of the soon-to-be honeymoon suite. The remains of a glass of champagne standing next to the cosmetic sundries might be a clue to Liz's lack of prenuptial jitters.

"Here you go." I displayed her new veil on the bedspread. "Irina made it for you free of charge. She even decorated the headband."

Liz scrutinized the workmanship of the substitute. "That woman is brilliant." She flashed a brilliant smile of her own. "Thanks, luv. You know I could never have pulled this wedding off without you."

We exchanged hugs, both tearing up. I left for my own makeup session knowing one thing was certain—if I had to choose between a diamond and Liz as my best friend, even in Bridezilla mode, Liz won hands down.

Two hours later, I was as gorgeous as one glass of champagne and the talented makeup artist could deliver. I smoothed my silver silk gown and preened in front of the mirror, wondering if the detective would notice my glamorous new look. With my luck, the only man who would compliment me tonight would be my gay friend.

I grabbed my lipstick, room key and hairbrush and tucked the tiny crystal that had fallen off Paula's dress into the pocket of my silver evening bag. Her scholarship event was coming up soon so the odds were high that I might run into her somewhere in the hotel.

My cell rang, displaying Stan as the caller. I had to be downstairs for the prewedding photographs in ten minutes, but he could be calling with his competition results.

"Did you win?"

In a voice barely above a whisper, he replied, "No, I haven't competed yet. I can't find Anya anywhere. I don't know if she's left the hotel or if she's still hiding. What if something happened to her?"

"Calm down, Stan. Where are you and why are you whispering?"

"I'm in the main ballroom. I don't know who to trust anymore. I ran into Gregor in the lobby. He was checking out of the hotel. When I asked if he knew where Anya was he shrugged and said they decided not to dance together." Stan's voice increased in volume and pitch. "And every time I make eye contact with Boris he does that thing with his finger like he's shooting a gun at me. He's freaking me out."

I heard a female voice in the background. "Who's with you?"

"Irina's sitting next to me." A few seconds elapsed. "Sorry, I moved away. I'm not sure whether to trust Irina either although she said she would compete with me if the judges let me make a substitution."

"What if she's the murderer?"

"Well, if Irina is planning on killing me, hopefully she'll wait until after the tango competition," he muttered. "Then you can drape my first place ribbon across my dead body."

"Hey, that's no way to talk. What's Anya's last name

again? I can try calling her room, but then I have to get downstairs. There's a wedding going on in a little over an hour, you know."

"Her last name is Taranova. Wait a minute. Omigod. Paula just arrived. You should see the crystals shimmering on her dress. That woman looks like a million dollars."

The phone went dead just as the door to my hotel room slammed shut behind me. I walked down the corridor then entered the elevator. I opened my purse and tucked the phone into the interior pocket.

"Darn." Paula's crystal fell out of the pocket and landed on the carpet in the elevator. I bent over, hoping I wouldn't have to crawl all over the carpet in order to locate it. As the elevator doors opened, the sunlight blazing through the floor-to-ceiling windows shone on the stone, which had rested next to my shoe.

I picked up the tiny object, held it between my thumb and index finger and walked up to the windows lining the lobby. Fresh snow gleamed on the stately pine trees like iced white frosting. The late-afternoon sunlight shone on the crystal in my hand, causing it to shimmer with color.

I stared at the winter wonderland lost in thought, wondering what exactly Stan meant when he said Paula's gown looked like a million dollars.

FORTY-SIX

I STOOD FROZEN IN THE LOBBY pondering how crazy would someone have to be to wear a diamond-encrusted dress in order to win a dance competition. Had Dimitry noticed his partner's affinity for priceless gems?

Across from the bustling lobby was the shopping arcade and facing me was a large tasteful gold sign for Genesis Jewelry. The photography session wouldn't begin for another ten minutes so I raced across the lobby and entered the store. The display cases were covered with wall-to-wall bling, but I didn't have time to drool over things I couldn't afford. And I had a question that was burning a hole in my purse.

Several of the sales staff were occupied helping customers. One salesman must have noticed my frantic look. He walked over to assist me. "May I help you?"

I plucked the crystal out of my purse. "Yes, thanks. Can you tell me if this stone is a diamond?"

The distinguished pinstriped suited salesman didn't even blink an eye at my unorthodox request. He picked up a jeweler's loupe and examined the stone. Within seconds he nodded. "It's definitely a diamond. You weren't sure? Was it a gift?"

"Long story," I replied. "Is there any way to tell what this stone is worth?"

He shook his head. "Not today. We'd need to have a certified specialist appraise it. It looks like a decent stone, though." He scrutinized it under his loupe again. "I was looking to see if it was produced by one of the well-known Canadian mines. Some of the larger mines mark their diamonds with minuscule polar bear or maple leaf marks."

"Oh, I didn't realize there were diamond mines in Canada."

"The first mine was discovered in the Northwest Territory in 1998. Canada now produces one third of the diamonds in the world."

"I had no idea. I thought most diamonds came from Africa."

"The Sierra Leone continues to be one of the largest sources of diamonds, but despite the Kimberly Process Certification passed in 2003 to regulate trading of conflict diamonds, there are still issues worldwide."

I remembered watching the movie *Blood Diamond*. That had been quite an eye opener.

The salesman was now warming up to his topic. I glanced at my watch. Five minutes past photo shoot time. I was about to interrupt his diamond monologue when he uttered something that absolutely got my attention.

"Of course, no matter what laws they pass, they'll never be able to totally eradicate diamond smuggling, whether it's for money laundering purposes or just the laundering of conflict diamonds."

He returned the stone to me and I gawked at him, my mouth open wide enough to shove my purse in.

Paula's husband had mentioned their financial windfall this year due to his commodity investments. At the time, I assumed Richard was referring to the surging prices of gold, silver and other commodities that had turned out to be a great investment vehicle. But diamonds? Talk about a one-of-a-kind commodity, especially the black market kind.

Had Paula discovered a way to make a fast buck to support her expensive dance habit?

And had Dimitry figured out their scheme? How desperate would they be to keep from having their smuggling scheme discovered?

Desperate enough to kill?

FORTY-SEVEN

I GLANCED TO THE LEFT WHERE the chapel was located, which was where I should be heading for the wedding photos. Then I looked to the right, in the direction of the ballroom competition. If Paula killed Dimitry and Yuri, had she also eliminated Anya? Was her husband involved in the smuggling? And the murders?

Liz might *want* to kill me for being a couple of minutes late, but I wasn't taking a chance on anything happening to Stan. Who knew how desperate Paula was at this point.

I called Stan to tell him about my discovery and to warn him to stay away from Paula. My call went directly to his voice mail. Darn. I forgot phones are required to be turned off during the competition.

Then I called Liz but she didn't pick up, either. I left a message telling her not to worry. I'd only be a few minutes late. Tom was next on my list. I called his number twice then finally gave up leaving him a message to meet me in the grand ballroom. Before a killer waltzed her way out the door.

As I raced down the hallway, my heart beat so loudly it sounded like a bomb ticking away the seconds. I dodged several dancers, turned the corner and ran into a mass of people all waiting to enter the ballroom. None of whom were willing to let the frantic woman with the crazed eyes cut in front of them.

I finally made it to the entrance and was stopped because I hadn't purchased a ticket for the day's events. I argued with the attendant that it was a life and death situation. Evidently that line had been used too often by impoverished dance enthusiasts.

Fortunately, I had a twenty-dollar bill in my evening bag so I went back in line to pay. The attendant stamped my hand and finally allowed me to enter. The audience was even larger than yesterday. Standing room only.

Throwing good manners aside, I shoved one couple apart to see if I could discover Stan, Irina, or Paula on the dance floor, or even sitting at one of the tables along the perimeter.

"Hey," squawked the tall, tanned female dressed in two pieces of glittery turquoise fabric, attached by what looked like strings of dental floss. I wouldn't even sleep in that meager outfit, much less shake my booty.

"Sorry, I need to find a friend of mine. Do you know which event is next?"

She rifled through her program. "They're running a little behind schedule. After this Viennese waltz there will be a tango then the gold scholarship event will begin." That meant Stan was probably ready to go on if he had found a partner. Paula's multidance competition would begin right after his event. I scanned the room in search of a familiar face.

The refrain of a Rascal Flatts top hit filled the room. Hmmm. Who knew my favorite country duo wrote songs you could dance the Viennese waltz to? I peered at the couples on the dance floor. No one from our studio. I glanced toward the opening where the couples normally entered onto the floor. The light from the chandelier reflected a glint of something metal. A pair of wire rimmed glasses under a receding forehead. Stan!

A jumble of male and female dancers waited for their opportunity to perform. The music ended and the dancers who were currently on the floor bowed and curtseyed. Then they exited as the new competitors walked on. Stan looked frightened, but so did several of the other participants. If there were not enough competitors in a specific age category then newcomers, intermediate and advanced students could all end up dancing at the same time. The only person who didn't appear the least filled with trepidation was Stan's partner.

Paula!

My buddy looked out into the audience. As soon as he saw me, his frozen smile morphed into a warm grin. He pointed at me and Paula glanced in my direction. Unfortunately, I don't have a poker face. Our eyes locked and her expression grew wary.

The music started and the couples on the floor executed the authoritative steps of the tango. Paula stumbled once, but I didn't know if it was because she couldn't follow Stan's lead, or if her thoughts were elsewhere. My eyes remained glued to the couple so I couldn't compare their performance to the other competitors.

I was more relieved than the dancers when the music ended. Stan and Paula bowed and walked off the floor. I moved in their direction, my intent to intercede and keep Paula occupied until the detective arrived. I glanced at my cell. Had no one noticed the matron of honor's absence and checked their messages?

Stan and Paula split up and she disappeared from sight. Bronzed bodies in a variety of shapes and sizes blocked all paths leading to my friend. The emcee announced a five-minute break before the scholarship dance competition would begin.

A few couples drifted onto the floor to practice, providing me with an opportunity to scoot across the parquet tiles and bypass the throngs along the sidelines.

"Stan," I yelled. Not discreet but definitely effective because he glanced up at once. He waved and met me in the middle of the dance floor.

"How did I do? Wasn't it great of Paula to step in? Since we couldn't find Anya, the organizer let me switch to the amateur/amateur category."

"Yeah, terrific. Have you heard from Anya?"

He shook his head. "Not a word. Did you try calling her before the wedding…?" His voice dropped off and he glanced down at his watch.

"Laurel, it's almost four-thirty. Shouldn't you be getting ready to walk down the aisle? Liz is going to kill you. And me, too, since you came here to watch me."

"The only reason I'm here is to make sure the killer doesn't harm *you*."

He jumped back and landed on the sandaled foot of a female dancer. "Sorry," he mumbled as she glared at him. We moved away to the edge of the floor.

"The killer is here? Who is it?" His near-sighted eyes scanned the audience for an unfriendly face.

The music ended abruptly and the emcee began announcing the scholarship participants.

As the men in black tails guided their lovely companions garbed in multicolored satin gowns out onto the floor, I pointed to the couple standing dead center.

Stan looked in that direction. "See, I knew it was Boris all along."

"No, not Boris," I said. "Paula."

"What about Paula?" He shot me a sideways look, making me wonder if that one glass of champagne had addled my brain. Was I grasping at straws?

From my purse I extracted the tiny crystal. He reached for it and I dropped it into his palm.

Stan rotated the stone in the light beaming from the overhead chandeliers. "Where did you get the diamond?"

"It fell off of Paula's dress. I think she's been smuggling diamonds on her ball gowns. Replacing some of the Swarovski crystals with real gems."

His eyes opened wide. "Paula's been smuggling diamonds? Is the killer after her?"

I wanted to shake Stan. Dancing seemed to have diminished his analytical abilities.

"No, it means the killer *is* her. At least I think she could be the killer. Anyway, we need to keep her occupied until Tom arrives to question her. I left a message for him so he should be here any minute."

"Once they finish dancing, she could disappear out of sight. For good," Stan said. "Tom will never be able to find her. You saw how crowded it was a few minutes ago. It's wall-to-wall bodies now."

I glanced around the room. He was right. Once she left the floor, we'd never be able to get close enough to stop her from getting away. Strains of a waltz began. Boris positioned Paula directly in front of us. He dipped her backward. Even upside down, she exuded complete poise.

Stan held up the diamond in front of her eyes. Paula blinked once then as Boris whirled her across the room, she sneered at me, her heavily lashed eyes scornful. The waltz music ended then the strains of a fox-trot filled the room. There was only one way to keep Paula from disappearing forever.

I grabbed Stan's hand and yanked him onto the floor. "C'mon, it's our turn to dance."

FORTY-EIGHT

IT WAS DIFFICULT TO TELL WHO was more stunned by our appearance on the dance floor: my partner, the judges, Paula, or me. Stan astutely realized that if we didn't start moving, we would be run over. Dancers don't let anything or anyone get in their way and a couple of clueless amateurs could become road kill in seconds.

We began with the fox-trot, which I easily followed, so my first thought was that Bobby's lessons finally paid off. Stan led me in a promenade past one judge whose jaw dropped down to the notepad he used for scoring. For one brief irrational moment, I wondered how we would be scored then my thoughts returned to the issue at hand.

Boris deftly partnered Paula who was making a valiant attempt to maintain the strict posture and head positioning required in standard dance, but every now and then she would briefly check out our location. Boris seemed clueless and intent only on leading and succeeding.

A cloud of pink feathers landed on my nose and I sneezed into Stan's shoulder. Who the heck selected a dress that included a marabou-lined cape? Was it designed for show or to eliminate the competition?

Stan maneuvered us into a position only a few feet from our quarry. The music switched from the upbeat fox-trot into the sultry tempo of the tango. My first tango.

I couldn't believe how easy it was to follow Stan. He had truly mastered the beautiful dance that originated in Argentina. We gradually caught up to Boris and Paula. Her

eyes were so dark with fury they matched the cobalt-blue
of her gown. Boris led her into a complicated maneuver.
Without breaking her stride, Paula stretched her leg out in
the shape of a fan, spun it around, and bam!

I crashed to the floor in a puddle of silver silk. One
would think the music would stop when a dancer is felled
by another dancer, but the other couples swept past, probably ecstatic that there was one less competitor to worry
about. Not that anyone would consider us to be competition. The emcee was yelling something over the microphone but we ignored him.

Stan jerked me to my feet just in time for the last dance
event. Quickstep. We needed to be speedy as well as vigi-
lant to ensure that Paula didn't quickstep out the door. Stan
discovered the only way I could follow him, without tripping him, was to skip around the room. A few bystanders
laughed and pointed us out to their companions. My ego
wasn't at stake here, but lives certainly could be. Boris's
long legs loped across the floor and Paula amazingly kept
up with him.

For a killer, she was one heck of a dancer.

Stan and I caught up to the dazzling pair right as the
music stopped. The men bowed and the females curtseyed.
So did I. Unfortunately, since I'd never been presented to
the queen, I'd never learned the art of getting back up from
a curtsey. It didn't help that the heel of my shoe caught in
the hem of my gown. Stan fiddled with my dress, removed
my shoe and finally lifted me up under the arms. By the
time I was upright again, Paula was almost out the door.

Since the scholarship event was the last competition
until later that evening, dancers and viewers swarmed
toward the open doorway. Stan grabbed my hand and I
followed as he veered through the crowd. He had definitely
missed his calling as a football half-back.

We reached the hallway. To my left, I caught a fleeting glimpse of a blue skirt. Paula must have ducked into the room where the dance costumes were sold. To my right, Tom Hunter, dressed in a black tux, was headed in our direction. With official help close at hand, I rushed into the costume room. Stan followed a few steps behind me.

Paula stood next to the table where Irina, seated in a chair, was sewing embroidery on a gown. I should be able to stall her until Tom arrived.

"The police are on their way, Paula. It's all over for you."

"It's not over until the fat lady sings, Laurel. And you're not going to be singing anytime soon."

Paula grabbed the sewing shears from the worktable and the next thing I knew, her arm was wrapped around my throat, the sharp point of the long metal blade caressing my neck.

FORTY-NINE

THE FIRST THOUGHT THAT CROSSED my mind as the blade of the enormous pair of sewing shears pressed against my throat was that nobody better move, especially me. My second thought was that Paula was a bitch. What was with that "fat lady" remark?

I shifted slightly and the dagger sharp point pricked my skin. I cried out when a crimson drop landed on my dress. Tom suddenly appeared in the doorway. Although my knight was dressed in a tuxedo instead of shining armor, I felt confident he would rescue me.

Tom addressed my captor in a soothing voice. "Paula, drop the scissors. You don't want to hurt anyone."

"It's too late for me," she responded. "And for her."

No, it wasn't. Not for me, at least. All she had to do was let me go and everything would be hunky dory.

Tom took a step in our direction. Paula tightened her grip and another drop of blood fell on my dress. I didn't need a mirror to glimpse the panic in my eyes. I could see it reflected on Tom's face.

"Let her go. I merely want to talk to you to clarify a few things. None of this is necessary, Paula."

She shook her head and her chandelier rhinestone earrings grazed my cheek. Ouch! Even her jewelry was dangerous.

"C'mon, Paula," Stan said, "if you hurt Laurel, the judges definitely won't award you the scholarship trophy. And you were the best dancer by far."

My captor loosened her grip. "Boris and I did do well, didn't we? If you two hadn't screwed everything up, I'd be accepting my first place trophy right now. First it was Dimitry, then Yuri. Why is everyone out to get me?"

I shifted my stance and Paula tightened her hold. She must work out a lot because I wasn't going anywhere. A familiar face appeared in the doorway.

"Darling, what's going on?" her husband asked. He stood there, a bemused expression on his face.

Paula sighed. "Oh, Richard, I'm so sorry. I did it for you, my love."

The pieces of this intricate puzzle finally fell into place.

"Dimitry figured out you were smuggling diamonds on your ball gowns, didn't he?" I accused her. "That's why you killed him."

Richard's face turned a mottled shade of purple. "What are you talking about? Are you accusing my wife of murder?"

"Darling, please calm down. I don't want you to have another heart attack."

She sounded so concerned I thought I might have misjudged her. Then she increased her pressure on the scissors resting against my carotid artery.

Her husband fell into an empty chair by the doorway. "I don't understand," he faltered. Confusion marred his face.

"I did it to protect you, darling. Dimitry became suspicious of my insistence on buying ball gowns only from Didier. One day he examined a stone that fell off a dress. That's when he realized that some of the stones sewn on the dresses were diamonds, not just crystals."

"He insisted on a piece of the action, didn't he?" Tom asked gently.

The hand holding the scissors against my throat quivered, which did nothing for the tremors coursing through my own body.

"He threatened to inform the police, so I gave him one of the dresses, hoping he would consider it payment for his silence. Then a month later, when we were in the cloakroom, he made another demand. He said he would turn Richard and me in to the authorities if I didn't give him more diamonds.

"I was disgusted with his greed and I totally lost it. I grabbed the first thing I could find—Laurel's shoe, which was lying on the bench. He turned away and I smacked him on the back of his head. Hard. He yelled and cursed then walked out rubbing his scalp. A little blood oozed out of the wound, but I never thought it would result in his death."

"You stuck the heel in his mouth, right?" I asked.

She nodded, which made the blade bobble against my chin. Maybe I should stay away from questions that resulted in an affirmative response.

"I never meant to kill Dimitry. When I saw him lying there in the parking lot, with all that blood pooling under his head, I freaked out. I stuck the heel in his mouth and hoped someone would think Anya or one of his other women hit him out of spite. I knew if the police found out I'd killed him, it wouldn't take long before they would discover we were smuggling black market diamonds and selling them to Richard's clients." She shifted her stance and I could tell her gaze was directed toward her husband.

"We would be ruined," she said, speaking so softly I could barely hear her. "Richard had a triple bypass four years ago, and I wasn't sure he could survive jail. Or a trial.

"I couldn't risk losing you," she implored her husband.

Richard's face was so pale I thought he might pass out. Or suffer another heart attack. Perhaps he should have considered his fragile health before he became involved in an illegal smuggling endeavor.

"What about Yuri?" I asked.

"Yuri saw me put the heel in Dimitry's mouth so he tried to blackmail me. I had no choice but to poison him," she said. "He was a bad person. You understand, don't you?"

I wasn't sure if she was now pleading with me, her husband, or the detective who was trying to talk her into putting down her weapon.

"Of course, I understand," I said. "You know I'm your friend."

A security guard popped his head into the room, his hand hovering over the gun in his holster. I wasn't the only person who noticed. Paula tensed up, her grip becoming even more of a stranglehold.

"Paula, we'll get help for you. I promise." Tom's soothing tone of voice reminded me of the actors who play hostage negotiators on television. He also sounded like that every time I got mad at him. Maybe dating *me* helped perfect the skills he needed to calm irate female killers.

Tom moved forward slightly. "Let Laurel go and we'll get everything worked out."

"You'll look fabulous in orange," Stan chimed in. "Honest, it's your color."

Only Stan could pick the most inopportune moment to offer fashion advice.

"I don't trust any of you." Paula's voice was fraught with hysteria and fear. "She's coming with me." As she inched her way to the door, I planted my feet in an attempt to slow down her escape, but that only resulted in a deep gash above my breast. My head swirled with dizziness as a tiny flow of blood seeped down the front of my dress.

Liz was going to be so pissed.

FIFTY

Tom FLIPPED OPEN HIS CELL, hopefully calling for reinforcements. He never once took his eyes off Paula or the weapon she held against my throat. The young security guard restrained Richard, cuffing his hands behind his back.

From outside the ballroom, a noisy rumble caused Paula to jump, the blade barely missing my jugular vein and nicking me on my chin. Next time I chased after a killer, I was bringing some of Ben's Snoopy Band-Aids with me.

A tear rolled down my cheek as I wondered if I would ever see my children again.

Through the plate-glass window, I noticed two snowmobiles park next to the exterior door of the hotel. The drivers, wearing Royal Tahoe Resort staff uniforms, must be part of the maintenance crew. It would be difficult to maintain the grounds of a huge resort like this without the assistance of some type of transportation. The men climbed from their double-seated vehicles, removed their helmets and bulky ski mittens, and headed in the opposite direction from the room we were in.

I sighed, disappointed. I'd been hoping for a SWAT team.

Paula pushed me forward and we moved in tandem toward the door leading outside. To a below-freezing snowy tundra. What was her getaway plan? And the bigger question—what was she going to do with her captive?

Paula grabbed a down parka hanging on a clothing rack. The scissors shifted momentarily from her right hand to the left as she alternated slipping her arms into the sleeves of the jacket. My mind briefly contemplated that ballroom dancing also taught agility to would-be killers.

She shoved me through the door and pushed me toward the unoccupied vehicles. I stumbled on a patch of ice, but with the scissors pressed against my back, and Paula urging me toward the snowmobiles it was obvious what her next move would be.

A blast of frigid wind turned my goose bumps into miniature moguls. My teeth chattered and my brain felt as frozen as the surrounding terrain. As Paula forced me into the driver's seat of the nearest vehicle, I realized I was far more likely to succumb to death from hypothermia than death by scissors.

Paula leaned forward, her cold breath assaulting my frost-tipped ears. "Get me away from here and I'll let you go. I promise." When I hesitated, she poked the scissors against my ear.

I've grown really fond of my ears and would prefer to have a matching set for the remainder of my life. If Paula trusted me to drop her somewhere so she could run away from the authorities that worked for me. All I had to do was ensure all my body parts remained safe from harm, plus thwart her escape. By then Tom would hopefully have brought in some official reinforcements and devised a rescue plan.

Having ridden on the back of a snowmobile with my ex-husband, I knew they were fairly easy to operate. The biggest challenge was avoiding rocks, trees and other obstacles. I pulled up the red "kill switch" and turned the key. Then I shoved the throttle forward and we took off.

Most snowmobilers are clothed in protective gear, boots and helmets, not in sheer silk evening gowns. Tears streamed down my unprotected cheeks as we whizzed down the icy path away from the hotel. At this point, I didn't think Paula was operating on all eight cylinders, if she ever had been. Killing Dimitry might have been an accident, but planting the heel in his mouth and subsequently poisoning Yuri were pure evil.

She had justified her actions to herself because she was worried about her husband's fragile health. But just because Paula was a loving wife, that didn't make her any more sympathetic. Or any less crazy. Especially since she was forcing me to drive a snowmobile through the snowy terrain, a lethal weapon grazing my ear.

I glanced down and noticed my hands and arms had turned an odd shade of blue. I didn't know if it was the cold or the reflection of the moonlight on my dress. Or if I was losing my mind.

Two victims had already died. Was I about to become the third?

FIFTY-ONE

OUR SNOWMOBILE ZOOMED ACROSS the icy patches of the deserted beach. I had no idea if Paula had an escape plan. All I knew was that my ears were ringing from the cold. Were those sirens in the distance coming to our rescue? Or could the end be near and the sound was Gabriel's horn, welcoming me to the pearly gates? My hands were frozen to the handlebars and my jaw felt like it was locked in place. Despite her down jacket, I doubted if my passenger was in much better shape.

Paula's knee nudged my back and I hit the brake, slowing the vehicle almost to a halt. The wind still roared, but the sirens were definitely growing louder.

"Pull over to that boathouse," Paula shouted.

"You want me to drop you off on the dock?"

She punched me on the back with her fist. "No way. I'm not leaving you behind. I saw the way that detective looked at you. You're far too valuable as a hostage. You and I are taking a little boat trip."

The verdict was in. My captor was truly nuts. There was no way I could survive a ride across that lake clothed only in a thin evening gown. It was time to take action.

As multiple sirens shrieked alongside the ferocious winds, I shoved the throttle forward and we sped in the direction of the snow-covered boathouse. Seconds before we reached the enclosure, I leaned to the far left and moved the handlebars in the same direction. We skidded almost ten feet and I worried that we would crash into the mountainous snowdrifts piled well above our heads.

I hit the brake and the snowmobile righted itself. Instead of stopping in front of the boathouse as directed, I accelerated again. We flew down the icy planks of the narrow wooden dock.

Paula shrieked at me to stop.

So I did.

I shoved the throttle back and hit the kill switch. The engine immediately shut off, but the snowmobile slid a few feet from sheer momentum. For a few seconds I thought my brilliant plan would work as the machine teetered on the edge of the dock.

It rocked to the left.

Then it rocked to the right.

Paula let go of the scissors and wrapped her arms around my waist, but her frostbitten hands couldn't maintain their grip on my slippery chiffon dress. When the snowmobile teetered to the left once again, she fell off, screaming for help as she slid into the alpine lake. I clutched the handlebars, valiantly attempting to maintain my grip and keep the vehicle upright.

Endless seconds ticked by as the snowmobile and I fought for control.

The snowmobile won. As it listed to the right, I continued to grasp on to the handlebars. Half of my body was submerged in the frigid water while the other half remained exposed to the freezing air.

A huge lightning bug appeared on shore, making me wonder if I was about to lose consciousness. I shook my head and tried to remain alert. Not a lightning bug. A man wearing a helmet and riding a snowmobile, its beacon of light aimed at me and at Paula. She thrashed in the water in an attempt to stay afloat, the heavy satin gown threatening to take her down to Davy Jones's locker.

A giant ran down the dock, his face hidden behind his helmet. His massive arms swooped down to grab hold of me. I reached for his outstretched hand and our fingers briefly made contact.

The sensation of his callused hand touching mine was the last thing I felt as I lost my grip and sank down into a watery grave. Down into darkness and a welcome sleep.

FIFTY-TWO

I OPENED MY EYELIDS. THE SUN burned through my eyeballs so I closed them again.

Much better.

"She's awake." The well-modulated tones sounded faintly like my mother's.

"Are you sure? I didn't see her move." The masculine voice also sounded familiar, but I couldn't place it. A maelstrom of memories swirled inside my head where a jackhammer had taken up permanent residency.

"Mommy, please wake up."

Okay, that voice I recognized. I squinted into the bright fluorescent lights beaming down from the stark white ceiling. I looked around the room, astonished to see that I was lying in a twin-sized bed in a small room with pale aqua walls. A small boy with a shaggy head of hair threw himself on top of my chest.

I patted his brown locks. "We need to get you a haircut as soon as we get home, honey."

"Mommy, you took a really long nap. I didn't think you'd ever wake up." Ben snuggled against me. The warmth of his body felt good. I felt cold inside. Like I'd spent a week trapped in a meat locker.

Familiar faces surrounded my bed. Mother and Bradford. Jenna and Ben. Tom.

"Where am I? What happened?"

Tom and Bradford exchanged glances. Tom spoke first.

"You're at Bertram Hospital in South Lake Tahoe. You've been here since last night."

Crazy thoughts filtered through my brain. I vaguely remembered driving a snowmobile. Did I even know how to drive a snowmobile? And I sort of recalled being on the beach with a friend.

My brain reeled. Not a friend. A murderer!

"Paula forced me to help her escape on the snowmobile," I said.

Five heads nodded in agreement.

Memories of the previous night returned in one horrific sequence after another. "I drove the snowmobile onto the dock and tried to hang on to the bars. I couldn't hold on any longer and fell into the water." I smiled at my hero. "You saved me."

Tom looked abashed as he shook his head.

"Nope, Detective Bradford rescued you," Ben piped up. "He jumped in the lake and lifted you up out of the water, just like *The Little Mermaid*. Next time you fall in the lake you should wear a tail, Mom. It would help you swim."

I wrapped my arms around my son and clasped him against me. "Next time I won't be swimming in Lake Tahoe in the middle of winter."

I stared at Bradford. "What happened?"

He flushed with embarrassment as my mother squeezed his hand.

"I called for reinforcements but the next thing I knew the two of you had taken off and were heading who knows where," Tom said, his face stark white and his expression serious. "I ran into Robert and your mother who'd been wandering all over the hotel looking for you. When we went outside, the maintenance guys were arguing about who would follow your runaway snowmobile. Robert grabbed one of the guy's helmets, jumped on the second snowmobile and chased after you. I contacted some of the local deputies and once they arrived we tried to follow along the highway, thinking it would be faster."

Tom moved over to the side of my bed and grabbed my right hand. "I can't believe I almost lost you."

Jenna plopped on the bed next to her brother. "Move over, Ben. My turn to hug Mom." My daughter gave me a hug I would remember for the rest of my life. My eyes filled with tears at the love surrounding me.

Which didn't stop me from asking questions. "What happened to Paula? Is she okay? The last time I saw her, she was thrashing in the water."

"She's in intensive care," Tom said. "Paula was in the water much longer than you since you were Bradford's number one priority. We weren't even sure she was going to make it. Her husband is under arrest and we have a guard posted at her room. The FBI is now involved because their diamond smuggling scheme crossed state and international borders. Richard would sell the diamonds to a few of his clients who weren't finicky about the origin of their glittering tax-free assets."

"He told me it had been a great year for commodities," I said. "Was it Paula's idea or his?"

"Mason is taking the blame for the smuggling scheme. He said he lost a ton of money in the recession. His real-estate and stock market investments were all under water. Then he had a heart attack, which cost him several hundred thousand dollars because he was uninsurable and didn't have medical coverage."

"Oh, that's a shame," I said sympathetically, even though I realized I was feeling sorry for two criminals.

Tom rolled his eyes and shrugged. "Yeah, well, if they'd lived a more modest lifestyle none of this would have happened. Paula knew Didier from her cruise ship days and was aware that he occasionally dabbled in some shady transactions apart from his costume business. She introduced her husband to Didier and the two men came up with the concept of transporting the diamonds on her gowns."

"Why did she agree to the scheme?"

Tom shrugged. "I gather she was so addicted to their expensive lifestyle and to her ballroom dance hobby that she was willing to do whatever it took to pump up their personal bottom line. According to her husband, his clients were furious with him because of some speculative investments he'd made with their money. Some of his clientele aren't particular whether their profits are obtained legally or not. And they are *not* the kind of people you want carrying a grudge against you. Anyway, he guaranteed that the diamonds were legit and they evidently accepted his explanation."

"Some of them may have guessed it wasn't on the up and up, but they didn't really care how their assets were obtained," Bradford chimed in. "The bump up in the price of diamonds was an additional boon. Not to mention it's a tax-free gain."

"What about that Didier guy?" I asked. "Did he confess?"

"The authorities are still searching for him. It's beginning to look like Didier established an entire ring of people transporting and selling diamonds in this country. He even provided fake certificates certifying that the black market diamonds were not conflict diamonds."

"What about the murders? Does her confession count?" My brain still felt waterlogged and foggy about what had actually transpired, but I was fairly certain Paula had admitted to murdering both men while I was at scissor point.

"As far as the murders, there were plenty of witnesses

to Paula's confession at the hotel. Not to mention your kidnapping and attempted murder. Twice."

I straightened up. "Twice?"

"We don't know for certain yet," Tom said, "but Paula was likely the one who shot at you. She picked up some interesting skills while she worked for the cruise line."

Smuggling and shooting. Some hobbies!

All of a sudden I realized something else I'd forgotten. "The wedding. I can't believe I missed it. Liz is probably ready to murder me herself."

"She was until she realized you would never intentionally miss her ceremony," replied my mother. "And don't worry. There was no way she was getting married without you by her side. She should be here any minute…"

An enormous arrangement of flowers and balloons appeared in the doorway. Liz peeked at me from behind an oversized bright yellow smiley face.

"You'd do anything to get out of performing that wedding dance, wouldn't you?" Liz dumped the arrangement in Brian's arms. "Oh, Laurel, don't ever scare me like that again."

She shoved Tom off the bed and took hold of my hand.

I smiled at my best friend. And my kids. At my mother and Tom.

Then I told them to move aside so the man who saved my life could receive a proper hug.

FIFTY-THREE

ONCE AGAIN I GAZED AT MY reflection in the mirror. My silver bridesmaid gown had been cleaned by the hotel, free of charge. Although technically it wasn't their fault, the Royal Tahoe Resort was embarrassed that one of their guests was almost murdered by another guest on the hotel's property. They comped my room for the entire length of my stay, which extended a couple of extra days while I recovered and everything was sorted out.

Paula remained in the hospital, her condition improving each day. Her faithful husband had hired the best criminal attorney in the county for both of them. Once she was well enough to be moved to the jail she would remain there, without bail.

Mr. Chandler, Dana and their son, Robbie, drove up to the hospital to visit me. They brought a beautiful floral bouquet, and tucked in among the greenery was my Christmas bonus check. In his usual gruff manner, Mr. Chandler thanked me for solving the case and getting him out of jail. Dana hugged me like I was a long-lost sister. I had a feeling we might eventually become good friends. Their arrival coincided with the departure of my children, who were leaving to grab a bite to eat with their grandmother.

Jenna took one look at Robbie and by the expression on her face, I had a feeling she wasn't doing calculus equations in her head. He grinned at her and it was delightful to see the sullen young man break into a smile. It couldn't have been easy having his father arrested for supposedly killing his mother's lover.

The elusive Anya eventually turned up in Los Angeles. She had not only played hanky panky with Dimitry, but also with a married California legislator. She met the politician while working as a stripper at the Platinum Club in Sacramento to supplement her modest earnings as a ballroom instructor. The government men who were after her were investigating said politician for a variety of reasons, and they needed Anya's testimony regarding some of his illicit actions.

She finally agreed to help them out when the case came to trial in LA. In the meantime, she and Gregor were auditioning to become professional dancers on *Dancing with the Stars*.

Boris admitted sending the threatening notes to Dimitry, hoping he would change his mind about opening his own studio. Boris also turned out to be the person who trespassed on our property and who sent me the nesting dolls in an attempt to woo me. He'd drawn the red mark in the shape of a heart but his artistic skills left much to be desired. While I appreciated the gesture, I was glad I wouldn't have to venture into the Golden Hills Dance Studio and encounter his presence ever again.

Stan had no such reservations about the studio. He planned on continuing his lessons with Tatiana. Despite the fact that his substitute partner turned out to be a killer, Stan won first place for his tango. He also found out that during our mad dash across the dance floor, we managed to beat out one of the other couples in the gold competition for, of all things, our fox-trot.

I picked up a stick of makeup concealer and touched up the scratches I'd suffered from Paula's deranged attack with the scissors. My wounds appeared to be healing nicely. With one last glance in the mirror, I grabbed a bouquet of white roses and lilies and set off for the elevator. It was hard to believe it had been only three days since I had made a similar trip in this same dress. I pondered the craziness of the last few days and hoped everything would return to normal. All I wanted was to lead a nice quiet life with my family and friends.

And maybe, just maybe, someday I, too, would walk down the aisle with someone special.

Preferably someone tall, dark and handsome.

For today, all I hoped was that the wedding nuptials would go smoothly and it would remain a cherished day for the new bride and groom.

A HALF HOUR LATER, I STOOD next to my children who were both participating in the wedding. The strains of Pachelbel's "Canon in D" filtered into the reception area where we waited. Jenna wore a floor-length forest-green velvet dress that complemented her auburn tresses. Ben looked grown-up in a suit that, with luck, would survive the wedding before he managed to ruin it.

Tears glittered in my eyes as I watched my two children walk down the aisle hand-in-hand. The church wasn't too crowded since this wedding was being held midweek. The bridal couple had decided they couldn't wait another day to become husband and wife.

I hugged the bride, careful not to mess up her coiffure and wedding attire. Her short blond hair was unadorned and she wore a long, elegant St. John's white knit sheath with a matching jacket. She looked like perfection, as my mother always did.

"I still can't believe Liz and Brian decided to put off their wedding," I whined. "I feel like it's completely my fault."

"Can you imagine Liz giving up that romantic prepaid

cruise to Hawaii?" My mother's eyes sparkled as much as the diamond on her left hand. "Plus, now she gets to plan another wedding. She and Brian just reversed things by taking the honeymoon first."

I rolled my eyes. "Which means more to-do lists for me when they return."

I clasped my mother's slender hand. "Are you sure you're ready to go through with the wedding? This isn't purely a kneejerk reaction to my almost being killed."

"Honey, everything that happened this week reinforced my belief that life is too short and far too precious for me to wait any longer. I love you and the kids, of course. But I love Robert, too, and we are ready to start our new life together. Whether you approve or not."

I grinned at my beautiful mother. "Are you kidding? The man jumped into Lake Tahoe to save my life. You're marrying a hero, and I couldn't be happier."

I looked around for the best man, who was supposed to escort me down the aisle. Bradford's former partner and friend. The man whose smile melted my heart and all of my vital body parts.

Now where was Tom Hunter?

The strains of "Here Comes the Bride" rang out from the chapel. My mother grabbed her bouquet then turned to me. "Oh, I forgot to tell you, there was a last-minute change."

Her words were lost as muscular arms enveloped me in a bear hug. At last, Tom had arrived. I looked up into the smiling eyes of a cuddly grizzly bear.

Boris?

His teeth gleamed under his stiff black moustache. I turned to my mother.

"Mom?"

She shrugged. "What can I say? Tom was called away on a case, and Boris fit into Tom's tux."

Oh, well. There was nothing I could do but accept the studio owner's proffered arm. The wedding was about to begin.

I'm never certain where my life is going to take me, but there is one thing I know for sure. The next time I pray for someone tall, dark and handsome to walk me down the aisle, I'm going to be a lot more specific!

* * * * *

REQUEST YOUR FREE BOOKS!

2 FREE NOVELS
PLUS 2 FREE GIFTS!

MYSTERY WORLDWIDE LIBRARY®
Your Partner in Crime

FAMOUS FAMILIES

YES! Please send me the *Famous Families* collection featuring the Fortunes, the Bravos, the McCabes and the Cavanaughs. This collection will begin with 3 FREE BOOKS and 2 FREE GIFTS in my very first shipment— and more valuable free gifts will follow! My books will arrive in 8 monthly shipments until I have the entire 51-book *Famous Families* collection. I will receive 2-3 free books in each shipment and I will pay just $4.49 U.S./$5.39 CDN for each of the other 4 books in each shipment, plus $2.99 for shipping and handling.* If I decide to keep the entire collection, I'll only have paid for 32 books because 19 books are free. I understand that accepting the 3 free books and gifts places me under no obligation to buy anything. I can always return a shipment and cancel at any time. My free books and gifts are mine to keep no matter what I decide.

268 HCN 0387   468 HCN 0387

Name   (PLEASE PRINT)

Address   Apt. #

City   State/Prov.   Zip/Postal Code

Signature (if under 18, a parent or guardian must sign)

Mail to the **Reader Service:**

IN U.S.A.: P.O. Box 1867, Buffalo, NY 14240-1867
IN CANADA: P.O. Box 609, Fort Erie, Ontario L2A 5X3

* Terms and prices subject to change without notice. Prices do not include applicable taxes. Sales tax applicable in N.Y. Canadian residents will be charged applicable taxes. This offer is limited to one order per household. All orders subject to approval. Credit or debit balances in a customer's account(s) may be offset by any other outstanding balance owed by or to the customer. Please allow 4 to 6 weeks for delivery. Offer available while quantities last. Offer not available to Quebec residents.

Your Privacy— The Reader Service is committed to protecting your privacy. Our Privacy Policy is available online at www.ReaderService.com or upon request from the Reader Service.
We make a portion of our mailing list available to reputable third parties that offer products we believe may interest you. If you prefer that we not exchange your name with third parties, or if you wish to clarify or modify your communication preferences, please visit us at www.ReaderService.com/consumerschoice or write to us at Reader Service Preference Service, P.O. Box 9062, Buffalo, NY 14269. Include your complete name and address.

REQUEST YOUR
FREE BOOKS!

2 FREE NOVELS
FROM THE SUSPENSE COLLECTION
PLUS 2 FREE GIFTS!

YES! Please send me 2 FREE novels from the Suspense Collection and my 2 FREE gifts (gifts are worth about $10). After receiving them, if I don't wish to receive any more books, I can return the shipping statement marked "cancel." If I don't cancel, I will receive 4 brand-new novels every month and be billed just $5.99 per book in the U.S. or $6.49 per book in Canada. That's a saving of at least 25% off the cover price. It's quite a bargain! Shipping and handling is just 50¢ per book in the U.S. and 75¢ per book in Canada.* I understand that accepting the 2 free books and gifts places me under no obligation to buy anything. I can always return a shipment and cancel at any time. Even if I never buy another book, the two free books and gifts are mine to keep forever.

191/391 MDN FEME

Name	(PLEASE PRINT)	
Address		Apt. #
City	State/Prov.	Zip/Postal Code

Signature (if under 18, a parent or guardian must sign)

Mail to the **Reader Service:**
IN U.S.A.: P.O. Box 1867, Buffalo, NY 14240-1867
IN CANADA: P.O. Box 609, Fort Erie, Ontario L2A 5X3

Not valid for current subscribers to the Suspense Collection
or the Romance/Suspense Collection.

Want to try two free books from another line?
Call 1-800-873-8635 or visit www.ReaderService.com.

* Terms and prices subject to change without notice. Prices do not include applicable taxes. Sales tax applicable in N.Y. Canadian residents will be charged applicable taxes. Offer not valid in Quebec. This offer is limited to one order per household. All orders subject to credit approval. Credit or debit balances in a customer's account(s) may be offset by any other outstanding balance owed by or to the customer. Please allow 4 to 6 weeks for delivery. Offer available while quantities last.

Your Privacy—The Reader Service is committed to protecting your privacy. Our Privacy Policy is available online at www.ReaderService.com or upon request from the Reader Service.

We make a portion of our mailing list available to reputable third parties that offer products we believe may interest you. If you prefer that we not exchange your name with third parties, or if you wish to clarify or modify your communication preferences, please visit us at www.ReaderService.com/consumerschoice or write to us at Reader Service Preference Service, P.O. Box 9062, Buffalo, NY 14269. Include your complete name and address.

SUS11